FOREVER *Home*

HOPE TOLER DOUGHERTY

Published by Scrivenings Press LLC
15 Lucky Lane
Morrilton, Arkansas 72110
https://ScriveningsPress.com

Printed in the United States of America

Paperback ISBN 978-1-64917-224-2

eBook ISBN 978-1-64917-225-9

Cover by Linda Fulkerson - www.bookmarketinggraphics.com

PRAISE FOR FOREVER MUSIC - BOOK ONE IN THIS SERIES

A delightful and important read: I enjoyed Josie and Ches's story as they both grew together and in their relationship with Christ. Ches, in particular, intrigued me as his character began to understand who he was and who he was supposed to be. The contrast between his family and Josie's played well in the story, and I loved how they helped to "put each other back together." I'd put the book down and then keep coming back for more. Loved the Charlotte setting also!

— JODIE BAILEY - WINNER OF RT REVIEWERS' CHOICE AWARD, SELAH AWARD, AND CBS BEST-SELLING AUTHOR

ACKNOWLEDGMENTS

Although I write fiction, I try to make my stories as real as possible. When I don't know information I need to know, I'm grateful for people who graciously spend time with me answering questions. The following people helped this story come to be and made it better than my solo attempts. Any mistakes are mine, not theirs:

Emily Evans Sorrel, BSW, Child Placement Supervisor, Johnston County Department of Social Services;

Terri Toler Sutton, beach music dance instructor;

Rick Heilmann, owner and general manager of WKJO, Clayton, NC, along with program director, Brody Smith; morning show co-host, Carlie Heilmann; and afternoon show host, Kristen Lawrence;

Dave LaBrozzi, Brand Manager of KDKA News Radio in Pittsburgh and former Senior Vice President of Programming and Content WABC, New York City;

Amie Harper, former radio personality on WSM-FM Nashville and member of the nationally syndicated show, Country's Most Wanted with Bill Cody;

Mark Hall, Campus Director (Goldsboro, NC), Hope Center Ministries;

the fabulous team at Scrivenings Press: Linda Fulkerson, Shannon Taylor Vannatter, Elena Hill, and Kaci Banks;

Lane and Quinn Dougherty, twenty-something men who let me pick their brains;

and early readers Kevin, Anna, and Hattie Dougherty, and Tiffany Bracco.

I'm indebted to family and friends who support this writing journey and pray for me along the way.

I joyfully praise God Who is my constant source of help every day, all day.

1

"You're not getting away with this. Millie left the house to me." Merritt Hastings schooled her features to give away nothing of the turmoil shredding her insides. Years of practice in front of taunting schoolmates and different foster families had honed her ability to hide her feelings. She buttoned the second-to-the-top button of her blouse.

Allison and Trey Billings. The great-niece and nephew who never called or visited in all the years Merritt had known Millie. The niece and nephew whose wrapped Christmas presents clunked in her car's trunk until she donated them to a homeless shelter. Merritt recognized them at Millie's celebration service from high school pictures collecting dust on living room bookshelves.

"You may have the house for the time being because of that so-called will Aunt Mildred cut and pasted together, but it didn't say anything about the contents of the house. As her closest living relatives," he smirked, "we get the contents."

If they'd ever made the two-and-a-half-hour drive from Raleigh to Charlotte to visit her, they would have known she hated being called Mildred. If they'd ever visited her, they might have received more from her will than the five thousand dollars they'd vowed to contest.

Or maybe not. Millie donated substantial gifts to the church, her alma mater, the public library, and the foster care support group in town ... with glee. The support group dinner. The invitation rested on the hutch. *Gotta RSVP if I'm*—"Hey! Leave that alone."

Allison and Trey inched the upright piano toward the front door. "Get outta the way, Merritt." He glared at her from the far end of the instrument.

"You cannot have that piano. It's my livelihood. You can't take it."

Allison's eyes flew to her brother's.

"We're taking what's rightfully ours." Trey pushed against the instrument.

"You've already been given what's rightfully yours." Merritt planted herself at the front door. "How am I supposed to make a living?" Check your voice. It's getting wobbly and high.

"That's not our problem. I'm sure you'll figure something out. You're resourceful like that."

"Don't take that piano."

"Or what? We'll hear from your lawyer? You'll be hearing from ours first." His gaze flickered passed her head and motioned to the two men who had just carried the couch to one of the waiting trucks in the driveway. "Move, Merritt."

PALMS FLAT against her bent knees, Merritt sat with her back to her bedroom wall, forcing calmness with deliberate, slow breaths. Her head pounded from useless crying. She wiped her wet cheeks and surveyed the room.

Clothes from the chest of drawers lay in sagging piles near the opposite wall. Crumpled sheets and the comforter covered the mattress and box spring. Her to-be-read pile sat between the markings the bedside table had made in the carpet along with a box of tissues, but the lamp was gone just like the bedroom suit.

She spoke the positives out loud, maybe to convince herself. "No furniture means I don't have to dust. They left the mattresses. I don't have to sleep on the floor. I'm not homeless."

At the base of her throat, she slid the gold chain out of her blouse until she cupped the Venetian glass heart. "They didn't get your necklace either, Millie."

She pushed herself off the floor to access the rest of the damage and peeked into Millie's room. Same vision of drawer contents on the floor, mattress and bedding, bedside table stuff in random piles except for the bean bag chair Millie vowed helped her sciatica.

The bare den held no couch or chairs or end tables. A few magazines littered the floor near the fireplace. Resting alone in front of an outlet, the cable box looked bereft. She could turn that in for a rebate.

Four African violets lined the bay window, and a few framed photos tumbled over each other, emphasizing the absence of the piano. The backs of her eyes burned. She clamped her teeth onto the side of her cheek. No more tears today. At least they'd emptied the piano stool of the sheet music and left the basket of music books.

Moving on, she surveyed the kitchen. Table and chairs ... gone as well. She could have her meals at the bar, but she'd have to do it standing. Would two wooden stools be worth the trouble of carrying them off and trying to sell them? Trey and Allison clearly meant business.

The door to the laundry/mud room caught her eye. She glanced inside and chuckled. "So, they didn't want you? Well, I do. Thank You, God, for old appliances!" She placed her hands flat on each one. "I love you, you gold washing machine and dryer. No trips to the Laundromat."

She padded back to her bedroom and flopped on the mattress, pulling the comforter around her. "Let's recap. I have a mattress, pillows, and bedding. Nice. The grocery store stoneware plates are safe in the kitchen cabinet. The pantry and refrigerator have food. I have clothes, appliances, and a warm place to live.

"The den. That's harder to be positive, God." She blew out a breath and gritted her teeth. Her garage sale-spinet piano had seen better days, but Millie had rubbed linseed oil into the dry wood panels until it shined and kept it tuned every six months. It had good sound.

It was a piano.

A mourning dove cooed from her nest on top of the back porch column. "What a sad song you sing, little bird." Leaning against stacked pillows, Merritt listened to the throaty murmurs with eyes closed. The melancholy sound matched her mood, provoking the genesis of a melody in her mind. Hoping to catch the tune before it evaporated, she pushed away off the comforter, muscle memory steering her toward her—she halted mid-stride.

Tight fists at her sides, she growled out loud. "The first thing I need is a piano."

Breathing hard, she clutched her necklace again. She itched to spend time with the punching bag still hanging in the garage but forced herself to delay the temper session.

Millie had always warned against rash decisions. Thinking through problems calmly had been one of the many lessons Millie Ayden stressed after Merritt came to live with her. Learning to cook and celebrating something every day also topped the skills-to-know list.

Yes, she needed a piano for her livelihood, but she should be judicious in her purchase. She couldn't afford a baby grand, but maybe she wouldn't have to buy the first one she came across either.

If she could find another place to give lessons for—she counted on her fingers May, June, and July—three months, maybe she could take her time in buying her first piano and have it ready to go when she began lessons again with the school year in September.

Aside from feeling assaulted, ravaged, and stripped bare, the prospect of choosing a piano, not just accepting whatever she could get by with, lifted her perspective just a tad.

Oh, Millie. *Thank you for teaching me to look for the blessings no matter how bleak the problem.* It's just so hard to do it without you.

Quick tears swelled in her eyes again.

I miss you so much.

She wiped her eyes and headed for her date with the punching bag waiting in the garage.

2

The melody of the Christmas carol worked its magic. Tension seeped out of Merritt's shoulders. Swaying with the rhythm, she let the familiar words fill her head. A wrong note miffed her sense of well-being, but she pushed her fingers to continue her keyboard therapy. Another sour sound jangled her nerves. Firming her jaw, she powered through two more measures. A third mistake fractured her calm and bounced her fingers off the black and white keys.

"Merritt. 'I Heard the Bells on Christmas Day' has no D flat. Just B, E, and A. Pay attention." She zeroed in on the time signature. "See. No D flat. Stop playing it."

Beginning the carol again, she played through the entire song with no mistakes.

"Better. Thank you." Talking out loud to herself, playing Christmas carols out of season ... People might question her sanity if they heard, but Friday afternoon in the church sanctuary was typically slow.

Good. No nosy ears around. Pastor Dunleavy had given the okay to hold her piano lessons and play whenever she wanted or needed to. Lately, she needed to quite frequently.

Finished with carols, she thumbed to an old hymn near the

back of the book, played all four verses, and ended her solo concert with "Amazing Grace." She stacked the hymnals in place on the piano stool and arched her back. Her fingers tingled with the exercise. A good session. Time to go home.

Home? Her heart pinched. Go back to the house.

She followed the corridor down the wing past the senior pastor's office just as the door swung open. Pastor Dunleavy held it to let Sam Daniels pass through. Freezing in place, she blinked at the pastor.

"Hello, Merritt. You're finished with the piano then? Everything good?"

"Yes. Thanks so much." She glanced at Sam before continuing down the corridor to the parking lot. Forcing her feet to walk and not run like a thief with contraband, she had no control over her kicked-into-high-gear heart rate.

Sam Daniels turned bugging eyes to Pastor Dunleavy. "I thought this was supposed to be confidential. Nobody was supposed to know." He backed into the study.

"Our sessions are confidential. I don't talk about my conversations with parishioners." The pastor closed the door again.

"She just saw me coming out of your office. She knows."

"She doesn't know anything. You could have been giving me the riot act over something I said in Sunday's sermon. You could have been donating a million dollars to the missions fund." He paused before adding, "Would you like to donate, by the way?"

"Ha ha. I'll let you know when I get a million bucks. Seriously. She saw me coming out of your study."

Pastor Dunleavy hiked a hip onto the edge of his desk. "There's nothing wrong with seeking guidance, Christian counsel, wisdom, whatever you want to call it from your pastor. What's the deal? You don't want people to know that maybe your happy-go-lucky demeanor isn't always so happy-go-lucky?" He shrugged. "Maybe seeing you talking with me would help someone else drop by sometime."

"Yeah, okay. That sounds fine, but what was she doing here? Who is she anyway?" For a split second, her big brown eyes had drunk him up. Then they'd dropped away like she was trying to disappear. She didn't want anyone to know she was here either.

"Merritt Hastings. Since she lost her piano, she uses the one in the sanctuary now."

"How do you lose a piano?"

"Can you say, 'confidentiality'?"

"Right." Sam raked his hand through his hair. "Gotcha. I just thought nobody'd be hanging around the church on a Friday afternoon. The secretary's gone ..."

The pastor raised his eyebrows.

"Yeah. Thanks again for coming in on your day off. I'll try to make it work on another day. If I need to come back."

"I'll see you anytime, Sam, but why is it so important no one knows you're here? What are you afraid of? That your bad boy act will unravel?"

"I'm not a bad boy, Pastor."

"No, but you cultivate a devil-may-care attitude. Doesn't exactly line up with worrying about what others may think."

Sam exaggerated a sigh. "It's tough to be cool."

"I wouldn't know." The pastor glanced toward the door. "The coast is probably clear now. You can leave without anyone seeing you."

"Hey, I'm good. It just threw me a little bit when the door opened, and BOOM, there she was with those big brown eyes."

"Big brown eyes, huh?"

This time Sam opened the door and glanced left and right before stepping into the hallway. "Thanks for today. I'll think about what you said."

Merritt rolled out of the church parking lot and headed for her house. Sam Daniels. At church on a Friday ... she glanced at the time on the dashboard. Almost Friday night. What in the world? Talking to the preacher instead of getting ready to go out?

Sam Daniels, a popular senior when she was a way, way, way under-the-radar freshman back in high school. A talented baseball player who dated the captain of the girls' soccer team, he also reported the daily announcements, always adding his odd little editorials that had everyone laughing at his observations or groaning at his puns. Teachers loved him. Classmates seemed to adore him. Crowned Homecoming King and Student of the Year, he was popular with peers and adults alike.

A green four-square ball bounced to the edge of a yard, and she tapped her brakes. The owner of the ball, a little boy in bright red shorts, grabbed the ball and waved at her. Smiling, she waved back and continued to her house, with more thoughts of Sam buffeting her mind.

One of those shining people who glided through life smiling and joking and leaving good feelings in his wake, Sam had walked her to a student council meeting one afternoon, fueling her daydreams for the rest of spring semester.

She hadn't thought about him in years. Wasn't he supposed to be in New York City? Doing something in ... what? On Wall Street? Yep. That sounded about right. His personality would be perfect in the Big Apple.

The garage door lifted as she idled in the driveway.

Interesting, running into Sam again, but really none of her business.

Getting her life back in order. That was her business.

3

Delicious aromas greeted Sam as he glided through the front door of his parents' house. "Smells like a feast in here, Jo Jo." He hugged his sister, Josie, then walked straight to the bookshelves in the family room, the family's Bassett Hound, Winston Churchill, following behind.

She called from the kitchen, "What're you looking for?"

"Nothing." He scanned the row of high school yearbooks with his index finger.

"Oh, so you're just avoiding the plates waiting for you to set the table, huh?"

"No." He pulled out one, flipped through the pages, and then exchanged it for another.

She came into the family room, wiping her hands on a tea towel. "What are you looking for?"

"None o' your beeswax."

"You've just made me more curious." Rising on tiptoes, she peered around his arm. "You're obviously looking for someone. Maybe I can help you." She rocked back on flat feet. "Who is it?"

His finger stopped at a listing. Merritt Hastings. Page seventy-six and two hundred twenty-two. Booyah. He flipped to the beginning of the book. Page seventy-six. Right in the middle of the freshman class school pictures.

Josie pulled his arm down to get a look at the page. "Who are you looking for? The freshman class? Jake Combs was a freshman when you were a senior. Remember him from youth group? Or Tim Rollins. Who do you need? I know people in that class, too, remember. I was with them for two years of high school." She glanced closer at the page. "The H's? Tommy Hinnant was in that class. He was on the baseball team with you. Oh, and Charlie Houston. He ran track."

Flipping to page two hundred twenty-two, Sam twisted away from his sister.

Josie peeked again. "A picture of girls in the library?" She drew in a breath. "You're looking for a girl? Who is it? Tell me."

"Nope."

She slapped hands on her hips. "Yes. I mean it. Tell me right now or I won't let you have seconds of the mashed potatoes."

"You're holding my food hostage?" He shook his head. "Tsk. Tsk. Not a real good Christian look, Joey."

She snorted. "You haven't been interested in a girl since—"

"Since ... still none of your business. I'm not sending out wedding invitations or even asking for a date. I'm simply trying to place someone." He slid the yearbook back onto the shelf.

"Who? And if the color tingeing your chiseled cheekbones is any indication, there's more to this story." She grinned. "Interesting that you brought up weddings and dates."

"The so-called color may be indicating irritation at my baby sister." He turned her toward the kitchen. "I don't have time to date anybody right now." *Especially if I buy WBEL.* "Now, let me set the table. I thought Ben and Heath would already be here."

"They're on their way, and then we can all video call with Mom and Dad before we eat."

"IS THIS YOUR BEST PRICE?" Merritt ran her fingertips along the oak table. Smaller than the one Trey and Allison stole, it had a leaf to accommodate eight people, but the flea market vendor had only four chairs.

"I can knock off fifty dollars." Chewing on an unlit cigar, the seller waited for her answer.

"But it isn't a complete set. It's supposed to have four more chairs."

For a flea market find, the table presented a beautiful front, polished to a high shine with no nicks or scrapes or water rings. Picturing it in front of the windows in the kitchen conjured images of lots of celebrations around it.

"We're at a yard sale, lady, not a furniture store." He tapped the hand-lettered sign taped to the table with his forefinger. "I'll minus fifty like I told ya, but that's it. Take it or leave it."

Destiny, a foster sister for about half a year when they were both ten and her best friend ever since, elbowed her, leaning toward her ear. "Negotiation skill number one. Be willing to walk away. Yes, it's beautiful, but you don't need a table yet."

Sighing, Merritt stepped away from the table. "Okay. Thank you."

"Hey. It's real oak." He knocked on the tabletop. "Solid wood."

"It's a handsome table." Merritt flicked one last glance to the table, hating to give it up.

"A beauty like this goes fast. May not be here for much longer." Determined, the man circled to the front of his stall, removing the cigar from his mouth.

Clutching her friend's forearm, Destiny nudged her away from the table. "Just keep walking." She nodded to the man, "She's sticking to her budget."

Merritt called over her shoulder, "But thank you."

"I think he really wants to sell it. Check back before you leave. He might be more inclined to make a deal. You know. Sell it as opposed to carting it back to wherever he came from." She adjusted her newsboy cap over teal locks.

"Yeah. We'll see. But I need a table for the bi-monthly birthday parties."

"Have a cookout. Ask people to BYOC—bring your own chair." Laughing at her joke, Destiny had made a face. "It'll be fun."

"Asking people to bring their own chairs will be fun?"

"You're asking people to your own birthday party. What's the difference?"

"Millie always said a back rub feels the same if you ask for it or if it comes of its own accord. Yes, my birthday will be celebrated this time along with three other people who have May and June birthdays. You still get to come even if you have to wait to be celebrated till next fall."

"Wish I could shop some more, but I gotta roll." Destiny checked her phone. "My eleven o'clock shampoo and cut just texted asking to bring her little boy in for a cut too. Wants to meet earlier." She kissed Merritt on the cheek. "This morning was fun, though." Raising her face, she sniffed. "Mmm. Maybe I'll get one of those elephant ears to go."

She flashed two fingers as she backed away from Merritt. "Peace out, Girl Scout."

After unlocking the kitchen door, Merritt pushed it open with her elbow. She lifted the card table over the threshold and rested one side on the floor while considering the best position for her recent purchase.

Not exactly what she'd gone searching for this morning, but this ten-dollar set with four chairs was a deal that would work until she could find the right dining table at the right price. She flipped down the legs and angled the square on the diagonal to take up more space in the empty spot, then sighed. She'd make it work.

A half-hour later, she scraped the last bit of the KFC mashed potatoes out of the cardboard bowl and leaned back against the padded, metal chair. Millie would not approve of eating straight out of a carry-out container. She insisted on making every meal special. Cloth napkins. Flowers or a candle. Merritt fingered the centerpiece of roses from the backyard. The warm, wet spring had produced early, prolific blooms on Millie's bushes.

"Allison took the crystal vase from the bookshelf in the den, but roses in a mason jar work, too, don't you think, Millie?" An old habit, whispering to herself helped curb the lonesome sometimes.

She traced the pattern on the red-tagged, never-opened tablecloth she'd found in a dollar bin at the flea market entrance. It dressed up the well-worn table, covering up the dings and scratches too. Bonus!

The teapot caught her eye. A cup of tea would be a nice finish to the meal. Could a double portion of KFC mashed potatoes and gravy be considered a meal, though? Maybe she'd eat an apple later if she got hungry.

Or not.

Her hands prepared the tea by rote while her mind cataloged her to-do list. Pastor Dunleavy's approval to practice and give lessons at church afforded her a bit of a reprieve on purchasing a piano. She could wait for a best option. Not settle on the just-come-get-this-old-thing-out-of-my-house pianos listed in online yard sale posts.

Piano students could walk one more block from their schools, doing their homework in the fellowship hall till their lesson began. Living close to the schools and her church had many advantages.

Waiting ... a definite relief. Extra dollars were already allocated for the property taxes. So the piano problem was taken care of for the present. Next up, den furniture. Company needed somewhere to sit. A couch, two chairs at least. An ottoman could work as seating and a coffee table.

See? Those home decorating and craft shows do come in handy.

Her mind returned to the needs in the kitchen. Leaning against the counter, she encouraged the card table in the eating space. "No, you don't look ridiculous, little table. You look brave. I appreciate all three feet of you in the twelve-foot space."

And I'm not ridiculous for talking out loud.

She really needed a dining table and chairs, however, if she planned on hosting birthday parties and holidays like in the past.

A vision of the wooden table for sale at the flea market this morning floated in front of her mind's eye. She blinked it away with a grimace. Gone when she checked at noon, it wasn't the right one. Clearly.

"A better one is waiting somewhere. Right, Millie? I keep trying to be positive."

Oblong and fashioned from oak, the flea market table exceeded her budget. A round table to seat eight, in a darker wood, and in her price range would tick all her boxes.

The bar part of the island grabbed her attention ... the naked bar with extending ceramic tiles jutting out over nothing. Two stools should be easy to find. Maybe next Saturday. No, next Saturday she'd scheduled the May/June birthday party. Too bad Destiny wouldn't let her cancel the party.

The whistling kettle jostled her back from her musings. She dropped an Earl Gray bag followed by a sugar cube into the hot water, a nod to Millie's every-day-should-be-a-celebration attitude.

4

Big books. Little books. Paperback and leather-bound books wedged themselves on every bookshelf in the study. *Twenty-five, twenty-six, twenty-seven—*

"Merritt?" Pastor Dunleavy called her out on her daydreaming.

"I'm sorry. I was admiring your books." She cocked her head. "How many do you have?"

He glanced behind him and shrugged. "I don't know. People who've helped move me would say too many." He smiled, then zeroed in on her gaze. "We weren't exactly talking about the contents of my library, though, were we?"

"No. You're right. I just don't like thinking about Allison and Trey. I try to be a positive person."

"From what I know about you, you are positive, Merritt, but stuffing down feelings won't get you where you want to be."

"And where's that?"

He dipped his chin. "Merritt."

Guilt pricked her. "Okay. Sorry. I get it. You're the one who asks questions."

"Ask any question you want, but they'll help if they're valid ones, not delay tactics."

She huffed out a sigh. "This is hard."

"Worthwhile things usually are. Where do you want to be?"

"I want to be back where I was before Allison and Trey ransacked my house." She pointed to her chest. "My house. Millie left it to me. Legally. The will says so." Her voice thickened. Biting the inside of her cheek, she breathed in and out long breaths.

Emotions under control, she continued. "I don't want to have to give piano lessons in the church even though I appreciate you're giving me the space. I want to be at my house, but I don't like going home to those empty rooms. I love my house, but now instead of bringing me joy, it makes me sad to be there. I am so mad—" She clamped her mouth shut.

Nope. Enough of that.

"Go on."

She glanced at the gold clock on the side wall commemorating twenty-five years of service. He'd been preaching for most of her life.

"Why did you stop talking when you got to anger?"

She shook her head.

"Anger is a valid feeling, Merritt. You have every right to be angry."

She may have the right, but she didn't like being angry. Or sad, either. Those emotions made her feel out of control. They reminded her too much of the little girl she used to be. The little girl who spent most of her time being mad or sad and not knowing how to change it. She'd be going several rounds on her punching bag tonight.

"Are you angry at Allison and Trey?"

"Yes."

"How about Millie? Are you angry at her?"

She narrowed her eyes. Was he crazy? Millie loved her, brought her into her home, supported her, believed in her, helped her. Millie wanted her. She could not, would not be angry with the one person who chose her. "Millie was the best person

I've ever known." Her voice hitched. She cleared her throat. "So, no, I'm not angry at her."

"I understand the closeness you two felt, but let's think about this for a minute." He threaded his fingers together across his waist. "Millie left you the house, but she wrote her own will. She didn't put 'and the contents' in the will. If she had, Allison and Trey couldn't have emptied your house." He gentled his voice. "If Millie had paid a lawyer, not just used a notary public, maybe you wouldn't be in the situation you're in now."

She studied the tweed-looking carpet, refusing to meet his eyes. The back of her throat burned with tears waiting for release. She was absolutely not angry at Millie. Maybe disappointed.

No, not even disappointed. Millie left her the house. Millie loved her; she loved Millie. She would not be angry or disappointed with her. A free spirit, Millie followed her own beat and expected others to do their own thing too.

"Merritt?"

She straightened in her chair. "Thank you for your help today, but I need to get going."

"Merritt, you're not being disloyal by admitting anger or disappointment with someone you love. It's absolutely acceptable, normal even, to feel those feelings."

Normal. Would she ever feel normal?

Normal was for other people.

Sam pulled open the door to the church, and Merritt Hastings plowed into him. "Hey," he steadied her by her shoulders. "We gotta quit meeting like this."

He chuckled, but she mumbled, "sorry," and kept going. He watched her slide into her car, but she didn't crank up. She rested her head against the steering wheel.

Vacillating between minding his own business and checking

on her, he hesitated at the door. His late lunch hour dwindled with every tick on his leather-banded Timex. If she was sick, she didn't need to drive. If she was upset, she didn't need to drive. He could spare a few minutes to make sure everything was good.

Releasing the door, he headed for her car. He knocked on the window with his knuckle. She started and peeked over her arm. Her watery eyes widened before slowly closing. He knocked again. She swiped a quick pass over her cheeks with her fingers and rolled down her window.

"Car trouble?" Sam motioned to the hood. "I could take a look for you."

"No."

"Are you sure? I know a few things about cars and car troubles." He flexed his hands. "I got some skills around cars." He smiled at her, hoping his dimple would work its usual magic.

She studied him for a couple of seconds. "My car's good." She hesitated, then raised her chin. "I just needed a few minutes by myself."

Now would be a good time to wow her with a snappy comeback. Instead, his mind focused on her brown eyes, so dark they reminded him of black coffee. The shape of her eyes curved exactly right, tipped up slightly at the edges. Her long, thick lashes, spiky with tears—

"But thank you." She dragged her teeth over her full bottom lip. "If I ever need someone with car skills, I'll call you." The corner of her mouth curled up. "'Cause I don't have Triple A."

He chuckled. "Well, you're gonna need my number then." He offered his hand, palm up. "I can tap my digits in your phone right now, and you'll be good to go."

She laughed out loud. "Your digits? Are you for real?"

Bingo. He grinned, the dimple forgotten. "Hey. I'm offering my number just in case you're ever stranded in the middle of nowhere and need a ride."

"Okay." She fished in her pocketbook, brought out her phone. "Just in case."

He tapped in his number. "I'm Sam Daniels, by the way."

"Right. Josie's brother."

"Ha. The correct way to say it is, she's my sister." He hit *save* and glanced at her. "My little sister." He offered the phone back.

She grabbed the end with her fingers, but he held his end. "And your name ...?" He watched her big, dark eyes blink.

Come on. Let's make this a real introduction.

"Merritt."

"Merritt. Nice." He released the phone and extended his hand. "Happy to meet you, Merritt ...?" He tipped his head, waiting for her last name.

She studied him. It was like pulling teeth with this girl. He raised his eyebrows and smiled.

Come on. Say Hastings.

"Hastings." She clasped his hand.

"Okay." He nodded. "Nice to meet you, Merritt Hastings." The weight of her hand felt good in his. Her long, thin fingers tapered to short nails painted an interesting purple. Perfect for piano playing. *Stop thinking about her nice hands. You don't have time to date.*

She slipped her hand from his. "Thanks for checking on me. I've got your number, so if I'm ever stranded ..."

"You be sure to give me a call." He stepped back from the car, an odd sense of disappointment enveloping him as she rolled up her window.

SNUGGLING into her bean bag chair, Merritt held the cardboard container against her chest. The warmth soothed the rough places from the day. She scooped a spoonful of mashed potatoes, dipped in gravy, and held the dollop on her tongue before swallowing. Her shoulders loosened, sinking like the potatoes to a cozy release of anxiety. Being home always dialed back her stress level.

The hour with Pastor Dunleavy felt more like a raking-over-the-coals meeting than a help-me-get-my-thoughts-straight session. Maybe tomorrow or the next day, his words wouldn't make her heart rate explode. She'd think about them later.

Or not.

Right now, though, thoughts of Sam crowded out every other image. She picked up her phone, scrolled through the contacts to Sam's entry, and read the numbers again. Her fourteen-year-old self would be turning cartwheels over this prize. Who was she kidding? Her twenty-something self wanted to turn a cartwheel or two.

Why exactly?

Because it looked like she had one more friend in her contacts list?

Because Sam had always been a cool person, and having his contact made her feel a little bit cool?

Because having a cute guy to call if she ever had trouble was a comforting thought?

Holding the spoon in her mouth, she pushed herself out of the bean bag and carried the empty carton into the kitchen. A cardinal perched on a crepe myrtle limb caught her eye from the back window. Thankful for a beautiful distraction, she watched him until he flew away.

Seriously, though. Would she really call him if she had trouble? Probably not, but having the option felt good. She strolled to Millie's bedroom to address the few items left in disarray on the floor.

Listing happy reasons to have Sam's number in her phone made her feel slightly comical.

No, more like pitiful.

Setting the phone on the window ledge, she surveyed the room and retrieved one of Millie's cardigans from a stack of clothes. She held it to her face and pretended it still smelled like her. A longing for her old friend threatened to dislodge the fragile uptick in her mood.

"Be positive, Merritt." She said it out loud, copying Millie's constant encouragement. "Think about your blessings."

Right. She had friends. Many friends, who looked forward to coming over to her house for dinners and celebrations. Her career both challenged and delighted her. She could change her own tire, thanks to Millie, but for more involved kinds of trouble, she could always call Jesse, her mechanic friend, for help.

Yes. She counted lots of blessings.

Tapping the screen, she found Sam's name again and smiled at the number. What would it be like to call him up, talk about her day, text a quick message between lessons? She swatted away her silly daydream. She'd never use it.

Still, it was nice to have it in her phone.

5

A talented nine-year-old slid off the piano bench and waved goodbye. Glancing at her date book, Merritt arched her back. The last two Friday afternoon students, a brother and sister, canceled today's lessons at the beginning of the month. They'd probably be at the beach by now. Good for them.

Now she was free for the rest of the day. The whole rest of the day, including Friday night since Destiny had an after-work blowout session for one of her best customers.

She wasn't booked to play piano at the Lamplighter until next week. Melancholy tiptoed up her spine and spread across her shoulders.

Christmas music. That's what she needed. She flipped open a hymnal to "Joy to the World." Perfect. She'd get a workout for her fingers, and she could pound the keyboard as much as she liked.

The familiar notes felt good beneath her fingertips. Her arm muscles tingled with the fast-paced exercise. She moved from "Joy" to "Silent Night," then "Away in a Manger." A few notes wobbled together on "It Came Upon a Midnight Clear," but she let them slide. They weren't true sour notes, just not perfectly clear.

A few measures into the last line of "There's a Song in the Air," her thumb played a natural E instead of an E flat. "Uh, uh!" flew from her lips. She rallied, though, finishing the line and repeating the song without any mistakes.

"Much better. Let's see." She turned a few pages. "What's next?"

"'Oh, Come All Ye Faithful'?"

She jumped straight up from the bench, her eyes searching for the voice. Sam. How long had he been listening? Heat clawed up her neck.

He strolled from the last pew toward her, smiling. "Do you always talk to yourself when you play?"

Gripping the edge of the bench, she blinked slowly. "Do you always scare people half to death? Do you always eavesdrop on private situations?" Breathing in through her nose, out through her mouth, she steadied her crazy heartbeat.

"Private situations?" He leaned against the arm of the first pew. "I didn't see a Do Not Enter sign on the church sanctuary door." A touch of irony tinged his tone. "I heard Christmas music and wanted to check it out. You do know it's May, right? Not December?" His grin took the snark out of his question. "You play very well, by the way."

"Thank you." She switched off the piano light. Pushing back the bench, she grabbed her satchel. "Well, it's all yours." Rising, she turned to leave.

"You don't have to go. I'm—"

"It's okay. I'm finished. Bye." Determined to leave the embarrassing scene behind, she strode for the sanctuary exit.

"Hey, I didn't mean to crash your party." Sam followed her retreating form.

"No problem." She called over her shoulder, waterfall curls bouncing off her back. "Have a good weekend." The door swung behind her.

He shook his head. "Way to go, Sam, my man," he muttered to himself. "Way to clear out a room—of one person." If he'd kept his mouth shut, she'd probably still be playing her solo concert, and he liked it even if it wasn't time for Christmas music.

Moving past the piano to follow in her footsteps, he spotted a yellow notebook on the music rack. He opened it. A date book with appointments. Her planner? He jogged through the empty hallway toward the parking lot. Three vehicles waited in their places, but Merritt's car wasn't one of them.

Man, she wasn't kidding about being finished. She'd hightailed it out of here.

The least he could do was take it to her, but where did she live? He turned toward the church office.

"Hey, Mrs. Carpenter, how are you?" He grinned at the new church secretary.

She smiled at him and straightened in her chair. "Good afternoon."

With purposeful strides, he approached the octogenarian smiling at the corner of the secretary's desk. "Hey, Ms. Connie." He reached down and enveloped her in a careful hug. "How ya doing?"

"Sam Daniels, I'm fine. Aren't you as handsome as ever?"

"I try, Ms. Connie. I really try."

Her laugh twittered through the office. "Oh, my. I'm sure all the young girls just love you."

"Well, I can't say that's true, but I can't say it isn't either."

"Sam, you are rotten. You know that?" She batted his arm with an offering envelope.

"Yes, ma'am. I've heard it once or twice." Wiggling the notebook, he glanced at Mrs. Carpenter. "I just found this on the piano in the sanctuary. I believe it's Merritt Hastings's. I can take it to her if you give me her address."

Mrs. Carpenter's wide smile drooped. "Sam, I'm sorry, but I don't think I can give out personal information. It's against church policy." She pointed to her desk. "You can leave it here, and I'll make sure she gets it."

Sam's lighthearted attitude deflated a notch. The idea of seeing Merritt again had fueled some of the teasing banter with Ms. Connie. "Well, I guess."

"Wait a minute." Ms. Connie arched a brow over her sharp blue eyes. "If that's her appointment book, it's important. She'll be worried about it. I know where she lives, and I don't have to follow a privacy policy." She grinned at Sam.

"Hold on, Ms. Connie." The secretary rolled her chair closer to her desk.

Waving away the protest, the older woman barreled ahead with her mission. "Linda, it's fine. I've known this young man his whole life. He may be full of blarney, but he's harmless."

Sam frowned. "Ah. Ms. Connie, I—"

Ms. Connie laughed. "I love to tease, Sam, and you're easy. She lives in Millie Ayden's house on Clover Street. Millie fostered her during high school, I think." Ms. Connie's smile faltered. "Oh, I miss Millie. A great woman." She sighed. "Go give that girl her book, Sam. The house number is two seventy-six."

Bending toward her, he kissed her cheek. "Thanks a bunch. I'll see she gets it."

6

Merritt poured the cold brew coffee over a scoop and a half of vanilla ice cream. The anticipation of the sweet treat helped to erase the sting of embarrassment in the sanctuary. Thank goodness she hadn't been singing too. That deserved another half scoop.

Leaning a hip against the kitchen counter, she stirred some of the melting ice cream into the coffee. Enough about Sam Daniels. She had other more important things to think about than a cute guy. Who popped up in random places. Who loved to tease.

No more thinking about Sam.

A sunbeam highlighted the card table and caught her attention. The floral tablecloth cheered it up but didn't hide the spindly legs. Yes, that's what she needed to think about—refurnishing her house. She still needed—

The sound of the doorbell jerked her out of her planning mode. She frowned. Late afternoon visitors weren't a usual thing. She hesitated in front of the door and peeked through the peephole.

Sam.

Her insides clenched. Questions clanged together in her

mind like bumper cars at the state fair. What was he doing here? How did he find her house? Sucking in a breath, she steadied herself.

Opening the door a few inches wider than a crack, she greeted him. “Hello, Sam.”

“Hey. Fancy meeting you here.”

She wrinkled her brow. “Because it’s my house?”

“Weak joke. Sorry.” He held up her notebook.

She gasped.

“Look what I found at the piano. It’s yours, right?”

“Yes.” She let go of the doorknob to retrieve the book. “Thanks. I didn’t realize.” She glanced up at him. “That’s very kind of you.”

“It looked important.” He grinned and stuck his hands in his back pockets. “I figured you probably needed it sooner rather than later. The secretary offered to keep it because she couldn’t give out your address. Good thing Ms. Connie didn’t have the same rule. She shared your address pretty quick.”

“Oh, Ms. Connie. She’s a sweetie.”

Hazel eyes lighted on her other hand. “Root beer float?”

“No.” She repositioned her fingers around the forgotten treat, the notebook cradled against her chest. “It’s an affogato.”

Scrunching his face, he huffed. “An avocado?”

She chuckled. “No. Affogato.”

“I believe that’s what I said.”

“Ahf-o-GA-toe. An Italian word.”

“Italian for root beer float?”

Another chuckle. “No. It’s supposed to be vanilla ice cream and an espresso shot. I used cold brew coffee in mine.”

“Gotcha. Hmm. I like coffee.” He glanced at her.

Did he want an invitation inside for an affogato? No. She stuffed the notebook under her arm and grabbed the doorknob. Certainly, he needed to be somewhere else?

But should she invite him in as a thank you for bringing her notebook? What was the proper etiquette rule for entertaining without furniture?

His eyes tracked over her shoulder. She stepped in front of his vision. Nope. Don't look at the empty room. "Well, thanks for bringing my book. I'd invite you in, but—"

Taking his opportunity, Sam stepped over the threshold. "Thank you." With a nod, he surveyed the room. "I like what you've done with the place. Very minimalistic. Very on-trend."

A snort escaped Merritt's mouth. "Thanks. I had help." Eyes widening, she flat-lined her lips. Her chin raised a notch.

Sam cocked his head. *Are you challenging me not to ask about your movers?* Interesting.

Trying for a casual approach, he glanced around the family room again. "So you're changing out furniture?"

"Something like that."

Hmm. A definite cool front just rolled in, sparking not-a-topic-of-conversation signals. Merritt definitely didn't want to talk about her furniture. Or lack of it. Which, of course, made his goal of the moment to talk about her furniture, by way of a back door maybe.

"Something like that? Sounds like a mystery." He grinned, making sure his dimple flashed. "Mysteries are my favorite genre. Ask me anything about the Hardy Boys. I know them all by heart."

She laughed. A real laugh with her mouth wide open. Well, her lips were parted at least. Bingo.

"All of them? There are about a hundred of those books."

"Nah. I'm talking about the real ones. The originals. I read my granddad's set."

"So you're a fan of children's books."

"This may surprise you, but I'm a fan of reading." Nodding to his left, he stuffed his hands in his pockets. "You got a nice full bookshelf over there."

Her gaze skittered to the bookshelves and then back to him. No smile.

"You must like to read too."

"Uh-huh."

"So ... is your new furniture coming soon?"

She blinked.

He waited.

Fingering the red heart necklace around her neck, she blinked again.

Hello? Was she ignoring him? *One thing you're going to find out, Miss Merritt, Sam Daniels is determined.* "The furniture. In your den. Do you have to wait long for it to be delivered?"

"I ... ah." She clenched her jaw. "I have to ..." Tossing her hair back, she pushed out a breath of air. "I'm working on buying some."

"Oh, gotcha." Awkwardness sneaked into the room. Time to make tracks. "Well, I just wanted you to get your planner."

She opened the door for him. "Seriously, Sam. I appreciate you bringing the book. You saved me time and a trip back to the church." A corner of her mouth lifted, highlighting a tiny scar branching from there.

Another question to add to the growing list about Merritt Hastings. What happened to make that scar? What happened to her furniture if she lived here with Millie? What happened to make her wary of visitors?

Or was she only wary of him?

Wanting to discover the answers to those questions kindled an interest that surprised him, but he tamped it down. Not the time for other distractions, buddy.

"Glad I could help out, Merritt. See you around."

7

Despite Merritt's initial misgivings, the cookout birthday party scored high marks for a gathering of friends. She glanced out the kitchen window and smiled at the guests congregating in the backyard. No one had complained or even asked about the lack of furniture except Eva, her former case worker. She'd accepted the explanation with an arched eyebrow.

"Truly, Eva. I'm looking forward to new furniture. I have ideas of exactly what I want. But you know what I do still have?"

Eva laughed. "You know it warms me every time you mention that card."

"It's always been special. I've kept it since my ninth birthday when you gave it to me. The first thing to go into my moving bag whenever it was time for a new family." She handed Eva a basket of chips. "Will you take this outside, please? I'll bring out the fruit tray and the card too. Go help Destiny beat Jesse and his father at ladder golf."

Jesse, a friend since fifth grade, shared a May birthday with his father.

"You don't have to bring the card out. I just love knowing it's in your memory box." Eva opened the back door and waved to

Destiny. "She put me on your team. I'll try not to make you lose!"

After weeks of turmoil with the stolen furniture, upended piano lessons, unsettling talks with the preacher, a happy time at Millie's house soothed her battered spirit. Laughing voices from the backyard prompted a grin.

Thank you, God. I needed a celebration with friends today.

Leaning over the kitchen sink, she watched the game from the window. Destiny grasped a bolo, one golf ball attached by string to another ball. Locking eyes on the plastic game ladder a few feet from her, she tossed the swinging balls through the air, trying for the string to latch onto one of the ladder rungs.

Her effort missed all three rungs and wrapped around Jesse's camp chair. A good sport, she laughed along with the rest of the players.

Merritt lifted the fruit tray and headed outside for the party.

Joining the party, Merritt laughed along with the others. "Hey, Destiny, maybe you'll have better luck with the piñata."

"Ha ha. You're real funny. You know I'm not an athlete. How 'bout you showing us how to play this game."

"I've already shown you how. We've got eight points to your two, the ones Eva scored." Jesse stood with his hands in his back pockets.

"Right. Merritt isn't an athlete either. She needs to try. Be a good host, Mer, and put your guests at ease."

With a sigh, Merritt fit the fruit tray between the condiments and basket of hamburger rolls. "Give me a bolo, and I'll show you." She squinted at the target and swung her arm back then forward, letting go of the ball with impressive force. Her bolo passed right by the ladder and knocked into a tree at the yard's edge.

"Wow. That's power." Jesse's dad clapped at her effort.

Merritt bowed, laughing along with her guests. "And don't forget it."

AT THE END of the Saturday afternoon, everyone left full of hamburgers, birthday cake, and piñata candy. Jesse's dad had swung the final blow, releasing an avalanche of gum balls, chocolate drops, hard candy, and everything in between.

Jesse and his father had loaded the foster care supplies in Eva's car. Semi-retired, she still had contacts with the Division of Social Services and always took whatever birthday guests brought in lieu of gifts to the party. This time everyone brought backpacks, drawstring bags ... any carrier more substantial than a plastic grocery bag in which foster children could pack their belongings.

The last to leave, Eva hesitated on the front porch. "These bags will be so welcome and useful, as I know you remember. Thank you."

"Of course, let me know what you'll need next time. We'll have supplies ready at the summer birthday party."

"Will do. Hey," Eva licked her lips and dropped her gaze. She pulled a brochure out of her purse. "I have something for you, but I don't want to upset you."

Too late, with an intro like that.

Bracing herself, Merritt waited for what would most probably upset her.

Eva handed the brochure to her.

HANDBOOK FOR FAMILY AND FRIENDS OF OFFENDERS

"Seriously?"

"Yes." Eva firmed her words. "Think about reaching out to your mother. She's at the Anson Correctional Institution ... about an hour's drive from Charlotte. Just think about it. Take this, and you'll have it if you need it. That's all."

Grinding her teeth, Merritt took the pamphlet with one finger and a thumb.

Eva pulled her in close. "I love you, Merritt. She does too." She backed away. "Thank you for a fun birthday party. As usual." With Merritt holding the pamphlet like a used paper cup ready for the trash can, Eva waved goodbye.

Thinking better of throwing it away in a fit of pique, Merritt dropped it into the junk drawer in the kitchen and headed toward the boxing bag Millie had hung in the garage years ago. Beating out her frustrations on that stoic bag?

Imperative, if she wanted to be able to sleep later.

8

The moderator raised the gavel and said, "If there's no more business—"

"Wait." Selma Perkins's voice halted the gavel's arc toward the podium and crushed hopes of a quick exit after the church business meeting. She rose from her pew and surveyed the congregation. "Why is Miss Hastings conducting business in our sanctuary? I've attended every business meeting for the last forty years, and we never voted on this matter."

Heads turned toward Merritt. Her heart drummed and pushed heat up her neck and into her cheeks. She had to speak. Everyone turned, expecting her reply, but what could she say? Could she give enough to satisfy without humiliating herself further?

She sucked in a breath and leaned forward.

"Mr. Moderator, may I?" Pastor Dunleavy rose from the first pew.

Nodding, Will Meyers opened the floor to the pastor.

Pastor Dunleavy sought Selma Perkins in the sanctuary and smiled. "Mrs. Perkins, we are grateful for your faithful attendance, participation, and wisdom." His eyes found Merritt. "Miss Hastings, if you don't mind, I'd like to explain."

Her fear wouldn't completely allow relief yet, but a flicker of hope helped her blink her eyes in assent.

The pastor nodded once and surveyed the crowd. "I'd planned to mention Merritt and the piano to you good folks tonight, but you beat me to the punch, Mrs. Perkins. Thank you for getting the ball rolling." He smiled at the older woman. "Friends, one of our own, Merritt Hastings, experienced a bit of a rough spot a couple of weeks ago. She had some trouble with her piano.

"Miss Hastings teaches piano out of her home. In an effort to help her provide for herself, I offered the use of our piano." He paused. "She did not ask for it."

Mrs. Perkins interrupted. "But the sanctuary piano?"

"Yes, we have other pianos in the church, but this beautiful one," he gestured toward his subject, "gets played only a couple of times a week usually. Musical instruments are meant to be played. Some of these children have never set foot inside a church. We're allowing them to come into God's house, maybe get comfortable, maybe get curious. Who knows? I do know we're helping our family member earn her living." He raised his eyebrows.

Mrs. Perkins firmed her mouth. "What about wear and tear on our building?"

"This is a temporary solution. Wear-and-tear is minimal. She has one student at a time for thirty minutes. Remember, the Girl Scouts meet in the fellowship hall weekly for no remuneration. The board of election holds voting here every two years. We have precedence for outside groups using our facilities. This time we're helping one of our own."

One of our own. Family member. Is that really how Pastor Dunleavy described her? A fluttery feeling swirled in Merritt's midsection.

Ms. Connie waved her hand. "I make a motion to let Merritt use the piano for teaching students as long as she needs it." A quick second sounded from a back pew.

The moderator tapped the gavel. "Call to order. A motion's been made and properly seconded. If there's no more discussion, we'll vote."

Little pleasure came from Merritt's bowl of ice cream after the church conference. Rotating her spoon in her hand, she contemplated her predicament.

"So, what's the big deal?" Jesse raked his spoon across his fourth scoop of homemade coffee chocolate chip ice cream. "A couple of people voted against you. So? The majority said, 'yes, come use our piano.' That's great. That's what you wanted."

"But I didn't want everybody to know. I didn't want people to have to vote for or against me." Chewing on the inside of her cheek, Merritt rubbed her heart necklace between her thumb and pointer finger.

"Churches vote on everything." Shrugging his shoulders, Jesse shoveled a loaded spoonful into his mouth.

"You're missing the point." Destiny licked her spoon. "You have a secure place to hold lessons. You can make a living. Stop dwelling on the two or three uninformed people in the crowd. J. C. didn't make everybody happy, you know." Leave it to Destiny to boil it down to the main thing.

Thank You, God, for these friends.

"I hear you. I just—"

"Wanted everyone to love you. But we know that's not possible."

The truth stung, but she didn't want to admit it. "Maybe I just want to wallow a little."

"You're wallowing a lot. What good does that do?"

"It's good for you. You get to eat my homemade ice cream."

"True that. It's delicious, as usual." Destiny scraped up the last bit of chocolate.

"Thanks. I'll get you the recipe."

"No, thanks. I just want to eat yours." Destiny pushed her bowl aside and tightened the ponytail holder on her pink hair. "So what's your exit strategy? Quit the church's piano. Get back to teaching at home." She raised her eyebrows. "Your plan?"

"I need to find a piano, the best I can afford now." Sliding her hand into her pocket, Merritt discovered the note passed to her during the business meeting. Ms. Connie had written, *Please come see me tomorrow, if possible*, and added her address. She hadn't given a time. Maybe she'd be home in the morning before her lessons began in the afternoon. She could stop by Ms. Connie's before her monthly visit to The Crossroads assisted living facility.

"Okay." Destiny slapped her thighs. "We start looking for a piano. As long as it plays, it doesn't have to be a Steinway."

"It won't be a Steinway."

"Don't put God in a box, Merritt." Leaning back in his folding chair, Jesse nudged her back to being positive with a few words.

"You're right. There's a piano out there for me. I just have to find it."

9

Placing her teacup onto the saucer, Merritt smiled at the sweet woman across from her. "Thank you so much for offering your home, Ms. Connie, but the church already voted to let me use the sanctuary's piano for lessons. You vouched for me, remember?" A vase of blue hydrangeas decorated the round table in Ms. Connie's cheerful kitchen dressed in blues and yellows.

An arched brow showed over a matching teacup. "I do remember. Thank you. I may be old, but I'm not senile." Ms. Connie lowered her cup, revealing a smile.

"No, ma'am. I didn't mean—"

"Of course, you didn't. Yes, I vouched for you. The church needed to let you use our piano, and you needed to hear them. Everyone needs to have family support."

Merritt's heart caught. Family. Yeah. Okay.

"I'm the only one playing my piano now, and it needs more attention than that. I'd love to have young people back in my house, filling it with music again."

"Some of my students are just starting out. You know what that means, I'm sure."

"Of course, I do. Plink, plink, plink. But those plinks add up, and they'll turn into beautiful music before long. I'm getting excited just thinking about it." She clapped her hands in front of her chest and giggled like a third-grader. "I'm not taking *no* because it'll break my heart if I do. Do you want that guilt on you?" Another smile escaped pursed lips.

Merritt laughed. "No, ma'am. I guess not."

"Great. What if you start next Monday afternoon? You'll have time to let your students know, right. You could send them a quick text, right?"

The octogenarian's house would be cozier than the intimidating sanctuary. It could be a good fit until she found her own piano. "Yes. I'll text them tonight."

"We better trade numbers too. Just in case we need to get in touch."

"Absolutely." Merritt bit her lip to hide a smile. The lady texted. What other talents did she possess?

SEVERAL DAYS LATER, the smell of freshly baked chocolate chip cookies wafted through the front door of Ms. Connie's craftsman-style bungalow. The aroma summoned memories of coming home from college to warm cookies shared with Millie. She squeezed her eyes shut and rapped the brass knocker.

"Well, hey, there." Ms. Connie greeted her with a quick hug before turning to the front room. "I've got your space all ready for you. A chair by the piano stool waited along with a TV tray showcasing napkins and a dessert plate of cookies.

"Ms. Connie, we can't eat in your living room."

"Well, why in the world not? A few crumbs never hurt a thing."

"Right, but we don't want crumbs falling between the keys or chocolate smeared on them. What if you give a cookie as the students leave instead?"

"Hmm. You may have a point. I'm just so excited about this adventure." She took a breath, considering. "Okay, but have one now. Your first lesson isn't for twenty-five minutes. I've got some water ready for tea too."

Despite Merritt's fear that Ms. Connie would hover and be a distraction to herself or to her students or both, she stayed well out of the way of the lessons after their quick tea party. Studying Merritt's schedule, she approved with her signature three claps. She seemed especially happy with the promise of Saturday lessons.

"That'll be perfect. Sometimes Saturdays can get to be a bit lonesome. Committees meet through the week, and Sundays have church, but not much is planned on Saturdays for my set. We have to drive that bus ourselves." She explained without a hint of self-pity.

"I'm hoping to find a piano as soon as possible, but in case the search goes longer than I expect, I usually take August off. Then we get back at it in September."

"No lessons in August. Got it. I'll enjoy you for the two months you're here. Anyway, I loved hearing the music today, even the beginning students. I'm thrilled our arrangement is working out."

"I am too. Thank you again. Now you know you don't have to bake every week, Ms. Connie. If you do, you might spoil my students and me too." Merritt grabbed her satchel and moved to the front door.

"One of the freeing things about my age is I can do just about whatever I want to do. Within reason, of course." She grinned and waved to Merritt as she walked down the driveway to her car. "See you next time. Toodle-oo."

"Great lesson, Sadie." Merritt stuck a gold star on the sheet of "Somewhere Over the Rainbow." "This one will be a good choice when we play at The Crossroads in a few weeks." The residents at the assisted living facility near the library loved for her students to play for them, and Merritt scheduled a mini-concert every other month. Cherishing the visits with young people, they didn't mind hearing replays if students didn't have a new song prepared.

"That sounded wonderful." Ms. Connie peeked in from the front hall. "I made snickerdoodles today."

"My favorite." Sadie slid off the piano stool and skipped to the cookie baker holding the plastic bag with two cookies.

"I'm partial to chocolate chips myself, but these are good too. See you next week, sweetie pie."

"Ms. Connie, you're spoiling me and every one of my students."

"Me too." Sam waltzed in, grasping half a cookie.

Her stomach seized. Why was Sam here?

"Guilty. And I love doing it." Ms. Connie lifted her shoulders and grinned. "Did that back step give you any problem?"

"No, ma'am. It's like new now, if I do say so myself." Sam popped the rest of the cookie into his mouth.

"You refused to tell me what you charge for odd jobs, so I have a roast beef in the oven just about ready. You two take turns washing up and meet me in the dining room for supper." She left humming "Somewhere Over the Rainbow."

Sam looked at Merritt. "Did she ask you to dinner?"

"No."

"Me either. Seems like it's mandatory, not an invitation, though." He shrugged. "I'm game. Smells like Heaven in here, if you ask me."

"You think Heaven smells like roast beef?"

"You got a better scent?"

Merritt laughed. "Roses. Baking bread. Freshly mowed grass," She shrugged. "I guess a roast works too." *Ms. Connie, you're a piece of work. You just pull people along into your plans. No questions, just come on along.*

Was Sam right? Did she have to stay?

Well, why not? Tucking the sheet of star stickers into her appointment book, she stood. “So ... we’re staying?”

10

The remainder of Sam's day just took an upturn. "A free meal that smells like Heaven? You know I'm staying." He gestured toward the back hall leading to the powder room. "Ladies first."

Following the enticing aroma to the kitchen, he found Ms. Connie with one foot on a step stool. "Whoa, whoa, whoa. What do you need? I can get it for you."

"I can too." Stubbornness added a punch to the woman's words.

Offering his hand, he helped her steady herself. "I'm sure you can, but let me be a blessing, Ms. Connie, as church folk say."

She planted both feet on the floor and pointed to the topmost platter on the highest shelf. Stretching beside her, he reached for the platter.

Shaking her head, she grinned. "You're as smooth as silk, young man. How do the girls stand it?"

"Well, I'm sure I don't know. Maybe we should ask somebody. Hey, let's ask Merritt."

"Ask me what?" Merritt waited at the threshold of the kitchen.

"Ms. Connie wonders how all the girls can stand my smooth-as-silk charm and debonair ways."

Merritt laughed with wide-open-mouth abandonment that raced Sam's heart. "So much to unpack in that statement."

"Sam Daniels, you surely must have kissed the Blarney Stone over in Ireland."

"Not yet, Ms. Connie, but it's surely on my bucket list."

"Oh, my stars. Asking you two to dinner is the best idea I've had since opening up my home to your piano students. Here're the plates. Be another blessing and set the table, Sam.

"Merritt, slice this tomato for the platter. My late husband bought it for me when we took a trip to see the Biltmore House for our twentieth anniversary. Have you ever been? We stayed in a cozy cottage over in Little Switzerland and shopped in every antique store we could find. I nabbed this beautiful platter that weekend, and it's been my favorite ever since."

The three carried on with laughing banter through the whole meal, and Ms. Connie shared stories of her courtship with her husband. If Merritt found the conversation suspiciously leaning toward matchmaking, she did a good job hiding any discomfort.

"Now for dessert." Ms. Connie rose and headed toward her refrigerator.

"Ms. Connie, you made me eat three servings of your delicious roast. I don't know—"

Merritt snorted. "Made you?"

"Rest a minute. Let your food settle, but you have to try this pie. It's my favorite. I've had this recipe since I flirted it off a cook in Atlantic Beach, back when I was singing with my girls." She set a lemon pie dolloped with whipped cream around the edge in front of them. "I love lemon pie but not with meringue." Ms. Connie wrinkled her nose. "Nope. I don't like that stuff in my mouth. Boiled egg whites, either."

"Wait a minute. You flirted it off a cook, and you sang with your girls. Your daughters?" Merritt folded her arms on the table.

"Oh, my stars. No. This was before I married. When I sang alto in the Wee Warblers."

Sam signaled a surrender pose. "Cut me a small slice, please, and do tell. You've got more stories than the Empire State Building."

"Oh, Sam. I've just lived a life, hon." Standing over the table, Ms. Connie sliced three wedges in the pie.

"The Wee Warblers?" With one hand, he motioned for her to continue; with the other, he dug into his lemon triangle.

"There were four of us, all with last names that began with W—Watson, Williams, Wellons, and Walker. We loved the alliteration of our names and the group name. We thought we were cool, cool, cool." She nodded. "Yes, we used that word way back then."

Merritt forked the tip of her pie, raking it through the whipped cream. "So you sang with a group at the beach?"

"We sang all over for about a year. We started at WBEL in Belmont. It's an AM station. You're probably not familiar with it." Ms. Connie pulled a saucer with a tiny sliver of creamy yellow in front of her.

Sam's head cocked sideways. "I know it well. In fact, I want to buy it." His insides seizing, he stole a glance at Merritt to gauge her reaction.

Why did that secret slip out of his mouth?

MERRITT MET Sam's glance and smiled, hiding surprise at his statement. Memories of his announcements over the PA system in high school deepened the smile.

Owning a radio station, huh? Sounded about right.

"Well, aren't you full of surprises, Sam?" Ms. Connie plopped a spoonful of extra whipped cream on top of her dessert.

"No, ma'am. You got me beat, hands down. Did you travel when you sang?"

"We sang on the radio mostly. During our busiest time, we sang every weekend. We'd get invitations to come and sing from the mountains to the coast. We had a church song list and a dance hall playlist. When we sang in the dance halls, one of our daddies would come with us and sit at the back."

"How old were you?" Merritt licked her lips, tasting a dab of whip cream. Intercepting Sam's stare, she blotted her mouth with her napkin.

"Oh, I was seventeen. I think the oldest was nineteen." Readjusting her glasses higher on her nose, Ms. Connie gazed toward the window for a moment, lost in thought. "Then we started getting engaged and married. It was a hoot while it lasted, but then we had other chapters to write."

"You didn't want to make a career of singing?" Sam focused on their host again.

"Not one bit. I wanted to have a family. Don't get me wrong, I loved singing to a crowd singing along with us or dancing around the polished floor, but I had different aspirations. I wanted to be a momma, and now I'm a great-grandmother. Goodness!" She looked at Sam. "Tell me about your radio station. I bet it's changed a lot since we sang in the booth."

"Well, first off, it's not mine yet." He cocked an eyebrow. "I just got a great idea. Why don't you come with me to see it sometime? You can check it out and tell me what you think. I'll see about setting up a time."

She clapped three times. "Yes, I will," she swung her gaze to Merritt, "but only if you come too. You be our chaperone. Or I'll be yours." She threw her head back with a guffaw that didn't match her church lady façade. "This is the cherry on top of my outstanding evening. I can't wait to see the station again. Let me know what time you'll pick me up."

11

The last chords of "In My Life" hung in the air, mingling with the tantalizing aroma of lasagna, the signature dish at the Lamplighter. Merritt arched her back and chose the sheet music for "As Time Goes By" as her next selection.

Stretching her fingers over the smooth keys, she began the piece and considered asking for a to-go carton of Chef Luca's lasagna. Homemade noodles, homemade red sauce, and homemade ricotta. Locally sourced beef and herbs from the restaurant's herb garden. No wonder the lasagna was so popular.

Yep, a portion would taste great for lunch tomorrow. Keeping the rhythm, she nodded in response to the good idea.

In fairness to the chef, people raved about all his dishes. His wife's desserts usually left in boxes with stuffed diners who didn't want to miss the homemade *tiramisu* or *panna cotta*.

Millie had been a faithful supporter from the first week of Luca's opening. She'd dined weekly, sometimes twice a week, bringing someone new to try the 'best Italian food I've eaten since Florence.' Luca had good-naturedly given Merritt a piano audition at Millie's prompting. Impressed with her range of titles, he added her to the substitute pianist rotation. Merritt occasionally played during college, securing his confidence.

Playing contemporary favorites mixed with perennial classics, Merritt had won devoted fans. 'Have something for everyone' had been Millie's advice. As soon as he could, Luca brought her on board as one of the regular dinner pianists. The deal included an hourly stipend, tips, and a to-go meal. She played several times a month, filled in for other musicians, and played at private parties. A great supplement to her teaching income.

Her fingers found the familiar keys without much concentration, the sheet music in place for insurance. Another memory of Millie's help in her life warmed her insides. She glanced from the music to the hostess station, and the smile froze on her lips.

Sam, waiting to be seated, locked eyes with her. Sam, standing beside a blond, smiled back at her. Sam, with his hand at the blonde's elbow, was on a date while she played for her supper.

Yes, sir. Comfort food in the form of Luca's to-die-for lasagna would definitely be the take-home menu choice.

THE HOSTESS SAID SOMETHING TO ... wait ...

What's her name? What's her name? Pia. Right.

Sam sucked in a breath to settle his insides. Man, seeing Merritt at the piano and then forgetting his date's name. Enough to crank up the blood pressure, for sure.

His date. Right. The next time Josie roped him into helping with her library, it better be for a 5K or a golf tournament or something besides a bachelor bid. He cringed at the memory of standing in front of a crowd of rowdy women flashing placards with dollar signs.

'It'll be fun,' she said. 'It's for a good cause,' she said. Right.

"Sam."

He blinked. Both the hostess and Pia faced him, waiting. "This way, please." The hostess led them right in front of Merritt, whose eyes were focused on the keyboard. Maybe he could say hello later.

He ran his finger around the collar of his button-down. This Pia was a bossy piece of work already. Beautiful but bossy. 'You're wearing the suit you wore for the auction, right?' 'We're going to the Lamplighter, right?' On the surface, these questions sounded like suggestions, but from her, they sounded like a heavy-duty request. Would she order his dinner, too? 'You'll have the sirloin tip steak, right?'

"This place is just as great as I've heard. No wonder it took months to get a table." Pia took a picture of the centerpiece. She'd already taken four selfies since he picked her up, directing each pose like a pro.

"Hey, tag the library in your pictures. My sister'll appreciate it."

"Oh, right. You're Josie's brother."

"Actually, she's my sister." No response from Pia, busy tapping on her phone. Not like the half-smile he earned from Merritt with the same weak joke.

The final notes of "As Time Goes By" slowed and faded, and Merritt began a new song. He peeked over Pia's shoulder to watch Merritt sway with the rhythm. Her face, angled toward the keyboard, showed peaceful ... determination tinged with ... sadness?

Comprised of big rolling chords, the piece—he couldn't place the name—created a mournful response in his chest, making him miss his parents. Shaking off the feeling, he concentrated instead on her face. The quiet countenance, the hooded eyes, her just-parted lips, tendrils of hair framing her cheeks ... all of it combined to give her an other-world presence. She played for the diners, yet she seemed removed from the room.

THE LASAGNA COOLED in the refrigerator, waiting for noon tomorrow.

Right now, Merritt needed serious comfort food. She opened the freezer, snatched a pint-sized Tupperware container, and popped the lid. Mint chocolate chip ice cream. Millie's recipe for homemade mint chocolate chip.

Merritt's first attempt at recreating Millie's ambrosia-like frozen delight missed the mark but ran a close second. She grabbed a soup spoon and headed for the den, swallowing the first spoonful on the way. Stopped short when she saw the half-empty room. The two wing-back chairs she'd procured from a local online yard sale didn't offer the comfort she needed.

She veered toward her bedroom and flopped onto her mattress.

Tonight had been surreal, playing while Sam shared a meal with a gorgeous blond woman in a beautiful form-fitting dress. Humoring herself during the date, she played a set of some of Millie's favorites, beginning with "The Impossible Dream." Playing vintage songs like "*Que Sera, Sera*" and "In My Own Little Corner" amused her.

Those old songs didn't get requested much these days, but she loved playing them anyway, pretending to send out secret messages. Tonight, the songs provided entertainment as well as reminding her to cool it with the daydreams of Sam.

Three more quick spoonfuls and pain cracked through her head. She pressed her tongue against the roof of her mouth to assuage the searing ache in her brain.

Slow down, Merritt. You have plenty of time. Enjoy the taste.

You don't have to share the ice cream with anyone. It's all yours.

12

A silver metal tower rose over the square-brick building, signaling the Belmont radio station. Biting her lip to control the adrenalin pumping through her body, Merritt found her heart necklace and squeezed.

Radio stations had always been her secret getaway from the chaos in the houses she lived in. While her foster parents' real children wanted only iPods or computer games, she'd treasured the forgotten radios. Turning to the lowest volume setting after bedtime, she could listen to all kinds of music from any place broadcasting a strong signal.

"Oh, my word. That tower looks like it could be a danger to planes. So much taller than I remember. But the building looks exactly the same, on the outside at least." Ms. Connie fiddled with her seat belt until Sam helped unbuckle it.

"Earl Lange increased the wattage back in the nineties and made some other improvements. Come on. Let's go in." He held Ms. Connie's elbow as they made their way to the glass front door, glancing at Merritt with a wide grin.

A tingle tripped up her spine.

Oh, that dimple.

A middle-aged receptionist greeted them as they entered the

building. "Sam Daniels. When I saw your name on Mr. Earl's calendar this morning, I said to myself, 'Self, it's going to be a good day.'"

"Well, thank you, Ms. Judy."

A man whose head just missed grazing the door frame joined them in the front office. Ceiling-leaning white hair edged his face, bringing to mind Albert Einstein. His welcoming smile revealed a slight gap between his two front teeth.

"Hey ho, Sam. So good to see you. And you brought these beautiful women with you. One look at me, and you know I'm in the right business." He hooked his thumb toward his chest. "The perfect face for radio, right?" His Adam's apple bobbed in time with his words. "Ladies, glad to have you visit our station."

Sam rubbed the side of his nose and made introductions. "They were looking forward to coming. Ms. Connie used to sing from here back in the day."

Mr. Earl's smile stuttered for an instant as he gazed at Ms. Connie. "Is that right?" He peered more closely at the tiny woman. "Are you one of the Wee Warblers?"

"I am indeed. I wondered if you'd recognize me, Earl. It's been a long time. Life seems to have treated you well."

Nodding, he folded his arms in front of him. "I've had my hills and ditches like everybody else, but I can't complain except lately. It's my Louise. She's got cancer." He whispered the last word. "It's not looking good."

"So sorry to hear your news. I suppose that's why you're wanting to sell to Sam."

"Thank you." He passed his hand across his chin, regrouping. "We'll take a tour of the station before you leave. We've got some snazzy equipment now, to be sure."

"Of course. Your daddy always kept up with the industry way back when. I'm sure you've carried on his business savvy."

"Well, I don't know about that. I do know he wanted you girls to keep singing. He was willing to back you too, but ..."

Ms. Connie nodded. "I know, but we just wanted to go home and start our real lives. It was fun while it lasted."

The two senior citizens traded news from the past decades for the next few minutes, and Merritt took in the black and white pictures lining the hallway.

"Look at all these famous people. There's the governor from back in the day." Ms. Connie tapped the frame featuring Terry Sanford. "Oh, look. My favorite baseball player, Catfish Hunter. Your daddy used to interview politicians, ball players, singers. Anybody with a good story. All these signed pictures tell the tale."

They moved down the hall, and Ms. Connie pointed to one near Mr. Earl's shoulder. "There we are. Barbara, Linda, Peggy, and me."

Stepping forward, Merritt got a better view. "Yes, look at your outfits. How cool. I guess you had to use some serious mousse and hair spray to get those swoops and curls to hold."

"Dippity Do worked really fine." Ms. Connie touched her cheek with her hand. "Oh, I haven't thought about that stuff in a long time." She rose on her tiptoes to gaze at the picture.

"Well, ladies," Mr. Earl glanced at Sam and gestured toward the back hall. "Let's go sit in my office and talk."

"Ah, Mr. Earl, these ladies came to see the station. Could they keep looking at the pictures for a few minutes?"

"Oh, I thought they were your investors."

Slack-jawed, both women swiveled to Sam.

Red rising in Sam's cheeks, he shook his head. "Nope. No, sir."

"We'll wait for you right out here. I want to find some more pictures of the Wee Warblers." Merritt hooked her arm through Ms. Connie's and stepped away from Mr. Earl's office door.

Silently thanking Merritt for taking control of the awkward situation, Sam held his breath and prepared himself for the impending conversation.

Earl dropped into the office chair behind a desk laden with loose papers, files, a bottle of Cheerwine soda, and an opened package of peanut butter crackers. Signed pictures of people holding guitars and banjos and microphones covered all four walls in his cramped office.

Motioning for Sam to take a seat, Mr. Earl rolled himself closer to the desk and clasped his hands on top. Eyes on the pack of crackers, he avoided Sam's gaze.

"Sam, I'm glad you came today. I've been trying to figure out how to tell you." He worked his jaw. "I've had an offer for twenty thousand over asking price."

Icy fingers gripped his insides, freezing trails all the way to his fingers. "Twenty thousand?"

"I couldn't believe it myself. We're small, but we've got a solid community of retail sponsors here. We're still a viable little station." He glanced at Sam and sighed. "I want to sell to you, buddy. I've known you since you were fifteen." Earl scratched the back of his head.

"Remember the first night you manned the evening shift by yourself? When you realized you'd allowed ten minutes of silence, you talked for the next twenty non-stop. Thirty minutes with not one note of music, but the people listening loved your jokes. Loved you."

Heat took over where the chill left off and climbed up his neck at the mention of one of the most embarrassing moments of his life. This one right now could probably be called the most devastating so far.

"Sir."

Mr. Earl rose from his chair, knocking his knuckles on the desktop. "That's a lot of money, son. We've got insurance but not the right kind. I want to take care of Louise at home. The buyer wants me to tell him something by the end of next week."

"Yes, sir." Sam shuddered.

"Hate to drop that on you now, but I wanted you to know. I know we talked about you ... I just ..." Mr. Earl shook his head.

"You're between a rock and a hard place, Mr. Earl." He should offer some sort of social platitude right now, but breathing took all his willpower, that and not smashing his fist in the wall. "Let's catch up with the ladies."

Nodding, Earl stood and exited the office. Sam leaned against the door jamb, hoping the solid wood might fortify him. He glanced down the hallway toward the group of three. Earl, already talking with the women, motioned around the corner to the control room. Connie proceeded with him, but Merritt waited for Sam.

Reaching for his arm, Merritt delayed him. "Are you okay?"

"Sure." He smiled but didn't meet her eyes.

"I don't believe you."

Chuckling, he scrubbed his jaw. "I, um, I just had a dream deferred, I think. My legs have just been knocked out from under me, so to speak." He blew out a breath. "He's had an offer for twenty thousand over his asking price. I didn't have the original amount, and I sure don't have an extra twenty K.

"We were supposed to hammer out a deal for me to work toward owning it." His throat worked as he turned from her. He nodded down the hallway. "Come on. Let's catch up."

Pointing through the on-air studio window at the afternoon D.J., Earl said something to Connie, then addressed Sam. "We hope you two stopped for a quick kiss back there." He showed the gap in his front teeth.

Ms. Connie clapped her hands. "I couldn't have said it better myself."

Red stain now colored Merritt's neck. She wrapped her arms around her waist.

"No, sir." Putting forth a weak laugh, Sam headed toward the other couple. "We were talking business."

Shaking his head, Earl tsked. "Wasted opportunity."

SMOOTHING the hem of her yellow window-paned skirt, Merritt crossed her ankles in the front seat of Sam's car.

"Hey. I'm sorry about Mr. Earl's comment." A cheeky grin playing around his mouth, Sam checked the rear-view mirror as they drove to her house.

In the time it had taken to finish the station tour and drop off Ms. Connie, he had shaken off the outward effects of the dream-busting announcement. Traces of the normal, teasing Sam were surfacing. Of course, he'd tease about Mr. Earl's suggestion.

"Which one?" She feigned innocence.

As the grin faded, Sam narrowed his eyes. "The kissing one."

"Oh, no worries."

"Judging by the color on your neck when he said it, I thought you might have been uncomfortable."

"If I blushed, it was because he caught me off guard, that's all."

"So kissing doesn't make you uncomfortable."

"Of course not. I'm a normal human being." Tugging the seatbelt away from her chest, she shifted in place.

"Maybe we should test the theory that you're not uncomfortable with kissing." The grin showed again.

She ignored the slight uptick in her heart rate, wrapping her purse straps around her hand. *Slow down, heart. Sam is being his teasing self.* "Thanks, but no thanks."

"Man. I thought you might want to console me a bit. You know, the part about a dream deferred and all that."

"I'll be glad to talk with you through the disappointment, listen to your woes, suggest some wisdom ..."

"Not your type, huh?"

"Exactly." Loosening the grip on the straps, she concentrated on the houses passing by her window.

"You don't like cute guys with buff arms and a sparkling

personality?" Releasing the steering wheel, he flexed his right bicep.

A laugh escaped before she could stop it.

"You're killing me, smalls." He turned onto Clover Street, the fabric of his heather green T-shirt stretching over those buff arms.

A picture of him dressed in his suit at the Lamplighter flashed through her mind.

Right, the date.

"My type is guys without girlfriends."

Sam slammed on the brakes, did a quick glance in the rearview mirror. "What?"

Lurching forward, she palmed the dashboard.

Releasing the brake, he proceeded down the street. "Sorry. But, seriously, Merritt. I don't—" At her raised eyebrow, his mouth dropped open. "Oh."

"Uh-huh." She repositioned her seatbelt. "You took your girlfriend to the Lamplighter."

"Right, but she isn't my girlfriend."

"Maybe not yet."

"Not ever. But seeing as you brought it up—"

"It really doesn't matter." She lifted her chin and counted blue hydrangea bushes in neighbors' yards.

"But you mentioned it, so I'll explain. You saw me fulfilling my end of a fundraiser for the library. For my sister."

Laughing outright, she hoped to squash the relief she had no business feeling. "You were in the bachelor auction?"

"I did my part to help my sister and my community."

"Right."

Just two houses from her driveway, a groan broke free before she could corral it.

"What's up?" Frowning, he split his gaze between her and her house as they approached. "You got company."

"Yes." She began her calming breathing exercise. "Hey, I enjoyed meeting Earl Lange. Thanks for the invitation. Ms. Connie had a ball too." She cracked open the door before Sam put the car in park. "You don't need to walk me to the door. I'll get out here. See ya."

Please leave, Sam. I can't deal with you and them too."

"Wait a minute."

SOMETHING WAS GOING on with Merritt. Her face paled when she saw the two people on her front porch. Her breathing had become slow and exaggerated.

"I'd love to meet your friends." Sam's words hit the passenger side door as she slammed it. Which fueled his interest in the people waiting for her.

"You're back. Finally." The guy at the front steps made a show of checking the watch on his wrist. "I emailed we needed pictures to put on the website."

"I didn't get an email." Merritt circled her waist with her arms.

"Well, I sent it." He rapped on the front door. "Come on. Open up. We need to get pictures up ASAP."

"This is my house, not yours."

"It's just a matter of time, Merritt." Cradling a camera in her arms, the woman fiddled with the snap closure. "We want to get a jump on this seller's market."

"You can't come in. Today isn't a good day."

Sam joined Merritt, a hand on the small of her back. "I think you heard the lady. No pictures today."

"Who are you?" Jutting his chin toward Sam, the man widened his stance.

Sam pulled his phone from his pocket. "Someone who's about to call the police to report trespassers before I put a call into Merritt's lawyer. That's who I am."

"Merritt has a lawyer?"

"I have one more number to tap before it starts ringing. Are you leaving, or do I give this address to the dispatcher?"

Hands on his hips, the man worked his jaw.

The woman swung her gaze from the man back to Merritt. "We'll leave now, but you are not going to win, Merritt. This house is rightfully ours as Aunt Mildred's only biological heirs." She tugged the man's arm and headed for their car.

"I'll move my car." Sam slid his phone into his pocket. "Merritt, I'll be back in just a minute." Steel undergirded his words.

By the time he'd allowed the couple out of the driveway and parked again, Merritt had entered her house and closed the door. *We're not done with today yet, Merritt.* He knocked on the front door. "I'm back."

She opened the door a crack. "Thanks again for the station visit."

"You already said that. We need to talk about other stuff. Do we talk here, or can I come in?"

"There's nothing to say, and I'm sure you need to get going."

"I'm free as a bird, as they say." He glanced at her hand on the knob. *That's how it's going to be, huh?* "So who were those two Welcome Wagon rejects?"

"Sam—"

"I may have misread your discomfort at the radio station, but I'm pretty sure I got it right now. You're breathing funny. You were stiff as a board out there. Your face has no color at all. What's going on?"

She sighed and swung the door back. "Fine."

He stepped inside. The front room had two chairs and a side table, new additions since the day he'd brought her appointment book to her.

"We can sit in the kitchen or in here." Her rigid jaw jutted forward.

"Lady's choice."

"The table."

He followed her into the kitchen, lit with the fading light of a summer's day. "Nice view. Your backyard's great."

"Would you like—"

"You don't have to play hostess, Merritt. Who were those people?"

Running the tip of her tongue over her top lip, she kept her focus on the table. "Trey and Allison Billings. They're Millie's great-niece and nephew." She pulled a cloth napkin out of a crystal napkin ring and began rolling it up like a cigar.

Sam nodded. "Okay. They want this house, but Millie left it to you, I'm guessing."

"You've figured it out in a nutshell." Unrolling the napkin, she began pleating it like a fan.

"If she left it to you, what's the problem?"

"They don't think the will is valid. Millie was kind of a free spirit. She wrote it up in longhand and then had it notarized. They're fighting it."

Reaching over the table, he freed the napkin and set it aside. "So, how are you fighting back?"

"I haven't had a chance to look into fighting back. I've been securing a place for my lessons, my livelihood. I guess I was hoping they'd let it go. But I know that's a silly pie-in-the-sky way to think." She glanced around the room. "That's why we're sitting at a card table on folding chairs. They swooped in and cleaned out the house."

"That's what happened to your furniture? They stole it?"

"They called it taking what's rightfully theirs." Pressing her lips together, she stared out the bay window into the backyard. "I hadn't heard from them in a while. I was kinda hoping ..."

"That maybe they'd changed their minds?" Sam shook his head. "They seem like the determined kind. I think you need a game plan, Merritt."

13

The rabbit that lived at the edge of the backyard hopped out of the butterfly bush and sat still, watching the house. This view had always calmed Merritt, brought her peace like no other place she knew. Knowing the house was her safe haven, Millie promised it would remain hers.

"I liked the game plan I had in May."

"What was that?" Sam threaded the napkin back through the crystal ring.

"Live here and teach piano lessons."

"And then what?"

"What do you mean?"

"What else do you want to do? Other aspirations for your life?"

She frowned. "What's wrong with my life?" Hackles rising, she mentally cataloged her life—working for herself with nice, upstanding families who respected her, owning her own home, friends who had her back. Yes, she had a life anyone could be proud of ... at least for the time being.

"Nothing, but I think you have more plans than that. You play at the Lamplighter. You like performing."

She turned her head away, heart beating a crazy rhythm. She played at the Lamplighter and weddings for extra money, not because she liked performing. Performing was a means to an end, keeping her house, her safe space. The sparkly life of performing held no interest for her.

"Yep. I know I'm right." Sam nodded, a satisfied smile lighting his face. "Listen. I know a guy who might be able to help. My sister's boyfriend, Ches, is a lawyer. We'll see what he says."

"Wait a minute. There is no *we* here. I appreciate you want to help, but I can handle this problem." As she always did.

"Like you've done so far?"

Merritt snorted. "Excuse me?"

"I thought I did a pretty good job of sending them on down the road a while ago. You're welcome, by the way."

As much as Merritt hated to admit it, he was right. And she also didn't want to admit that having someone else push back against Trey and Allison felt nice. Sam could have left when he dropped her off. He had his own wounds to lick, but he'd stayed to fight for her, defended her without knowing the full story.

Millie had always supported and shielded her. Lately, Ms. Connie stepped into that role, and now Sam ... Warmth filled her chest.

Dipping her chin, she conceded. "You're right. Thank you." She chuckled. "I admit I liked the shock on Trey's face when you mentioned my lawyer."

"I'm supposed to see Ches soon. I'll find out what he thinks."

Merritt sighed. "Thanks for getting rid of Trey and Allison, but you don't have to stay involved. I'll figure something out."

"Asking Ches is no big deal." Studying her face, he smiled. "You're getting some color back. Good. For a minute, I thought you might keel over or something." Sam leaned back in his chair and stretched his long legs in front of him. "What if we change the subject? I'm kinda wondering again about your type. I think you were about to describe it when we drove up to your house a while ago."

SHOCK BROUGHT MORE color into her cheeks. Good job. Sam glanced at his phone. "Hey, what say I order a pizza and continue this conversation over a few slices?"

Merritt opened her mouth to speak, but the doorbell rang, followed by two people bursting through the front door.

"We're here. Time to eat. Who's hungry for fried chicken and mashed potatoes?"

Seeing Sam sitting with Merritt at the table, they stopped full tilt at the kitchen's threshold. The man carrying a large bag emblazoned with a fast-food logo bumped into the woman who carried two smaller ones.

"Oops. Sorry for busting in, but it's Thursday Night-Game Night." Her dark hair dyed blue at the ends, the woman waved at Merritt but kept her eyes on the interloper.

Sam sat upright in his seat. Merritt rose to take the food from the man dressed in black jeans and a Harley Davidson T-shirt. He, too, had dark hair, but pulled back into a shoulder-length ponytail.

"Hey, man." Stretching out his right hand, the man approached Sam. "Jesse."

"Sam."

"Hey, Sam. I'm Destiny." The woman eyed him up and down.

Please let me pass whatever test she's giving.

"Nice to meet both of you." Mentally crossing his fingers, he hoped for a dinner invitation. Getting to know Merritt's friends could prove invaluable, and spending more time with her? The extra shot of espresso in his coffee. Plus, going home to brood about the radio station had zero appeal.

"Good thing we got the family-sized special. It was two

dollars off this week. I hope you like chicken." Destiny, glancing at Sam, set her bags on the counter.

Raising his eyebrows, Sam summoned his dimple in hopes it would secure an invitation. Merritt hadn't spoken since the two had entered. Since he'd asked about her type again, actually. Maybe he should just go with Destiny's assumption that he was staying.

"I love fried chicken, especially with mashed potatoes." Volleying the loaded statement, he held his breath and waited.

"They're Merritt's favorite too. She eats them at least once a week, especially if she's stressed."

"Perfect for today then." He bunted that comment to see what would happen. "Where're the plates? I can set the table."

"What happened today?" Opening a cabinet, Jesse pointed to the plates.

If looks could kill.

Merritt opened another cabinet for glasses. "Trey and Allison stopped by, but no harm. No foul."

Jesse muttered under his breath.

"So what happens next?" Rearranging the items on the tabletop, Destiny placed the box of chicken in the middle.

Sam grinned. "Funny you ask that. We were just discussing her game plan. That and what her aspirations are."

Hiding behind the freezer door, Merritt filled four glasses with ice.

"Oh, did she tell you about her songs?"

"Her songs?" Sam forced his eyes to stay on Destiny. Didn't want to experience any more death daggers coming from the lady of the house. "No. She talked about her students."

Merritt moved around the kitchen, grabbing serving spoons and a pitcher of water, ignoring the conversation.

"She writes music." Avoiding eye contact with Merritt, Destiny flicked a quick look at Jesse.

Dealing the napkins out like cards, Sam stilled, his gaze flying to Merritt. "Wow—"

"Okay. I'm right here, people. Let's give it a rest. Everything's ready. Let's eat before it gets cold."

Sam narrowed his eyes. *Fine. Table this discussion for now, but we'll get back to it. And to your type too, Merritt.* Those thoughts, along with the impromptu invitation to dinner, prompted a satisfied smile.

Looking forward to it, Merritt.

14

Somehow the dinner conversation covered everything but her house and her aspirations. *Thank You, God.* The good-natured talk spilled over into the game of Outburst after dinner. Sam fit in well with Destiny and Jesse. An interesting, quick thought, but not one for Merritt to dwell on for long. A nice impromptu evening but not likely to happen again.

Destiny closed the lid on the game box. "I need to peace out. I've got an early dye job and cut tomorrow."

"I'm shoving off too." Offering his hand, Jesse pulled Destiny from the floor.

"Hey, we do this every Thursday night, Sam. Come back next week if you want to lose again." Destiny's wicked grin stretched across her face.

"Don't you mean if you want me to show you how it's done?"

"You've got swagger. I'll give you that, especially after you lost every round tonight." Jesse nodded with a friendly smirk.

"I've been told that's one of my strengths. Swagger, not losing." Unfolding himself from his floor pillow, Sam stood and stretched.

The three burst out laughing.

A lightness swirled around Merritt's chest and dispelled the last twinges of dread Trey and Allison had worked earlier in the evening. Laughter and food and fun ... the house had missed these essentials for weeks. She had too. Tonight happened without a real dining room or kitchen table. They'd shared food on a wobbly card table. They'd sprawled on the den floor to play the game, the guys enjoying having room to spread out.

The group moved to the foyer, but no one opened the door to leave.

Merritt took a deep breath. "Hey, thanks, everybody. I needed tonight more than usual."

"Glad to be of service. You know you can always count on us, Mer." Destiny hugged her.

After a couple of awkward moments of silence, Destiny flashed a peace sign and pushed open the glass storm door. Jesse followed with a "See ya."

Shifting his posture, Sam stuck his hands in his pockets. "Interesting couple."

"They're not a couple." Merritt leaned against the door jamb.

"They may not be now, but they want to be."

"And you know that how? You met them two hours ago."

"Yep. Plenty long enough to pick up on the vibes between those two."

Merritt refused to confess she agreed with him. Sam didn't need fuel to stoke his hearty ego. She'd always wondered about a mutual attraction between the two, but their timing never synced. They'd either been involved with other people or going through bad breakups.

"I guess time will tell."

"Known them long?"

"Destiny and I were foster sisters for about eight months when we were ten. We kept up with each other at school once we were separated. Jesse was in my homeroom in fifth grade."

Nodding, Sam focused on her words. "Gotcha." He waited for more in vain. "Well, I guess I'll call it a day, too, unless you want to finish the conversation about your type now."

Merritt covered her mouth for a fake yawn. "Not really feeling it."

"Another time then."

Her heart squeezed with the thought of more time with Sam. Would he keep pressing her on her type, though? Why? Just being nosy? Just teasing her? What about that girl from the Lamplighter?

Stop, brain, thinking about Sam and his possible girlfriend. But could she be more than a library obligation?

Stop, heart, doing that squeezing thing. Falling for Sam is not in the plan.

Moving toward the door, he turned back toward her. "Tonight was fun, Merritt. Thanks for letting me be part of it." He held her gaze for ... how long?

She couldn't think about time while his hazel eyes demanded all her attention. Reflecting his lapis-colored shirt tonight, they looked as blue as some of Millie's Italian pottery.

Stop, eyes. Stop staring into his. Nothing good will come of it. He has at least one sister, maybe others. Families and you don't work well.

Breaking eye contact, she glanced out the front door as if she were checking the weather or looking for a Girl Scout selling cookies.

"You're welcome."

"They invited me to come again." Shrugging, he raised his eyebrows. "But it's your house."

"We have a standing date on Thursday nights unless work happens. Then we pivot. It's usually takeout, but sometimes, if I'm feeling it, I'll cook something or make a dessert at least." She shrugged back, pretending nonchalance but hoping he'd come again. "Sure, if you'd like takeout and a board game, come join."

"I appreciate the invitation, and you can bet I will."

Despite early admonishments for her heart to remain neutral and her eyes to stop gazing, her lips lifted of their own accord at the thought of another night like this one. Sam's dimple rewarded that breach of will, and her heart squeezed again, rebelling too.

WATER DROPLETS from the steamy bath clinging to her, Merritt wrapped herself in a plush, yellow towel. The baths, the thick towels, even the color yellow were all perks that added deep pleasure to her life as an adult.

Her favorite color, yellow, deemed unpractical in her childhood because it showed dirt, appeared throughout the house now. Padding into her bedroom, she checked her phone. A text from Sam ramped up her heart rate.

Athlete?

Huh? Did he send her someone else's text?

I'm sorry. What?

Your type. Athlete?

Athletes are fine.

Just fine, huh. Okay. Musician?

Of course musicians are good.

Good, huh? How about brainyacs.

Is that how you spell it?

Spell check didn't give me another option.

Seriously? You think I'd like dummies?

So, smart dudes?

She texted a laughing emoji.

Let me see here. I'm working up a profile.

So far I check all the boxes, just FYI.

Sam ticked off lots of boxes, but his self-esteem didn't need her to confirm it.

You want to talk about this with texts?

In person is even better. How about a date?

You're asking me on a date with a text?

Good point. How about we talk at Ms. Connie's?

Maybe Tuesday?

Sure. I have lessons till six.

Great. See you then.

Smiling to herself, Merritt waited a few minutes to see if another text came through just in case before turning the phone to airplane mode. This new course in their friendship ... spending time together, teasing each other, texting ... made her spirits float. She could get used to it in a hurry, which is exactly why she shouldn't get used to Sam or how he made her feel.

She glided to her bedroom, wavering between wanting more time with Sam and anticipating the crash and burn.

SAM WOKE up in a cold sweat and groaned. His heart beat out a sick rhythm from the nightmare, but the nightmare, unfortunately, was real. He rolled onto his side and checked his phone. Eleven fifteen. He'd been asleep for only forty-five minutes.

His jaw ached. Grinding his teeth again. Maybe some milk would help. He trudged to the kitchen and blinked at the bright light bouncing off every angle. Heath, still awake, sat at the kitchen table with his laptop.

"Hey, Sleeping Beauty. What's up? You said you were calling it an hour ago." Heath typed a few keys, then closed the computer. "Hey, man. Really. What's the matter?"

Shielding his squinting eyes with one hand, Sam extended his other in front of him. "Do we need all these lights? They're blinding me."

"Why, yes, I do. I was checking the books, remember? Trying to pay a few bills." Heath considered his brother. "You must have had a nightmare, little bro. You haven't slept long enough to get up on the wrong side of the bed."

"What's it to you?" Sam hunted in the refrigerator for the milk jug.

"Clearly something's got your shorts in a wad. Wanna talk about it?" Heath leaned against the ladder-back chair.

Sam poured milk into an empty pint jar. "Want some?"

"Glad to see you still have manners." But Heath shook his head. "What's going on?"

Sam sat at the table with his head in his hands. "The radio station. The bank." He blew out a long stream of breath.

Frowning, Heath folded his arms across his chest. "Radio station?"

Tell him. He'd find out soon enough anyway, but as soon as he confessed the problem to his brother, the whole family would know. Would know of his stupidity. He could hear Ben now, 'Why did you have to move so quickly? Why didn't you get a contract signed? Why did you quit before ...'

Heath reached across the table and grabbed his arm. "Sam. Seriously. What's the matter? I'll help. Ben'll help. Just tell me."

"I quit the bank a while ago. Earl Lange was going to let me work to own the station. I was working on the down payment he needed, but we hadn't signed any papers. He's had an offer for twenty thousand over his asking price. It's crazy. That little radio station nobody's noticed in years, and now somebody wants it so bad he's willing to pay over the asking price?" Sam guzzled all the milk with a few swallows.

Heath let out a breath. "Let me get this straight. You quit your job—your well-paying, benefits-paying, job—for a radio station? And now you need to come up with the whole cost plus twenty K?"

"Wow. You catch on quick."

Heath zeroed a hard gaze, every inch the big brother tonight. "You're in no position to throw sarcasm, Samuel."

Keeping his eyes on the table, Sam wiped his mouth with the back of his hand. "Sorry."

"Why in the world would you quit—"

"Because of Ches."

"Ches made you quit?"

"No. Working at that big dollar law firm was killing him, then his boss did a number on him. I saw what was going down with him, and I quit."

"You just quit, huh? No, plan, no job, no talking it over—"

"I talked with Pastor Dunleavy a couple of times."

"He told you to quit?"

"No. He asked questions. Helped me sort everything out."

"Is he helping you pay for it?"

"Now who's being sarcastic?"

"Sorry." Heath scrubbed his jaw. "So what's your plan?"

"My legs have just been knocked out from under me. I don't have a plan. I'm trying to figure out how to stand up again."

"Have you talked to Ben?"

"No." *Not in the mood for any lectures from Ben.* "You're the only one who knows."

"Maybe he could help you get your job back."

"I don't want my job back."

Leaning against his forearms, Heath softened his voice. "What do you want?"

"I want the radio station." Sam twirled the milk-coated glass in his hand. Getting his old job at the bank would be going backward. He wanted to move forward and buy the radio station. Start to make it his own with his ideas in the program lineup.

"Then make a plan to get the station."

"Okay. One. Buy a lottery ticket. Two. Win a million bucks. Three. Buy the station."

"Stop wallowing and think of something you really plan to do that doesn't involve compromising your values and throwing away your money at a gas station." Heath tossed him a notepad and ink pen. "You've got a healthy bank account from your stint in New York, and you don't waste money."

"And..."

"Broker a deal with him."

"I thought we had one."

"But you didn't sign a contract."

Sam glared at his dense brother. "As I said, no. He knew I wanted it and was working on the arrangement for the down payment and the payout scale for five years. He didn't list it for sale. I don't know how this other dude got in on it."

"Don't worry about that. Think about what your path forward is going to be."

"Pretty weedy, it sounds like."

"We'll figure this out. Maybe start thinking outta the box. We got your back, Sam."

"I know ... Thanks."

15

The pigtailed eight-year-old held the last notes of "Let It Go" and turned to Merritt with a spotty grin, showing a few new teeth that looked too big for her petite frame.

"Excellent, Violet. You played the whole piece very well. I'm so proud of you."

Swinging her legs under the piano stool, the little girl dipped her head. "Thank you, Miss Merritt."

"This piece will be great for our concert at Crossroads next month." She cocked her head. "You know, you even have time to memorize it if you want. What do you think?"

Grinning wider, Violet nodded her head like a bobble dog on steroids. "Mommy says I'm a good memorizer with my spelling words."

"You'll be a good memorizer with this song too. Okay, Ms. Connie has your cookie in the kitchen. Good lesson today." As the little girl slipped off the stool, she high-fived Merritt and skipped toward the kitchen.

Merritt checked her phone and read a text from Sam that had come through during the lesson. Her heart rate picked up speed.

Sorry. Something's come up.

Gotta cancel. Rain check?

And her heart rate subsided back to normal. Her cheerful attitude sank too. No wonder he hadn't dropped in, munching on one of Ms. Connie's peanut blossom cookies. Something came up?

Something ... or some*one*?

Her fingers hovered over the keypad. Be calm and collected. One text will not reveal how long she stood in front of her closet evaluating the possible outfits, how she'd begun to look forward to seeing him here today and on their future date. She sighed and considered the reply.

No worries.

Promising herself a carton of mashed potatoes and gravy on the way home, followed by ginger snaps and milk, she sent the text, hating how her body had been buzzing all day in anticipation of seeing Sam.

He asked for a rain check. He didn't blow you off completely.

True, but a rain check had no specific time attached to it. Just sometime in the future. She shook her head and dropped the phone into her satchel.

A quick knock, and the front door opened. Jared, a sometimes-surly fourteen-year-old, ambled into the living room and melted onto the piano. Six months ago, she'd expected him to quit taking lessons every week, but he kept coming and bringing his too-cool-for-school attitude. Turns out his mother bargained social media time for piano lessons and practice.

Merritt tried ever since then to bring interesting music to show how fun playing could be, but his attitude stayed the course. He didn't quit, though.

Little successes.

"How're you doing, Jared?"

"Fine." He placed his three books on the piano and opened the top one to the piece he'd worked on for two weeks. Placing his hands over the keys, he began to play.

He'd improved markedly since the first time he tried it. Merritt listened without drawing attention to sour notes. The piece had maybe only two or three.

"Well done, Jared. You've really learned this one well. You'll have no trouble polishing it for the concert."

Slumping his shoulders, he sighed. "Do I have to? It's so lame. All those old people ..."

"Jared. Come on now. They love when we come. Remember all those smiles. Remember the ice cream social we had last time? I saw you get a second sundae."

"Yeah. I was starving, and they had at least twelve toppings."

"Right. They know how to enjoy ice cream, for sure. Also, you can leave after you play, but you'd miss the ice cream and all those extra minutes for your social media. Plus, staying till the end shows solidarity with the other students and respect for the audience."

His shoulder lifted and sank.

"You don't have to decide yet. I'll get a final count to the director later. But, hey, look what I got for you." She slid a glossy new book of U2 songs.

A quick spark widened his eyes before disappearing under hooded lids. Ah ha. He did like this group.

You don't have to show me, Jared. Just play and enjoy.

"Why don't you take this book home and see if there's a song you might like to try out. If you like it, we'll start working on one next week. Unless you want to start early and show me what you can do with sight-reading."

He took the book from her and flipped through it. "They got 'American Soul' in here."

"I think the book has most of their hits. Do you see your favorite?"

Scanning the table of contents, he stopped on a song. "Page thirty-three."

"Cool. Let's take a look."

He skimmed the time signature. "Three sharps. Ugh."

"You can handle three sharps."

"I'd rather play flats."

She nudged his shoulder. "You and me both, buddy. Well? Want to try it for a week? See if you like it?"

"I guess. Thanks."

"You're welcome." She forced her mouth to stay in a neutral line even though she wanted to laugh out loud and high-five this student too. Exchanging his first book for the one behind it, she opened to "Drops of Jupiter." "We've got time for this one before you get your cookie. She made peanut blossoms, a cookie with a chocolate kiss. Probably the most genius cookie."

Nodding, he grinned at the piano book.

A spark and a grin in one day. Nice job, Merritt.

The cookies had become a hit. She might have to continue offering a sweet snack once lessons resumed at her house with her own piano.

Her piano. She needed to ramp up the search for one. Ms. Connie's hospitality might have an expiration date, although Merritt knew she loved the music and chatter and the baking too.

Her house. Until ...

What would Trey and Allison's next move be?

TWISTING HIS WRIST, Sam sneaked a peek at his watch. Mr. Earl's call yesterday morning with an appointment to meet Doug Gillespie at WDVY had sent him scrambling to prepare for it, but he appreciated the old man's effort in helping him even if he couldn't sell his station to him.

Thank You, God, for Mr. Earl's intro.

If things went in his favor today, maybe his radio career would be revived. He brought his ankle up and rested it on his other knee, nodding along with Doug's explanation of the format. The meeting had gone way longer than he'd expected or allowed for.

"So we do news and sports, sports and news. I have my talk show from six to ten Monday through Friday—commentary, jokes, news, sports. Then we play beach music early evening through overnight."

Wait. What? He must have zoned out for a second. "Do you mean a beach music program on some nights or—"

"No. Every night. Beach music. All night. Our listeners love it. It's the most popular music in North Carolina."

Sam ground his teeth to keep in his mouth the statistics that disproved the last statement. North Carolina's rich history of bluegrass, country, jazz, and blues as well as pop could easily disprove Doug's conjecture, but he wasn't in a place to debate the man.

"So whaddya think, son?"

Think about what? "Ah, beach music?"

"The station. You've seen it top to bottom. Heard my spiel. Earl recommends you with high marks. I can help you out if you want to come on board. You could start with dubbing commercials, then we'll see how you'll fit in." Doug leaned back in his office chair. "What's it gonna be? Want to be part of the WDVY family?"

THIRTY MINUTES LATER, Sam glanced at the time. Should he call Merritt to see if he could salvage something of today? Maybe see if she wanted to get a quick bite to eat? But he didn't really want to do a fast food with her this early in their—what?

Nope. Not going there right now. He let that question ride. He'd think of it another time. His brain was exhausted, and he was starving too. Maybe he'd grab a quick chicken sandwich, and then ...

A fabulous idea flashed in his weary mind.

Yep. He smiled at the quickening in his chest. A good plan, for sure.

16

A text came through Merritt's phone. Setting aside the granny square she crocheted, she read the screen. Sam.

Are you still awake?

It's eight o'clock.

Is it too late for ice cream?

It's always a right time for ice cream.

Are you decent?

Seriously?

Yes. I'm serious. Can I come in?

Merritt's breath caught in her throat. Decent? Yes, but the T-shirt she wore for comfort after her last lesson ... Calling it ratty might be a compliment. What could she throw on fast? The doorbell chimed.

Rats.

As she hurried to the door, she pulled on the hem like that might make it more presentable. As if.

Sam stood in the doorway, sucking on a straw and offering her a milkshake too. He swallowed and smiled. "I hope you like coffee milkshakes. I thought it might be a safe bet after the avocado thing."

Accepting it, she took a swig. Bliss. "I do. This is delicious. Thank you." Turning toward the den, she gestured to one of the wingback chairs and claimed the one with her granny squares.

Settling into the opposite chair, he rested his ankle on top of the other knee. "Crocheting? Josie crochets too." His eyes met hers. "Am I forgiven for bailing on you this afternoon?"

"There's nothing to forgive. You didn't stand me up me on a date."

"I told you I'd see you at Ms. Connie's."

His apology took most of the disappointment from this afternoon. The milkshake erased the rest.

"Things happen." She could attest to the old adage from an early age. She'd learned to enjoy a milkshake in the present and not count on promises.

"Yeah, well." He stared at the top of his cup for a moment.

In his reflective mood, he didn't come across like the goofball, here-for-a-good-time guy he projected in high school. In fact, most of these last months she'd known him, he'd been helpful, kind, supportive even. He'd had flashes of the clown, of course, with a quick quip here and there, but he seemed to be a solid human.

An idea popped into her mind. "Are you seriously a musician?"

He jerked his gaze to her. "What? Yeah, sure. I mean, I can play. Not sure you'd call me a musician."

"What instrument?"

A corner of his mouth tipped up. "Piano. Want to give me lessons?"

"Maybe. If you need them." She took another taste of the chocolaty treat. "How many years did you take lessons?"

"From second grade till I graduated high school. A loooong time."

"Then you must play pretty well."

"Truth be told, I can hold my own on the ivory keys."

"Cool." She studied him. "Then I have a favor to ask."

"You've seen me in action with the house bandits. Ask away."

"I'd love for you to come meet a fourteen-year-old who plays very well but thinks piano is lame. Maybe play something you like for him." She moistened her lips with her tongue. "Maybe even play a duet with him."

"Most fourteen-year-old boys camp out on that page. I hated practicing, but I love to play now ... when I feel like it. Have you given him good music, fun music?"

She smirked at him. "He's got scores to movies, and I just gave him a U2 book today."

"Impressive. Solid choice."

"I know he likes Train because I saw a quick smile before he hid it."

"Who doesn't like Train? He's just being a fourteen-year-old. He wants to seem cool. Maybe he's got a crush on his teacher? I know I would have."

His statement raced her heart a bit, but she ignored it. "His mom makes him practice for social media time, so he's improving every week."

Sam chuckled. "Sounds like the deal I had with my mom, but I practiced for time on the ball field and minutes on game boy."

"So, will you do it? Maybe play a duet with him ... or something by yourself at our next program at The Crossroads Assisted Living facility."

"A recital?" Scowling, Sam stirred his straw. "That's upping the game a bit."

"Nothing so formal. We go and play for the residents about

every other month. They always have a party for us afterward. Usually ice cream with lots of toppings."

"Trying to bribe me now, huh?"

"I think seeing a regular man, not someone on TV, playing the piano and enjoying it would give him a boost. Help him see this is a talent he can enjoy the rest of his life."

"Just so you know, I'm no regular man." Sam took a long sip of his milkshake and swallowed before answering. "What do I get out of this bargain?"

SURPRISE LIT MERRITT'S EYES, and Sam liked it. She'd been wary since he walked in. Were they still on for a date? He hated not following through at Ms. Connie's, but the radio meeting had turned out pretty good.

"Who said anything about a bargain?"

"I think I just did."

"You get the satisfaction of helping a teen who needs a positive role model in his life. You get to showcase the talent God gave you. You get to—"

"Right. Those are great things, but I think you can sweeten the pot, as they say."

"What do you mean?" Setting aside her milkshake, she'd grabbed the ball of yarn, twirling it between her palms.

"I mean we didn't get to plan our date this afternoon. I still want to find out about your type."

"We don't have to have a date for you to find out my type. I—"

"Wait. Hold up. That's the bargain." He slapped his thigh. "We go on a date, and I find out your type."

She squinted her eyes. "Why?"

"Why go on a date?"

"Why are you so interested in my type?"

"Curious about what the ladies are into these days."

"The ladies."

Nothing. Not one change in her demeanor. *Note to self, don't play card games with her.*

"Particularly one."

One slight quirk of an eyebrow.

"So let's review. I add my musical talent to your show at the old folks' home, and we chat about your type over a nice dinner."

"It's an assisted living facility, for your information. Some really cool people live over there. I met a ninety-nine-year-old World War II vet last time we were there. He cracked jokes the whole time we ate ice cream and clapped the loudest for every student, even the youngest ones who played one note with each hand."

"Good to know. So do we have a deal? A duet for a date?" He nodded. "I like the sound of that."

Pulling in a breath through her nose, Merritt agreed. "Which means, of course, attending some of his lessons on Wednesdays to practice."

"Of course. Which means more dates."

"Let's have one first."

Chuckling, he stirred the remnants of his milkshake. "You slay me, miss."

Rising, he offered his hand and helped her stand, holding her gaze for an extra beat. "Well, I need to get my beauty sleep. See you Wednesday, if not before."

17

The sun beams shining through the kitchen window were welcome additions after a night of fitful sleeping. If Merritt didn't believe it when Trey and Allison emptied her house, their last visit followed by a curt voice mail message with the new date of their photography session proved they were continuing the fight.

Not long ago, a quick ten or fifteen minutes workout on her piano would have washed the blurriness away. Would have lightened her spirits and readied her for the day. But now ...

Millie. She stopped there. No use wondering about all the what-ifs and whys. The reality of the empty space where the spinet used to sit gaped at her every time she entered the living room. Millie.

Pray.

I know I should pray, but I just don't—

Pray.

Okay. *Lord, I'm praying. I don't know what to do. I need a piano and probably a new place to stay. I don't know how to fight Trey and Allison or even if I should. Would it be a losing battle? Right. I know. Not if You're leading the charge, but are You leading this charge? Should I fight them or let it go?*

She shuddered. She couldn't think of letting go of this house, this respite from years of moving and living with people who had no real place for her, or saw her as someone to pity or who brought in a monthly check. Draining the last bit of strong coffee, she savored the slight taste of the sugar cube and smiled.

Thank you for teaching me about making every day special, Millie. And thank you for loving me.

A few hours later, she waited at Ms. Connie's front door, the smell of brownies welcoming her. Someone else seemed to have a soft spot for her too.

"Hooray. You're here early, but the brownies won't be finished baking for another few minutes."

"I'm not here for a brownie, but thank you. I'm early to practice for myself. Is it still okay?"

"Oh, my. Yes. I love that you're going to play. You can serenade me while I finish my correspondence. How lucky am I?" Ms. Connie clapped three times and disappeared down the hall.

Merritt began with some of her favorites she knew by heart. Her fingers glided over the keys, and she swayed with the rhythm, losing herself with the memories the melodies evoked. Coming to the end of "Claire de Lune," she slowed the tempo and held the last note with a fermata.

"Beautiful." Robust clapping sounded from the doorway.

She jumped two inches above the piano stool.

Sam.

"We have to stop meeting like this."

"You have to stop scaring me half to death."

"I can't believe you didn't hear us. Ms. Connie almost choked. She was laughing so hard at one of my jokes."

"I didn't hear you."

He nodded to the piano. "Student bail on you?"

"No. I'm practicing until my first student arrives. Jared's lesson is after that one."

Ms. Connie appeared at Sam's side. "That was just lovely,

Merritt. I finished my regular cards and wrote two more people. How about a brownie before the lessons start?"

Sam covered his heart with his palm. "I can attest. They're delicious."

"No, thank you. Maybe later." Merritt waited for her host to return to the kitchen. "I didn't realize you'd be here this early."

"I'm fixing a column on her back porch, then I'm meeting Jared, and I'll be on my way to fulfilling my part of the bargain, which leaves ... your part." Wiggling his eyebrows, he grinned. "I'll leave you to your piano now and see you later."

TRUE TO HIS WORD, Sam appeared in time for Jared's lesson. The introductions over, Jared remained aloof, waiting on the piano bench for Merritt to reveal the duet choice.

Sliding the sheet music onto the piano, she held her breath to gauge Sam's reaction to the piece she'd selected for the duet. Shock might be too strong an adjective. Definitely, surprise captured his face.

"'Blackbird'? You want us to play a Beatles song for the concert?" Sam cast his eyes from the lines of music back to Merritt.

"A lot of the residents there were young adults in the sixties. Some of them probably watched the Beatles' first appearance on TV. They liked rock and roll back in the day, and they still do. They'll love it. Trust me."

Please like it.

She'd spent a lot of time looking for a piece that would capture Jared's attention and maybe even excite him just a bit too. She'd also put herself out there with Sam's part.

"So, Jared, you like the Beatles?"

"I guess."

"And here I thought you'd pick a Broadway musical song or something."

"Musicals are good." Sifting through her satchel, she found Sam's part.

"Are you kidding me? They're great."

Skepticism prompted an eyebrow to arch. "You know musicals. You like them?"

"I love a good musical." He smiled at her. "You know, there's more to me than my pretty face and charm."

A laugh escaped before she could confine it. "Right."

Jared snickered but quickly remembered himself and broke off the sound.

Bending over Jared's shoulder, Sam studied the sheet music. "This looks pretty okay. Just one sharp. What do you think, Jared?"

Sulking on the piano stool, Jared shrugged. "Whatever."

"Hey, man, get excited. Ms. Hastings says you're terrific on the keyboard. I got skills too. Together, we'll blow their socks off." Patting Jared on the shoulder, Sam sought Merritt. "So, where's my part?"

She handed him the pages of sheet music. "Here you go."

Studying the first page, Sam frowned. "Wait. Where'd you get this arrangement? It looks—"

"I arranged it. I couldn't find one I like, so I—"

"So you arranged your own? Merritt, that's great." He scanned over the pages. "Wow. This looks really good."

He smiled at her, and her stomach did backflips.

"Okay, Jared. Show me what you got. I'm ready to be impressed."

After the lesson, Merritt packed her day planner into her satchel, smiling at how well Jared had clicked with Sam.

Brushing crumbs from his fingers, Sam swallowed the last of his brownie. "Mmm. That's good. I think it's my favorite. Jared's really good. He sight-read 'Blackbird' with little problem.

He'll have it ready soon. I'm going to have to bring my A-game."

"I told you he's good. Thank you for doing this. I want him to love piano, and I think—"

"Merritt, you can't make someone love it. Maybe we can spark more of an interest, but ... just don't get your hopes up too high."

She sighed. "Believe me, I know how to keep my hopes low, Sam."

He tilted his head and thought for a moment. Opening his mouth to speak, he apparently changed his mind. "What if you and I play a Broadway musical song?"

Breath catching, she startled at his suggestion. "You and me? Play a duet?" *Playing a duet. A much better topic than my low hopes.*

"Why not? Worried I'll show you up?"

She threw him an are-you-kidding-me glance. "A duet could be fun. Any song in particular?"

Lifting both hands palms up, Sam scanned the ceiling. "I don't know. So many to choose from. 'Singin' in the Rain,' 'If I were a Rich Man,' 'One Day More'..."

"Les Miz? Who are you?"

"Just a man who loves his musicals. We watched at least one a month, sometimes two a month. Friday night at our house meant movie night and pizza." He checked his watch.

"Gotta be somewhere?"

"In a bit." He waved his sheet music. "You've got another talent, Merritt. This is a good arrangement. I foresee a side hustle for you."

"I don't know." She chewed her bottom lip.

"I do, and I know some people in the business. I could make some calls—"

Her heart seized. Could he really help her?

Nope. Stay in your lane, Merritt. Focus on keeping the house and the students. A good life. Chasing anything more than that ... She didn't want it. "No, thank you. I'm good."

He tapped his watch. “We can talk about this again, but I have to roll now. Later.”

18

Blueberries clustered on every branch. Impressive for July. Merritt added a handful of the blue orbs into her bucket. A bumper year for blueberries, Ms. Connie had assured her when she asked for help to pick her berries. Blaming her shoulder problem, Ms. Connie excused herself from picking. Asking Sam for his help with the harvest, she cited, 'many hands make light work.'

Yeah, right, Ms. Connie. I know what you're up to.

"Some of these blueberries are the size of dimes." Sam popped one into his mouth. "Mmm. Sweet too."

"A blueberry fan, huh?"

"Who isn't? Blueberry cobbler, blueberry smoothies, blueberries on peanut butter toast, blueberry—"

"I get it. You like blueberries." She adjusted the string around her neck. The repurposed gallon milk jug fashioned to keep both hands free for picking grew heavier with each handful she added.

"You know she's probably making a treat for us right now." Tilting his hand over his bucket, Sam let the berries fall like a cascade of water.

"I already had a chocolate-dipped shortbread after lessons."

Two berries fell to the ground as she stretched for them. "Oh, man."

"She shows love through food."

"Uh-huh. I've noticed."

"My sister docs the same thing."

They picked in silence for a few minutes.

"You've got an interesting schedule. I can't figure out when you work. What gives?"

"Thinking about me, eh?" Bending a branch out of his way, he grinned at her.

She made a face at him. "You've been off in the afternoons here and at the church sometimes. Not exactly bankers' hours."

Moving to a new bush, he answered her quietly. "Yeah, well, I'm not a banker anymore."

Oh. Foot in mouth.

"I didn't realize." More silence except for the thumps of blueberries landing in the milk jugs. "What happened?"

"I gave notice."

"Did you quit because of the radio station?"

He sighed. "I didn't quit. I gave a two-weeks' notice with a plan for the next phase. I don't quit things, FYI. When I commit, I'm in for the long haul."

That statement took Merritt's breath away. So many people had quit on her, she'd need at least four hands to count them all. What would it be like to have someone, someone in addition to Destiny and Jesse, commit to you, have your back, fight for you for the long haul?

"But ... your job."

"I never planned to work there fifty years and leave with a gold watch. It was a great place to land after I got home from New York, but now it's time for a change. And that change is radio. I was making a commitment to radio, but the original plan died."

"What—?"

"Yoo hoo. Looks like you two are on the last bush. Come on

in. I don't want to wear you out the first time you pick. Let's have a treat."

Sure enough, when they entered the kitchen, Ms. Connie had the makings of a cobbler on the countertop. Merritt glanced at Sam. Her heart flipped at his smile and quirked eyebrow, a shared joke between them. What would it be like to share more jokes, to share other experiences?

"Oh, look at those beauties. I'm going to take about three cups to make this cobbler, and you two can divide the rest." She eyeballed the amount of berries she needed and rinsed them in a bright green colander.

"I laid out dish towels for you on the kitchen table. Empty your jugs and pour out your berries. Pick over them and then put them into the quart-sized freezer bags. I never wash my blueberries before freezing them. Just wait till you're ready to use 'em."

With the blueberries sprinkled over the batter in the baking dish, she slid the cobbler into her oven and adjusted the temperature. "Who's ready for some lemonade? I made a fresh pitcher for you."

"That'll hit the spot, Ms. Connie. It was toasty out there." Sam fanned himself with the bottom of his faded red T-shirt.

"Pull the chain for the ceiling fan, Sam. I'm so appreciative of you all helping me with these berries. You two are such blessings." Selecting two cut-crystal glasses from a cabinet, she set them on the counter beside the refrigerator. "Sit at the table, and I'll bring over your lemonade."

They sat across from each other, rolling the berries, picking off little stems, and discarding not-quite-ripe purple berries.

"Don't forget to write today's date on the bags." She pointed to the marker beside the freezer bags. Turning on the oven light, she peered at the baking dessert. "Looks good. I upped the temp, so it'd cook fast. I'm sure you have places to be." The faintest grunt passed through her lips as she straightened. "Well, did you solve the world's problems out there?"

"I don't know about the world's problems. I'd be happy to solve some of my own." Sam threw a few berries into his mouth."

"Well, three heads are better than one, I'd say. What's your problem? Let's give it a go." Moving to the table, she sat across from Sam. "Does it have anything to do with leaving the bank and the whole WBEL mess?"

Sam's hand stilled over the berries. "What?"

"I may be old, Sam, but I can still pay attention. Just so you know, I don't participate in gossip myself, but if someone says something in front of me before I can stop them, I hear it."

A warm, buttery scent wafted toward the table.

"Mmm. I can smell the cobbler. Won't be long now. Well, Sam?" Ms. Connie crossed her hands on the table, her worn wedding ring showing on her top hand.

"Yes, ma'am. I'm working it out, I think."

Squishing the air out of her bag of berries, Merritt zipped the two sides together and waited for Sam to expound on his dilemma.

"And what about you, Merritt? How's the hunt for a piano coming along? Don't get me wrong. I'm happy as a kitten eating tuna fish from a crystal bowl with you and your students using mine, but I know you want your own. Any leads?"

Whiplash. Just like that, she was on the hot seat.

WHEW. His turn in the spotlight must be over. *And Merritt looks about as happy as I was.*

"Well, I haven't found anything yet." A stray blueberry from Sam's pile rolled off the table, and Merritt bent to retrieve it.

Ms. Connie donned two lime and turquoise oven mitts and opened the oven, backing up to avoid the wave of hot air. "I heard through the grapevine that those people who ransacked Millie's belongings were back at your house the other day."

Red crept up her neck toward Merritt's flat-lining lips.

I've seen that angry look before. Would she leave before Ms. Connie could scoop ice cream onto the steaming dessert?

Opening her mouth to speak, Merritt closed them before uttering a word and breathed through her nose instead.

"Like I said, I don't gossip, but other people do, and sometimes you can't help hearing things." Ms. Connie set the cobbler on a cast iron trivet between them. "Sam, get the ice cream out of the freezer, please."

Covering Merritt's hand with her own, she made direct eye contact with her. "You look like you could just about spit nails, but listen. People empathize with you. They hate that this has happened to you, sweetie."

"They're determined to have Millie's house. My house. They've already texted me when they're coming back." Merritt's throat worked, but she kept her cool.

What should he do? Play the clown, as usual, or try to comfort her? Indecision glued him to the linoleum.

"Wonderful, Sam. Thank you." The older woman motioned for him to set the carton on the table. "Let's crack that open. We need some ice cream quick." She scooped a generous portion of cobbler onto a blue and white saucer.

Ms. Connie to the rescue. Thank goodness.

"Yes, ma'am. Ice cream is good medicine." He peeled off the top of the carton.

"I like the way you think, Sam. Put a scoop on Merritt's cobbler." She piled more dessert on another saucer and slid it in front of Sam. "For you." She lifted a tablespoonful of blueberry deliciousness onto a saucer for herself. "I'm watching my girlish figure."

She shook her head at Sam until he had just a tad of ice cream on the scoop. "That's good. Thank you. Now. Let's do the best thing for these problems you two have, hmm? Let's pray." She grabbed their hands and stared until they join hands too. "Close your eyes and let's talk to God."

ENJOYING A GOOD, wide yawn, Sam headed for WDVY, his happy place. With WBEL in his rearview, WDVY held heart-revving possibilities for his dream of owning a station.

Lately, he'd been burning the candle at both ends with handyman projects for Ms. Connie, duet practices with Jared, working any shift, and doing anything from producing commercials to sweeping floors at WDVY. But if this exhausting schedule led to his own station ... his heart thumped a crazy beat.

He squeezed the steering wheel and prayed.

Dear God, please let this happen. Please let this be Your will. But if it isn't ...

Nope. He couldn't think that way. He took a hard pass at sliding closer to any more negative thoughts.

Circling back to the piano lesson, he chuckled at Jared's bored and this-is-beneath-me vibes. The teen might be a hard nut, but, always up for a good challenge, Sam had plenty of tricks to crack his duet partner. *Yes, sir, buddy, you'll be begging for another duet in a couple of weeks.*

Maybe Merritt could surprise them with another cool duet choice, maybe using her own arrangements as she'd done for his part. A smile accompanied the welcome idea.

He rubbed his chin as he nudged onto I-77. Her arrangement showed skill as well as creativity. What if he sent a copy to Marty in Nashville, see if he could do anything with it? Yes, of course he should. Why wouldn't she want to pursue a side career of arranging music in addition to teaching?

After parking, at the far end of the lot, Sam grabbed his backpack and tossed in the snack bag of Ms. Connie's cookies. Maybe they'd bolster him with a bit of courage later. At the front door, he punched in the enter code and relished the cool slap of heavy-duty A/C. Bracing air should help quell last-minute nerves before setting in motion his covert mission.

He trudged down the hall to the on-air studio. Felix, the evening DJ, waved him through the door.

"Well, hey, Sam. Perfect timing as always." Felix greeted him from behind the control board. "Catching up on some work?"

"That's exactly right. I gotta produce some commercials. I don't mind being here at night by myself. It's quiet."

"Yeah, I hear ya." Felix adjusted a couple of sliders on the control board before standing and stretching, crackles and pops sounding from his neck. "Man, they say sitting is the new smoking, and I believe it. I need to find a way to kick this habit, too, I guess, but what can I say? I love radio."

"I know what you mean." Why would he give up a good-paying, respectable job if he didn't love radio? Thinking about putting in his notice at the bank made his stomach flip again. He ejected the traitorous thought and focused on his colleague.

"I just double-checked the overnight, so everything's good to go till morning." Felix glanced over the board again and grabbed his satchel under the side table. "That's all I got, so I'll leave you to it then." He saluted Sam and whistled his way out down the hall.

Flicking his gaze over the programming monitor, Sam scanned the scheduled music. Beach music. Beach music and more beach music. A shudder shook his spine.

He retraced his steps down the hall to the production studio and dropped his backpack beside the table. Digging inside the pack, he found the copy for two new sponsors, then voiced the commercials on his to-do list.

Completed. Now for the fun part.

Diving into his backpack again, he retrieved three of his own CDs. He spread them on the console with shaking fingers and blew out a breath.

Calm down, racing heart. This is where I'm supposed to be. Okay, technically, this time of night isn't when I was hired to work, but I'm not doing anything illegal.

Irritating to the owner, maybe, but not illegal.

He opened the cases and pushed the discs into the production computer. Adrenalin wrecked the rhythm of his lungs. Not too much longer before the sweet music of local musicians hit the airwaves.

Sitting in front of a mic, he never questioned his life's purpose. Being in a radio station was absolutely where he was supposed to be. The hard part? Convincing an owner to sell to him and figuring out the financing.

Depending on the deal, Sam could probably swing the purchase price with a little grace and financing on the owner's part too. If he wanted to sell. Saving most of his salary during his time in New York City had padded his bank account. That money combined with a generous loan might afford him the station and a menu beyond ramen noodles for the next thirty years.

He'd posed a question over the air once or twice a week for a few weeks. A music question first. A sports question another night. Politics, a perennially hot topic sure to bring chatter, left him hanging too.

Armed with this loose research, he set his plan in motion. Tonight, Operation Become an Interesting Radio Station began. Jazzed with the prospect of going rogue with the format, he dropped and did twelve pushups.

Back in front of the studio mic, he focused on his task. "Good late evening to you. That last song, 'Carolina Girls' by General Johnson and the Chairmen of the Board, is one we know and love here in Charlotte. We think our girls are special, all right.

"Now we're gonna highlight some talented local ladies with a real sweet song by Bloom Reel. Listen close, and you'll hear a dulcimer. You'll hear a mandolin. You'll hear the best harmonies you've heard in the past six months, probably longer. Here we go. Enjoy."

Heart pounding in his ears, Sam clicked the start button on his monitor to release "Cherry Blossom Daze" into the world. At least, the local world around Charlotte. He leaned back in the swivel chair and breathed in slowly. The haunting chords of the melody he first heard a few years ago at SpringFest washed over him. He swiped his face and laughed out loud at his shaking fingers.

Well, the deed's done now. Let's see what the fallout will be.

As the last notes of the song filled the studio, Sam rolled up to the mic and waited for the final sound, not willing to talk over the beautiful melody. "There you have it, folks. That right there is a song. Did it get you down deep? If I'm honest, it gets me every time. You can hear it live next weekend at the Lake Wylie Amphitheatre. How lucky are we, we can catch this great local band in person, right? Get tickets at the door next Saturday night for Bloom Reel."

On the computer screen, he highlighted the next song Felix had programmed earlier. "Okay. Back to regular programming for all you beach music fans. Get your dancin' shoes on for 'Be Young, Be Foolish, Be Happy' by the Tams.'"

We'll see how foolish I'm being pulling this stunt. Glancing at the strobe light for incoming phone calls, he chewed on his cheek for the entire Tams' song and two more beach music favorites. The light stayed dark.

He grabbed his backpack and headed out the front door, his grin shining the whole way home.

19

Stepping in front of Merritt, Allison angled her body toward the fireplace and twisted the viewfinder on her Nikon. Very expensive. Very extravagant, especially when almost every cell phone took quality pictures these days. She spoke while she focused. "Merritt, you really should go ahead and start looking for a new place. You're not going to win this battle. My brother's determined."

Gritting her teeth, Merritt counted to ten and then eleven and twelve. "You seem pretty determined too. You're taking pictures of my house."

Allison lowered the camera and dipped her chin. "Mildred's house. He's the one in charge, but I agree with him. Mildred left this house to my mother in her 2004 will. We're acting on behalf of our mother, her biological niece." She emphasized biological as if Merritt might miss the reference.

"She updated her will three years ago and left you money. Be happy with that and let go of this greedy-grabby escapade. Not a good look. You don't even want to live here. I do."

Trey entered from the hallway with a measuring tape and clipboard. "The so-called will you speak of is a piece of paper. It was never filed with the county, so, therefore, it's not valid. By rights, this house is going to be ours. We'll list it, and you can bid on it like all the other people who are beginning to see potential in Clover Street."

A knock sounded from the front door seconds before Sam burst through. "Hey, hey. How's everybody doing today?" He sauntered toward Merritt and winked.

Relief or pleasure or a mixture of both ballooned in her insides before reality stole the rush. *Don't get used to Sam swooping in to stand beside you. Don't get used to this feeling of solidarity.* Still, she could be thankful she didn't have to face Trey alone right this minute.

"Hey." She involuntarily stepped toward Sam. "Trey and Allison need pictures to post on the real estate agency's website."

"You're doing the agent's grunt work?"

Hands on his hips, Trey grunted. "I'm a licensed agent. I don't get why you're here."

"You don't have to get it." Surveying the room, Sam swung his gaze toward Trey. "You 'bout finished here? 'Cause we've got stuff to do."

"We just got started. We still need pictures of the bedrooms and baths."

"Well, I'd hurry it up if I were you. You got fifteen minutes to take your pictures."

"Now, wait a minute. Merritt knew we—"

Sam folded his arms in front of his chest, planted his feet. "You're wasting time. Fifteen minutes." He glanced at Merritt. "Mind if I have a glass of water while they're finishing up?"

Merritt led him into the kitchen and lowered her voice. "Are you kidding? I doubt they'll leave in fifteen minutes unless you carry them out."

"I thought you noticed these guns when we were picking blueberries." He held up both arms and flexed his biceps, grinning. "Don't worry. They'll get outta Dodge. Just wait and see. He may be a bully, but bullies fold when they get some push-back."

Stop staring at his biceps. Stop relishing this feeling that someone else is helping. Remember, two people are taking pictures to sell the only home you've ever known.

She reached for the bottle of club soda in her refrigerator.

"Uh, just plain water's fine. Not a fan of bubbly water."

"Really? But it's like a party in a glass."

"They tickle my nose, make me sneeze. Let's see. I think your glasses are ..." He opened a cabinet. "Yep. Right here." Turning on the faucet, he filled his glass halfway. "This'll be fine." He took a sip. "Delicious and no sneezing."

Smiling, Merritt poured a glass of sparkling water for herself, sliced a wedge of lime and dropped it into the glass.

"Ooh, fancy."

"Millie believed every day deserved a celebration." She licked the lime juice from her finger. "She made every day special."

Heat coiled in his gut. To stop staring at her lips and fingers, Sam gulped the last of his water. "Good stuff." He angled away from her to set the glass in the sink, forcing himself to stop thinking about the tiny scar at the edge of her mouth.

"I appreciate you're here, but how did you know—"

"Ms. Connie texted me. You must have mentioned they were coming at your last lesson. She's got your back." He leaned his hip against the counter.

Merritt glanced away, body language indicating a cool down in the room.

Placing his forefinger along her chin, he nudged her back to him. His thumb found the scar of its own volition. "Hey. What's up?"

"I'm not used to people in my business." She moved her chin, and his hand fell to her shoulder.

"She's not in your business. She cares for you. She prayed for us the other week. For our problems, remember? She thought you might need some moral support."

"Well, don't you two look cozy? Sorry to interrupt. Not." His hand on the threshold, Trey leaned into the kitchen. "We've got the pictures. You'll be hearing from our lawyer." Allison stood behind him, avoiding eye contact.

Sam pointed to the time on his phone. "Look at you. Four minutes to spare. I knew you could do it." Digging into his back pocket, he pulled out his wallet, extracting a business card. "Here's Merritt's attorney's card."

Flipping the card from front to back, Trey read it. "Ches Windham, huh? His name sounds familiar."

"I'm sure you've heard of him. He's a great lawyer. A bulldog, you might say."

Trey quirked an eyebrow. "You are full of yourself, aren't you?"

"I can't agree with you, Mr. Billings. I'm here helping the lady. You're here threatening to take her home away from her."

Trey handed the card back to Allison. "The law is on our side."

"We'll see about that."

Shaking his head, Trey left without a goodbye.

"You're good at stalling Trey and Allison, but I can't afford a lawyer." Merritt held her glass to her temple.

"You don't need to pay anything yet. We're going to talk to Ches right now. I set up a consultation meeting." Taking the glass from her, he set it on the counter. "He's with my sister at my parents' house."

She rubbed her eyebrows. "Um, your parents?"

"They're not there. They're missionaries in the Dominican Republic for the next year or so." He pushed off from the counter. "So grab your purse or whatever you need, and let's hit the road. Oh, bring a copy of Millie's will."

"We're going to your house?"

"Are you unconscious? Yes. We're going to my parents' house to talk with Ches. Josie's cooking dinner and will make you eat, so expect to stay for a couple of hours at least. Maybe we'll end up playing a game over there too. Never can tell."

20

Heart racing, Merritt repeated cautionary words like a mantra to herself. *This is not a date. This is not a date. This is NOT a date.*

It was hard not to think about it being a date, however. He swept in and stood up to Trey and Allison. He made her laugh. He touched her chin, and even though she shrugged it off, she could still feel the heat of his hand when it fell to her shoulder. Now ... driving together to his house

This is not a date.

"If Josie is having us to dinner, I feel bad not bringing anything like a side dish or a dessert or even flowers."

"Josie'll have it all covered. Believe me. You can bring something next time."

Next time.

This is not a date.

He turned into the driveway and parked behind a black crossover. "Good. Ches is already here. We can get started." He held her elbow as they climbed the front stairs.

She blew out a breath. *This is not a date.*

"Hey." Softening his voice, he halted her. "Don't be nervous. Ches's a good guy."

"What if there's no case? I'll lose my house. What if there's a case, and I can't afford him? What if—"

He gripped her shoulder. "Slow down. We'll have a nice meal. He'll look over the will. Maybe play a game. Maybe not in that order." He dropped his hand. "Ches will shoot straight with you. If he can't help you, we'll start plan B."

Again with the *we*. *This is not a date.*

He flashed a warm grin and opened the door. "Honey, we're home."

When they entered the kitchen, Josie was smoothing her hair down, and Ches moved to lean against the counter with his hands in his pockets.

Sam swung his gaze between them, chuckling. "Well, sorry to interrupt you two, but this is Merritt Hastings. We brought the will I told you about."

Taking the will from Merritt, Ches offered her an encouraging smile.

"Hello, Merritt. It's nice to meet you." Josie's face shone with an eager friendship, lighting up her eyes. "Why don't you boys take the will into the family room, and we can get to know each other in here."

Merritt made a mental note. One more thing to add to her prayer list: joy that radiated from every part of her face.

"I'm so sorry about your house and your piano." Leaning against the island, Josie focused all her attention on Merritt.

Merritt's insides tightened. Smile bigger. Make sure she knows it's no big deal. "I'll figure something out. I appreciate that Ches is willing to read the will."

Reaching forward, Josie clutched Merritt's hand. "He'll do whatever he can to help you, don't worry. He loves cases like this."

"What do you mean 'like this?'" *Pitiful people? Poor people? People who—*

"Helping people who need representation. He used to work

for a humongous law firm, and it was eating him alive. He quit and works for a nonprofit now."

"Sounds like he took a pay cut."

Grabbing a spoon, Josie lifted a pot lid on the stove and peered inside. "Yeah, but money isn't everything."

Easy to say when no one's trying to grab your house out from under you. "Right. I'm sure he has a good heart."

"The best." Another joyous grin.

Merritt smiled back instead of groaning. This girl was easy to like.

"I hear Ms. Connie is letting you use her piano." Laying the spoon in the rest, Josie turned to Merritt. "Isn't she the sweetest thing?"

"Uh-huh." *About as sweet as you are.*

What would it feel like to have grown up in a home like this one with parents who loved you, with siblings who loved you? Yes, Millie tried her best to give her a happy family experience as long as she lived, but ...

Merritt fingered a picture of Sam with Josie and two other guys who looked like siblings. Two brothers and a sister, the photographer caught the foursome mid-laugh. Love and fun shouted from the silent picture.

Scenes from her own house flooded her mind. Playing *Name That Tune* on the piano, she'd call out, 'What's this one, Millie?' Listening to a few notes, Millie would answer by singing the song at the top of her lungs. Sometimes off-key, she never missed a song.

And Millie dropping sugar cubes into her coffee, using cloth napkins every day, bringing home daisies from the florist just because.

Merritt clutched the red glass heart at her neck, rubbing the smooth back with her thumb. *Oh, Millie, I hurt with missing you sometimes. Why didn't you make that will ironclad?*

Sam and Ches walked into the kitchen with the will, their

faces inscrutable. Her stomach bottomed out. Trey and Allison would have the house. They'd get that sweet little house and sell it to the highest bidder. The smell of the baking chicken turned her stomach. She held her breath so as not to heave.

"Quit looking like fun suckers, you two. What do you think, Ches? How will you help Merritt?"

All of a sudden, Ches grinned and shrugged. "This will looks solid to me. She has everything written clearly. She signed it, and she's got three witnesses, including a Pastor Thomason."

"But it isn't notarized." Calm down, heart.

"To be valid in North Carolina, a will doesn't have to be notarized. It needs two witnesses, and she has three. Plus, the testator, Millie in this case, has to have been in sound mind. Was she?"

"She was always a free spirit, but she was sharp as a tack, as they say." Her words floated out of her mouth with a feathery quality, her lungs fighting with her racing heart. Something light like relief and joy began swirling in her chest. Could this news be true? "But Trey said she didn't file it at the courthouse."

"You don't have to file it. It's still valid." He scratched the side of his nose. "Do you know this Pastor Thomason? Or any of the other witnesses, Joe Peabody or Lisa Gunderson?"

"Lisa was a college friend. I met her at the funeral. She's probably in Millie's address book. I don't know the others."

"We'll do a search, see what we can come up with. If Trey and Allison push it, the witnesses would probably have to testify about Millie's mental state at the time of the will."

At the mention of another *we*, Merritt's heart squeezed so hard she flattened her hand against her chest. Did these people say *we* when they actually meant *you*, or would they really help her out of this mess? Tears sprang to her eyes, and she bit the inside of her cheek to get a grip. It was enough to know that her will was valid. If she had to proceed on her own, she would.

She had lots of practice at doing that.

Backing out of his driveway, Sam punched on the radio to his favorite country music station. A classic George Strait song filled his crossover. He stretched his arm out across the top of Merritt's seat, disappointed in the slight stiffening he detected in his companion's spine.

Don't worry, Merritt. I'm a gentleman. Just stretching here. No hanky panky.

"Is this station okay? You like country music?"

"Sure. It's fine."

"Fine? George Strait is one of the masters. He's more than fine." He lowered the volume. "What do you listen to? Classical?"

"Sometimes. It depends on my mood."

"Gotcha. But country?"

"Yes. I listen sometimes." She considered him. "One of my all-time favorites is Patsy Cline."

"Ooh. Old, old school country. 'Walkin' After Midnight,' right?"

Merritt chuckled. "Right. And 'Crazy.'"

"Okay. I believe you now."

"Now?" A temperature change in the car accompanied her lone word.

Great day, she was prickly. "Hey, hey. No aspersions on your sterling character. I only meant you proved your point. You weren't just saying you were fine with country to go along with me."

The twang of a steel guitar filled the car, and they drove in silence for a few minutes.

"So what's your mood tonight. Before you got bent out of shape at me just now, that is."

"I'm not bent out of shape, and how do you know I have a sterling character?"

"Now that's a leading question if I ever heard one." Pulling into her driveway, he coasted to a full stop and turned off the engine. Would they talk in the car for a little while? Would she invite him in? Maybe if he repaired the damage he'd done with his careless comment. "I know about your character because I've been around you for more than ten minutes. I've seen the way you treat Ms. Connie. The church voted to let you use the sanctuary. My sister likes you."

"Josie likes me?"

Chuckling, Sam made a face. "Are you kidding? She smiled at you all night long, even when I was beating her pants off in Yahtzee. She thinks you're brilliant for including me on the duet. Unfortunately, she found out about the piano gig because I have to practice at home."

Her fingers closed over the passenger side door handle. Okay, the car chat was over.

"Wait. I'll walk you up."

Key in hand, she turned at the front door. "Thank you for tonight. It was fun."

"I thought you might be happier. You just got great news, right?

"Right. I still have a lot on my mind, a lot to deal with, with Trey and Allison. But, yes, tonight was a lot of fun."

"Even when Josie and I were going at it? You know she cheats at board games."

Merritt laughed. "She said you cheat."

"Baby sisters. Large pains."

"You don't mean that."

"Oh, the stories I could tell you." He opened his mouth to say more, but the longing in her eyes pulled him up short. He couldn't move. He could only hold her gaze. Should he kiss her? Did he want to? Yes. Yes, he did. Keeping his eyes locked on hers, he began a slow descent to her mouth just as a moth dive-bombed between them from the porch light, landing on her chin.

She jumped back, flailing her arms.

"He's gone. We're fine."

The lucky but time-challenged moth escaped the swats.

"Sorry. Not a fan of moths." Focusing on the keyhole, she shivered.

"Especially when they land on your face, huh?" He crammed his hands in his jeans pockets.

Trembling, Merritt missed the lock twice with her key.

Hmm. His disappointment in the lost moment transformed to curiosity. Did the moth do this number on her? Or ... was it the possibility of a kiss? Did she want one too? Or was she freaked out when he leaned in for one? Curiosity turned to frustration. Figuring this one out might take some time.

The third try succeeded in unlocking the door. "Well, thanks again, Sam. Good night."

"You're welcome. Hey, when we doing this again?"

"What?' The keys slipped out of her fingers.

Rising from retrieving the keys, he served up one of his most mischievous grins. "We still haven't made plans for a date. I'm working on my part of the bargain practicing with Jared." He raised his eyebrows.

She nodded, her eyes searching for the doorknob.

Enough teasing tonight. The emotions from the day scattered like dice on a Yahtzee play. Her need to be inside her home radiated from her body.

"We'll talk about it soon, okay?" He tipped an imaginary hat and descended the steps to his car.

RECLINING against three pillows on her mattresses, Merritt replayed the evening in her mind. The shock and joy of finding out the will was valid. The intense competition of the Yahtzee game. The time-stopping moment between her and Sam at her front door. The nosy moth landing on her chin. She shook off the creepy feeling brought on by the memory of the moth and focused on the almost-kiss instead.

Had he been heading for a kiss? Would she have let him? Fun to think about, but a kiss between them might not be the best thing. She'd probably read more into it than he intended. A guy like Sam had fun wherever he went, but was he ever serious?

Maybe she needed a little fun. Millie would encourage her toward fun, for sure.

But he let the moment go and didn't press her even for a visit inside. Was he playing or really interested?

Her cell phone, charging on her lap desk, vibrated against the wooden top. She glanced at the screen, her breath freezing. Sam.

Waiting for two minutes to open the message, she read what he had written.

Just checking to see how you're doing.

Wondering when we can have another date.

Another date? He counted tonight as a date? Zings raced up and down her body.

Another date? When was our first?

Hellooo. I picked you up. We ate dinner. We played a board game. I took you home.

You never asked me. You told me we were going.

I didn't even know you were stopping by.

Thanks for reminding me. I helped you out and then took you to dinner.

That your sister cooked, btw.

Ouch.

He added an emoji with huge, wide eyes, and Merritt laughed out loud.

That reminds me. Thanks for helping with Allison and Trey and for showing the will to Ches. I can't tell you how much it means to me.

You can tell me when we go out again.

Are you asking?

You're tough.

Merritt, would you like to go on a date with me?

Where?

He sent a laughing emoji.

I'll surprise you, but it won't be to my parents' house.

I like your parents' house. Okay. Yes.

Fantastic. Are you at Ms. Connie's tomorrow?

Yes.

Let's talk then.

Okay.

Get some sleep. Night.

A date. With Sam? It'd be fun, of course. As long as she kept her head and heart securely in check. Easier thinking it than doing it, especially since her eyes had already scanned her closet for the perfect outfit for the date and what to wear for tomorrow's lessons.

Oh, girl.

21

Ms. Connie appeared at the doorway to the living room with a dish towel in her hands. "Guess what? I think I've found a piano for you."

A dip in her happy disposition surprised Merritt. She needed a piano, or at least she thought she did, but she'd come to enjoy giving lessons from Ms. Connie's living room. The cookies were a great draw, but seeing the senior saint five or six days out of the week added color to her life. It felt like having Millie back ... almost.

"Oh, wow. Really? Where?" Merritt bit her bottom lip. "How much?"

"Well, that's the thing. A friend of a friend has a piano she's kept in her front room, silent for years and years. No one in her family plays, and she's got arthritis." She tipped her head. "What a tragedy, don't you think? Anyway she's ready to downsize. She needs to sell it. Only thing is, it's been in that front room where she's turned off the heat and A/C.

"Who knows what shape it's in, but it's one of those old player pianos, she says. Taller than a spinet to make room for the player workings." Ms. Connie wrinkled her nose. "Might be in questionable condition. May not work at all for you."

"Okay." A blue feeling settled on her shoulders. Would this piano be worth the trouble of going to look at it? Kept in a room with fluctuating temperatures? Would she be inviting more problems into her life? Everything was going well with Ms. Connie, unless she was overstaying her welcome.

"Listen. I almost didn't tell you about this. I love you and the children and the music and baking for them, but I know you want your own piano. I'm happy as a puppy with a new bone with our arrangement as long as you are. But if you want to check out this piano, I'll call Francine and set up a time to see it. And just because you see it doesn't mean you have to buy it."

Tracing her fingers lightly across the keys, Merritt released a breath. "You're right. Thank you for helping me, Ms. Connie, with your piano and the one for sale."

Reaching for her, Ms. Connie gave her a quick shoulder hug. "Happy to do it, sweetie." She straightened her dish towel across her forearm. "I've got my famous ginger cookies today. Won a red ribbon at the county fair with that recipe."

Merritt chuckled. "Then I'm sure they're delicious. I look forward to tasting them."

Two hours later, voices carried from the kitchen as she closed her appointment book. Sam's deep laugh filled the house. Her heart jumped into a higher gear. *No. Nope. Slow down. We're not doing this. Get your mask in place before he sees …*

Sam sauntered into the living room, offering a saucer of ginger cookies. "These are the bomb. Have one. You'll want more." He flipped a bitten cookie into his mouth and smiled. "These might be my new favorite."

"Haven't you said that for every cookie she's baked?" She reached for a golden cookie with ginger bits dotting the top and sampled it. Delicious. This one definitely deserved a place on her Christmas cookie menu.

"Ms. Connie says she's found you a piano."

The award-winning baker joined them. "Possibly, Sam, but

she doesn't have to choose it. I called Francine, honey. She's free all weekend if you're interested and can go check it out."

"Want me to come with? Maybe Sunday?"

Despite her command to have a poker face, Merritt's eyebrows raised. Yes, of course, she'd like him to come with her. Would be grateful for another set of eyes. But would this outing take the place of a date? He hadn't mentioned Jared today. Was he rethinking their bargain?

WHAT DID those raised eyebrows mean? Shouldn't she have smiled bigger if she'd been happier to see him? Or was her little smile for the cookie instead? How to read this girl.

"I mean, you don't have students on Sunday afternoon. If you want company—"

"What a marvelous idea. You two go together. Four eyes are better than two, and I have a standing commitment on Sunday afternoons. I'll go phone Francine right now. Shall we say two or three o'clock?"

"I say the lady chooses, if she wants company, that is." Sam studied her. Would she let him come along or not?

"Two o'clock is fine. If you give us the address, Ms. Connie, we can meet there, Sam."

"Let me pick you up. Saves gas." And it's more fun to go together.

She toyed with the red heart necklace always dangling just below her collar bone. *Stop staring at the skin underneath that red heart.* Was she seriously contemplating whether or not to let him come?

"You two figure out the arrangements while I call Francine." Ms. Connie left them alone.

Sam cleared his throat. "Sunday afternoon's good, but I can't make game night this week. Something's come up."

Her eyes snapped to his before she ducked her head to gather her appointment book.

Was that disappointment she'd tried to hide? *Way to go, bro.* "Yeah, sorry, I was really looking forward to crushing it on Clue or Bananagrams or whatever, but I can't make it work."

"No worries. How's your practicing coming?"

"Fantastic. Jared and I are going to bring down the house." He grinned. "That reminds me. The other part of the bargain. We need to pick a date night. You got your calendar, right? Look in there and see if you're free next Saturday night."

She flipped to the correct page. "I'm playing at the Lamplighter that night."

"Friday then."

"That's open."

"Cool. We got a date for a date." He chuckled at his lame joke.

She shook her head. "You didn't check your schedule."

"Don't worry. I'll make it work. I'll text you when I'll pick you up after I get a reservation. Got a favorite place, or do you want me to pick the restaurant?

"I'll let you choose."

"This time." Maybe there'd be another time if he could keep her interested.

22

Dragging his hand through his still-damp hair, Sam followed the scent of coffee into the kitchen. His brother leaned against the counter, regarding him.

"Already back and showered? How was the run?" Heath blew over the top of his steaming coffee mug.

"Too short." Sam dropped a piece of bread into the toaster.

"You've been a little more squirrelly than usual. What's the deal?"

Stretching his arms for the ceiling, Sam grimaced at the pops and cracks. "Squirrelly, huh?"

"You're hardly ever here. What's the deal? Something's up. For sure."

"Miss me?"

Heath thumped him on the head. "Like missing the sound of a mosquito buzzing around my ear? Yeah."

"Real funny." The toaster popped up the slice of toast. Grabbing it with his thumb and forefinger, Sam tossed it onto a saucer. He slathered the bread with a chocolate nut butter.

"You know that's like candy for breakfast, right?"

"I'll have eggs, too, but what's the difference between this and a chocolate donut? I'll tell you what. This is healthy. It's whole wheat."

Shaking his head, Heath dropped another slice into the toaster slot. "Josie was bent out of shape with you blowing off dinner the other night. What gives?" He poured two glasses of milk while he waited for his toast.

"I got a new job, if you must know." Sam bit the corner of the chocolate toast.

"Hey, man. That's great news. What're you doing? Did Ben get your job back for you?"

"No, he didn't because I don't want it back. I told you I'm done with banks. Well, working for one anyway." He licked chocolate from his finger. "I'm a DJ at WDVY in Mount Holly."

"Like what you did in high school?"

"Like how I began my career in radio." Adding a little concrete to the words, Sam folded his arms, refusing to break eye contact with his brother.

"I didn't know you had a career in radio. I knew you liked fooling around on the air, making announcements, playing music, cracking jokes. I didn't know you'd leave a stable job to do all that."

Sam gritted his teeth. "I left a stable job when I thought I would be working toward owning WBEL."

"Yeah, now we know why written contracts are a thing. Earl—"

"Stop. Don't say anything about him. He's a good man. He felt like his back was up against a wall with Ms. Louise being so sick." Sam curtailed his brother from speaking ill about Earl Lange, but he couldn't stop unwarranted negative thoughts from knocking on his own brain sometimes. "He got me in at WDVY."

He exhaled. "Anyway, you've heard me talk about it before. Banking was sucking the life out of me. Ben loves it. He's good at it. Good for him. Not for me. Radio is for me."

"Okay. You want to be a DJ when you grow up."

"Stop making fun." Pushing away from the table, Sam stood.

"Wait. Sorry for how that sounded." Heath studied him for a second. "Help me understand."

Raking his hand through his hair, Sam dropped back into his chair. "I want to own a station. Plan my own programming. My own format."

"Is this even a viable business?"

"Yes. I've researched it. It's a healthy station."

"I mean, are radio stations going to survive podcasts?

"You're talking two different things." Leaning on his forearms, Sam urged his brother to take him seriously. "Podcasts speak to certain people on a certain topic. Radio stations offer a broader range of information and services."

"I hear ya, man. I just ... I don't want you to sink your money and time and effort into something—"

"Gotcha. I don't either. I've done my homework. I'm fine."

Heath reached over and squeezed his shoulder. "All right."

"Thanks, though. I appreciate you keeping tabs on me."

CLIMBING OUT OF HER HONDA, Merritt surveyed the wraparound porch. A vine, maybe Virginia creeper, climbed up one of the columns flanking the steps. She glanced at her phone. She'd texted Sam she was on her way to Francine's since she was already out. No reply yet. No worries. She didn't need him to evaluate a piano.

It'd be nice to see him, though.

She glided up the steps, noticing a crack on the second one. Her heart skipped at the thought of perhaps buying her own piano. Would this one be a find or a disappointment? She pressed the doorbell, and chimes rang through the door. Quick, short steps clicked on what sounded like a hardwood floor.

"Well, hello there. You must be Merritt. Connie has told me all about you. Where's that young man of yours?" The short, plump woman peered around Merritt's forearm. "Couldn't Sam come today? I so wanted to meet him too."

"He's supposed to come, but—"

"Come in. Come in. I'm so excited you might be interested in my piano. I hate to give it up, but it's time. I'm moving closer to my grandson, and the apartment doesn't have room for all my stuff. I say giving up my piano to live closer to my brand new great-granddaughter is a mighty fine payoff. Don't you think?"

"For sure." Maybe.

"I'll get to see her every day, and truth be told, my fingers aren't what they used to be." She held up arthritic hands and pointed to her temple. "It's all still up here, but it gets lost somewhere before it gets here." She wiggled her gnarled fingers. "Follow me. Let's go see the prize."

Ms. Francine waddled toward a front room off the hallway. "They're calling her Frankie, after me. My grandmother used to say you weren't supposed to name babies after people who hadn't been dead for more than a year. I'm still kicking, but I love having another Francine in the family."

Merritt sucked in a breath.

The piano held court on the back wall in all of its green glory. The piano was green. Not a Kelly green, thank goodness, but more of an avocado green. Merritt opened her mouth to respond, but no words tumbled out. Or stumbled either. She nodded instead.

"Here you go. My late husband, Van, refinished this for me to match my living room furniture in 1971. All the wooden pieces were antiqued an avocado green. The fabric pieces had beautiful greens and pinks, and my couch, the focal point, was white. Oh, it was stunning." She clasped her hands, lost in thought for a moment. "I'll leave you alone for a minute. Take your time. Open the cabinet. I want you to be satisfied that it's a wonderful instrument." She toddled back toward the hall just as the doorbell rang again.

How was she going to get out of this sticky situation with

this sweet little woman? Quick? Kind? Firm? However she did it, she could not have this piano in her house.

"Look who just got here." Ms. Francine had her arm threaded through Sam's. "Your handsome man. Just in time to help you evaluate it. I'll leave you two to it then."

Sam's grin blossomed. "Sorry I'm late, but am I ever glad I came. Wouldn't have wanted to miss this. Wow. I don't recall ever seeing a green piano before."

Merritt shook her head.

"You're speechless, huh?"

"Sam, what am I going to do? I can't ... I don't ..."

"What does it sound like? Have you tried it yet?"

"I couldn't get past the color."

Sam sat at the piano and played several chord runs. "Not bad. It needs tuning, but you'd have to tune it anyway after the move. Close your eyes." He moved into 'I'll Fly Away.' An oldie but a goodie.

"Nice. You've got that hymn memorized?"

"One of my favorites, actually." He played a few more chord runs. "I think it sounds decent. The color doesn't affect the sound quality." He stood to open the cabinet for a look inside. "The sound board's intact. The strings are good, not rusty. Don't worry about the color. We can change that. Come on and try it." He slid across the piano bench. "How 'bout a little 'Chopsticks'?" He began playing the low part to the old song.

She snorted and joined him on the stool. "Cliché much?" She added the top part.

"It's a cliché because everybody knows it. Even people who don't play the piano can play 'Chopsticks.'" Swaying with the beat, he nudged her shoulders with his. "See. I knew you could do it. Yeah, girl. You got it." He nodded to the beat like a rock star.

She added some flourishes, and he responded with some of his own.

"We're good. We could take this show on the road."

Francine appeared at the door. “It’s so good to hear my piano sing again.”

Concentrating on her fingers, Merritt demanded her shoulder to stop tingling from his touch.

“My grandson keeps pestering me to advertise my piano, but I wanted it to go to someone special. Connie says you’re a piano teacher. She loves your students. With you two playing duets on it and children learning on it, my piano will be so happy again.”

She cocked her head. “If you want it, I’ll make you a deal. How about two hundred dollars? Can you swing that amount? I know teachers aren’t rolling in money. Will two hundred work for your budget? I’ll let you chat for a few minutes.” With that, she disappeared.

“What’re you thinking? Sounds like she’d probably go lower. You could get a sweet deal. Forget that it resembles a giant vegetable. We can fix the color.”

“I’m not going to bargain with a little old lady. She clearly loves this piano and the man who wreaked paint havoc all over it.” She raked her teeth over her top lip. “I guess a coat of paint would be pretty easy, but ...”

“But what?”

“I had a cherry wood veneer in mind when I thought of a piano. That’s what Millie—”

“Okay. We’ll strip it, stain the wood whatever you choose, and it’ll look like new.”

“We? You know how to refinish a piano?”

“Don’t worry. I’m your man. With a solid plan.”

23

"No texting at the table. You know this."

Roused by his sister's snapping fingers, Sam glanced up from his hands.

He slid his phone aside. "I'm not texting. Anyway, we've finished eating."

"What are you doing then?"

"Finding videos about refinishing furniture."

Heath leaned his chair onto the two back legs. "Random."

"Not really. I need to brush up on my skills."

Chuckling, Heath tossed his napkin at Sam. "Refinishing skills? How 'bout getting some skills."

Sam batted the napkin back at his brother. "Remember the side table we helped Dad refinish back in the day?"

"And by 'help,' you mean watched and sometimes fetched a new piece of sandpaper."

"But he explained what he was doing as he did it. Seems pretty easy."

Leaning in, Josie folded her arms onto the table. "Why do you need to know how to refinish a table?"

"Not a table. A piano."

Heath dropped the front legs of his chair down with a plop. "A piano? Are you kidding or crazy?"

"We know he's crazy." Josie smiled—then gasped. "Did Merritt find a piano?"

"She did indeed, and it needs some work."

"And you're going to do it after you watch some videos?" Heath's cocked eyebrow shared more of his thoughts on Sam's new endeavor.

"Yep."

"Oh, Sam, she needs a good piano. You can't—"

"Don't worry, Jo Jo. I'm helping her dream come true."

"Don't you think you should start on something small and less complicated like, I don't know, a grandfather clock, maybe?"

"Funny, Heath. How hard could it be?"

RIFLING THROUGH HER JUNK DRAWER, Merritt searched for—the corner of a takeout menu stabbed her knuckle. She freed it from the odds and ends and froze. Not a takeout menu. No, the jail pamphlet Eva had forced on her at the birthday party months ago.

Mood melting, she shoved the offensive brochure back inside and slammed the drawer with her hip. Calm down, Merritt. It's just a piece of paper. It has no power over you. *I'll think about it another day.*

She strode to her crochet bag and plopped into a wingback chair. Grabbing some periwinkle yarn and a hook, she began a pattern she knew by heart. The repetitive rhythm of the stitches soothed her ruffled disposition.

As she finished off the third granny square for the evening, a text buzzed Merritt's phone. She exchanged her hook for the phone. Sam.

We can borrow Heath's truck to pick up the piano.

Tuesday.

Great!

You've got an empty bedroom, right?

Yes.

What if I refinish your piano in that room?

Her piano. In spite of the horrendous color and the wait time to get rid of that color, Merritt's insides pumped with joy. Her piano. After weeks of playing on borrowed instruments and being at the mercy of others … her piano.

Okay.

I could bring over supplies then.

Or wait till Saturday. Whatever works.

Thursday night game night?

Waiting for a response, she held her breath, letting it out way after the screen went black.

I'll let you know about game night. I hope I can.

Not an excited, positive response, but not a hard *no* either.

No worries. Show up if you can. We'll have plenty of food.

Will do.

Another wait after the screen darkened. Okay. The last text

must have been his sign-off. She dropped the phone and grabbed a crochet hook and a variegated ball of yarn. She'd joined the beginning chain and crocheted two stitches when the phone sounded again. She powered through the beginning round of the new granny square before looking at the text. Destiny. She blew out a disappointed breath.

Hey, girl. Thursday's on you.

Gotcha. Tacos.

Mexican Train then for game time?

Destiny sent a laughing face with tears along with her text.

You crack yourself up.

See ya then.

Another text came through before she released the phone. Sam.

The duet was fun.

Yes. You're good. Better than I thought.

Thanks, I think.

Was it the Chopsticks or I'll Fly Away that impressed you?

She texted a laughing emoji.

I'm happy you're helping Jared.

Glad to. What're we playing for the concert?

Surprise held her fingers still. Did he mean Jared or …?

Blackbird.

I mean you and me.

You haven't found a piece for us yet?

So he was serious about a duet with her.

I promise I'll find something.

You mentioned a musical the other day.

Another pause in texting. Three minutes later a new text popped up.

Yeah. That's good.

Choose something our audience will like.

Maybe avoid Guns and Roses.

You'd be surprised at their interests.

Okay. Surprise me.

Night, Merrit.

24

Merritt's week turtled by after Sam and Heath dropped off the green piano on Tuesday. Wednesday. Thursday. Finally Friday. Now that their date was on, however, minutes seemed to click in rhythm with her racing heart.

Slow down, time. I want to enjoy this special evening.

Twinkle lights embraced the lower branches of the dogwood and crepe myrtle trees, transforming the patio into a fairytale setting. She'd driven by this tiny restaurant for years and never known this magical outdoor room existed.

"I hope this is okay." Sam, handsome in his cornflower blue button-down and black jeans, fidgeted with the rolled-up utensils.

Smoothing the hem of her floral sun dress over her thighs, she relaxed. The dress was the perfect choice for tonight. The light in Sam's eyes when she opened her door earlier redeemed all those minutes vacillating in front of her closet trying to decide what to wear.

"Are you kidding? It's beautiful. I never knew this place existed back here."

Not exactly a customer magnet, a rusty sign touting the name, Harmony Honey, dangled askew over a faded green door.

"Alan likes to keep it that way. He plays most things on the down-low, as proven by the dive-bar look of the front. You'll never see this joint make any of Charlotte's top ten lists, but the ones who know about it are loyal and keep his business steady. I had to pull the friend card to get a table at short notice. "

Dive bar. That's exactly what this little building looked like. She'd forced herself not to show the disappointment when she thought Sam was bringing her here for a hot dog and fries. "If the food's as good as the dining area is beautiful ..."

"Just wait. But here's the deal." Bouncing his knee, he leaned in. "I don't know what he's serving. He didn't know until he went to the store today. Always cooks only what's in season. It'll be delicious, I promise."

Ugh. A promise. She didn't do well with promises. They sounded good, but most times they turned out to be very fragile. "As long as the food's recognizable, I'm usually pretty good with trying new things." She'd had to be, growing up in different homes with varied cooks, abilities, and grocery budgets.

A waiter appeared with two carafes of water. "This one is the sparkling one, for the lady."

She glanced at Sam and allowed a small smile. He'd remembered.

"And still water for the gentleman. I'll be back with bread and butter."

"So we don't find out what we're eating until the food arrives?"

"You got it."

She chewed on the side of her cheek.

"What's the matter? Worried we'll get snails or something disgusting like that?"

"I hadn't thought about snails." She made a face. "I was thinking of the cost."

"No worries. It's in line with other nice restaurants in town. Plus, I had a coupon."

She widened her eyes, prompting a loud guffaw from him.

"Teasing. I'm not using a coupon on our first date. I may when we start ordering pizza delivery." He dipped his head. "Just so you know."

Raising an eyebrow, she challenged him. "Oh?"

"You're cutting me to the quick. No future dates?"

"Let's finish this one first." She slid a braided clover chain from around the rolled napkin.

"That's right. I may not be your type." Smiling, he raised his glass of water. "What is your type, by the way?"

"You're like a kitten with a skein of yarn."

MOVING ASIDE the vase of zinnias, the waiter set a basket of rolls the size of golf balls in between them. Sam grabbed one, swiped it over the pot of butter, and popped it into his mouth. The warm, yeasty flavor blanketed in butter ... mmm.

Swallowing, he rolled his eyes upward. "So good. Get one while they're hot and before I scarf up all of them." Reaching for another one, a thought occurred to him. "You're not gluten-intolerant, are you?"

"No. You're just enjoying them so much ..."

Already pinching another roll, Sam counted the remaining ones in the basket. "Six left. I've eaten one, and this makes two. If I'm doing my math right, you get four, and I get two more."

"Clearly, you love these. I'll have one just to experience this culinary delight, and you can have the rest." Choosing a roll, she broke off a small piece.

He shook his head. "Once you taste them ..."

"Do you always count your food?" She popped the piece into her mouth, her eyes lighting.

"See? I told you they're delicious. And, for the record, I

absolutely do count my food, especially if my siblings are anywhere near, and I want my fair share."

Chuckling, she reached for another one. "I'll stop with two to save room for the main course, but you're right. These rolls are fantastic."

The waiter returned with two small bowls. "Cucumber soup with yogurt and dill."

Merritt glanced at Sam, who was staring at his bowl. "Thank you." She nodded to the waiter.

Sam groaned.

"You don't like cucumbers?"

"I don't like cold soup."

"You haven't tried it yet."

"Josie made cucumber soup one time back when we were in high school, trying to be fancy. Epic failure. She's a good cook—don't tell her I said that, by the way—but soup by its nature is supposed to be hot."

"I don't need to tell her. She seems confident in her kitchen skills." She picked up her spoon. "Try it. Don't hurt your friend's feelings."

Taking a taste, she cocked her head and closed her eyes for a moment.

"Trying to make yourself swallow it?"

Eyes popping open, she shook her head. "No. I was enjoying the flavors. It's delicious, Sam. Try it."

He stirred the drizzle of yogurt into his soup, scooped up a teaspoon full, and studied the light green concoction.

"Go ahead. It's refreshing too."

He sipped a tad of the soup and winced. "Just like I thought. Tastes like watery cucumber."

"Sam, you're horrible. What about the other flavors? The dill, the—"

"Want mine?" Seeking help, he turned on a look that usually made Josie succumb to his will.

Not moved, she shook her head. "You have to try more. You barely tasted it." She had another spoonful.

"There's a reason for that." He paused and smiled. "I got an idea. I'll put a dent in my bowl, so to speak, and you can tell me your type."

25

Merritt's stomach tightened. "Your determination is impressive. Why are you interested in my type again?"

"I'm interested in people. I minored in psychology in college."

"Did you really?"

He laughed and shook his head. "No. But I should have. People are fascinating."

"So, what did you major in?"

"Business with a minor in communications, but don't sidetrack me. We're talking about you, remember?" He rubbed his chin. "Let's see. I asked you about athletes, musicians, brainiacs. What's another type? Career-driven, type A?"

Should she just jump to what she truly looked for in a person to date? If she did, maybe they could dispense with the discussion of her preferences and simply have a regular conversation. A regular conversation with her not on the hot seat would be nice.

"Okay." She leaned on her elbows. "Here's my type. I'm looking for someone who doesn't have a family."

His mouth fell open. "Random."

"Not really."

"You're looking for an orphan? You'd put that on your dating app profile. 'People with family need not apply.' Definitely a new category here." He frowned. "What do you have against families?"

"In my experience, family comes with baggage."

"That's kind of unfair. Family also comes with a boatload of good."

"Says you who has a tight, loving, fun, supportive family. How many foster kids have you ever talked to? Really noticed?"

Silence.

"Uh-huh. That's what I thought. I'm your first, right?"

He pushed his half-eaten soup to the side. "I'm thinking a foster child would want a family."

"I do. I just want to create one of my own."

Closing his fist over his fork, Sam traced the pattern on the handle with his thumb. "Forgive me because I'm probably going to put my foot in my mouth, but I'm having a hard time following you. If the person you date and eventually marry has a family and you have one together, you have lots of people to call your own."

The waiter appeared and removed both bowls. He arched an eyebrow at Sam's bowl. "The main course will be ready momentarily. Do you need anything?"

"Please tell Alan I'm saving room for the entree." Leaning in, Sam dropped his voice. "Alan'll be fine, but that waiter's condescension ..."

"I'm surprised other people's opinion affects you."

"That's definitely another topic for another day. Back to the no-family rule. I mean, my family can be a lot to take. I've wondered about future spouses reacting to all of us, but Ches has been a great addition." His gaze pierced her. "I just don't know. Something's off here." Cupping his jaw, he studied her. "What happened?"

"What do you mean?"

"Something happened to bring you to this decision."

"Oh, yeah. I was a foster child, remember?"

"I get that. But something else is behind your resolve." He narrowed his eyes. "What, I wonder?"

Hot and cold pings leapfrogged up and down her body. *Cool it, Merritt. He's fishing. He has no clue what he's talking about.*

Carrying two loaded plates with pasta noodles, the waiter led a waitress to their table. He set down the plates and took a block of Parmesan cheese from the waitress. "Tonight, we have a pasta with pesto and sun-dried tomato sauce. The chef picked the basil from his own garden this morning." Gesturing with the cheese and a grater, the waiter smiled at Merritt. "Cheese, madam?"

"Yes, please." Merritt breathed in a calming breath. *Thank you for Parmesan cheese and a break from Sam's scrutiny.*

Sam agreed to more cheese as well.

"Chef Alan says he hopes you like the pasta." Smirking, the waiter grated cheese over Sam's plate.

"I know I will. It smells great. Thank you."

"I'm sure he'll be thrilled to hear." Sarcasm sprinkled over Sam's pasta along with the cheese.

"What is it with that guy? I've said please and thank you. I smiled at him. Not eating that soup isn't a judgment on him or this restaurant." Shaking his head, Sam grabbed his fork. "*Bon appétit*, as they say."

Interesting. With all his cheeky bravado, he'd always put forth a nothing-bothers-me attitude. This new insight into his personality swirled warm tendrils around her heart.

But let's keep talking about the food instead of my type. "The sauce does smell wonderful. Farm to table is the bomb."

"Yeah, that's always how we ate at my grandma's." He stabbed some noodles and transferred his gaze back to her.

Chewing the flavor-exploding pasta, Sam considered his next move. Judging by Merritt's concentration on her food, she didn't want to continue the earlier conversation. Fine. Maybe the topic landed too close to a painful memory or a taboo subject. No worries. They could enjoy this heavenly food and the twinkle lights now and revisit the no-family rule later.

"Well, what do you think? A thumbs up?"

Her eyes peeked over her fork for a quick look. "Definitely two thumbs up. This dish could be my new favorite. Do you think he'd share his recipe?"

"We can check. On second thought, I'll ask Alan later. Not sure the waiter would deliver our message ... or Alan's recipe to us."

"You're letting our waiter get in your head." She chuckled. "Like the song says, 'let it go.' It's a beautiful place with delicious food. Don't let him spoil your night."

"You're right. I won't. 'Cause we're having fun, yeah?"

"Mm-hmm."

As much as he wanted to revisit the interesting conversation before the pasta arrived, he liked the relaxed version of Merritt more than the tied-in-knots one. He could bide his time and wait for another opportunity to ask about her story. All in good time.

He sipped his water. "So."

Fingers tightening on her fork, she lowered it to the plate. She raised her eyes and met his stare.

"Do you like to cook?"

She blinked and narrowed her eyes. "What?"

"You want the recipe. I guess that means you like to cook. Are you any good?"

"I do like to cook. Millie taught me how. We used to cook together when I was home from college. She was great." She picked up her fork again, pushed a noodle through the sauce. "I like to experiment with old recipes and try new ones. I especially like to bake desserts and cookies."

"And I love to eat them. Sounds like we could be a good team."

Her smile, though unsure at best, boosted his confidence.

"I'm a pretty good cook myself."

"Frozen dinners?"

He spread his palm over his heart. "Wow. You're tough, did you know that?"

"I've had to be, Sam."

Her simple words sobered him. *Say something, man. Something wise and kind and heartfelt.* His brain, unfortunately, forgot to telegraph words to his mouth. He concentrated on the vulnerability in her eyes he'd bet she'd rather keep hidden. Sliding a hand across the tablecloth, he leaned—

"I might have known you wouldn't like the cucumber soup. Barbarian. Looked like you barely tried it." Stepping up to their table, Alan slapped Sam on the back. His timing rivaled the cucumber soup ... both terrible.

Stretching against the back of his seat, Sam looked up at his friend. "I definitely tried it. Merritt can vouch for me."

Smiling, Alan extended his hand to Merritt, and she returned his smile. A movement in his chest caught Sam off guard.

"The soup was delicious and refreshing too."

"Thank you." Alan grinned at Sam. "The lady has taste, for food, that is. Don't know how you scored a dinner with her. Must be kindhearted." He smiled back at Merritt.

"We were just talking about how tough she is before you interrupted us."

"That's my cue to get back in the kitchen. The dessert will be right out. Homemade lavender ice cream with chocolate honey truffles." He ruffled Sam's hair. "Good to see you, Sam. Don't be a stranger." Turning back to the kitchen, Alan waved goodbye to Merritt.

"Lavender ice cream?" Merritt turned her attention back to Sam. "Sounds fantastic."

"You think? Sounds a little foo-foo to me."

"Lavender smells wonderful. I have a couple of plants at—" She broke off, regrouped. "Wonder where he gets his honey?"

You are tough, Merritt. Enough thinking about Millie and the house you want to keep. We're going to have fun the rest of the night.

He glanced at his watch. *Yes, ma'am. More fun. That's a promise.*

SPRAWLING like a flat jumping jack on top of her duvet, Merritt burrowed her head into her pillow. The date had gone well. The food had been delicious—all of it—despite Sam's opinion of the soup. Yes, the unexpected texture and temperature took a few sips to get used to, but the overall cold-soup experience was positive.

Sam's comments rejecting the soup had endeared him to her. Steeling herself not to melt under his puppy-dog-eye stare at the table, she let herself enjoy the memory in the safety of Millie's house. His pitiful eyes counterbalanced the cheeky dimple winking beside his grin, summoning a smile of her own now.

For the most part, Sam had steered the conversation to fun and interesting topics with a few mentions of his siblings, like when he counted his rolls. Counting to make sure everyone received an even amount? Not a memory from her childhood. Her foster siblings most times grabbed what they wanted, and if anything was left over, lucky for her. She rarely had siblings working together for a common goal.

She blew an imaginary kiss to Destiny. *Thank You, God, for her.*

Alan had even given her a small box with two chocolates to take home. Toward the end of dessert, however, Sam had become increasingly distracted. Still attentive and cracking silly jokes at times, he'd had something else on his mind. A bit of awkwardness surfaced as they stood on the porch.

Rolling over, she searched for the time. Millie's clock radio mocked her. Eight forty-six. Home alone after a date at eight forty-six. Clearly, Sam needed to be somewhere else ... or with someone else. Was that why he hadn't kissed her at the front door? Did the kiss on the cheek signal a gentleman's restraint or a gentleman's lack of interest?

Opening the petite box of chocolates, she chose one and nibbled the corner. Should she give in and eat it or save it till tomorrow? She nibbled again and then bit the piece of chocolate heaven in two. Holding the chocolate against the roof of her mouth with her tongue, she put the other half back in the box and closed the lid before she could change her mind. The candy, safe in the box tonight, would be waiting for her tomorrow.

26

Operation Piano Rescue, as Sam liked to call it, progressed better than he'd hoped for. They'd already disassembled the whole thing and stripped the individual pieces of the hideous green. Merritt's smiles at the naked wood fueled his determination to make this piano shine.

The next step, the sanding process, would take time to get the wood as smooth as glass, the perfect excuse to visit more often with the lovely new owner. As the foundation layer, sanding was an important part of the transformation. Yep, several days—

"You know, you play really well." Merritt's compliment surprised him out of his reverie.

"Thanks. I try 'cause I enjoy playing." Dragging the sandpaper over the side piece, Sam focused on the grain of the wood. "All of us play, in fact. Our parents insisted and paid for lessons. Plus, my mom knew how to keep our interest with fun music, not just the boring classical stuff."

"You're killing me."

He chuckled. "Plus, we had a male teacher. That helped, I think."

"Hello, you know who you're talking to, right?"

Teasing her was fun. "This guy was retired Air Force, a fighter pilot. He wore cowboy boots but could tear up a piano ... in a good way." He blew dust off the wood and rubbed his hand over it. "Nice." Looking up from the wood, he quirked an eyebrow. "It's like what you want me to do with Jared, I think. Show him that piano players can be cool guys like *moi*."

"Funny too."

Yeah, Sam, always default to a joke. He concentrated on sanding and kept his mouth shut for a few minutes.

Looking up from her piece, she stopped sanding. "Hey, is something wrong?"

"No. It's all good. Your piece is looking right. How does it feel?"

"Wait. Let's go back a bit. You got all quiet. I thought you were making a joke."

Ugh. She wouldn't let him slide.

"Yeah. I guess I was." He tapped the sandpaper against his jeans. "It's just ... I wanted to explain about Mr. Jennings. I didn't have to bring it back to me."

Chancing a quick peek at her, he startled at her dark brown eyes zeroing in on him. His heartbeat kicked up under her gaze. Was she waiting for him to continue? Maybe if he opened up to her, she'd share more things with him too.

He licked his lips. "I've always been the clown of the family. People expect me to make a joke, be the silly one. Sometimes it gets a little old, and I find myself doing it when I don't mean to."

"You fall into a pattern and do what you think people expect you to do."

"A lot of times."

Nodding, she smoothed a rag over her piece of wood, capturing sanding dust. "I get it. People expect certain things of foster children."

Inspecting his worn piece of sandpaper, he tossed it onto the tarp covering the floor. "Like what?"

"Like they expect us to lie. Be angry."

"You're not like that." He chose a new piece of sandpaper, folding it to get a better grip.

"Thank you. I used to have anger issues, but you're helping to make my point. We're not always like that, but sometimes we put on an act to protect ourselves."

"Do you mean from physical abuse?"

"Emotional abuse is probably more common." Pausing, she traced the piece of wood with two fingers. "Have you ever heard the term respite parent?"

"No."

"When the foster family wants to take a vacation or just take a break from the foster child, they can leave the child with a respite parent for the time they're gone. It can be kind of traumatic."

Stilling the sandpaper, he processed her words. Dump the kid if you don't want to deal with him? He swallowed. "Did that ever happen to you?"

"No, but it did to Destiny. The family traveled out of state for Memorial Day Weekend and didn't take her."

Sam's mouth dropped open. "I can't believe it."

"Believe it." Though she kept her focus on the wood in her hands, residual pain for her friend seeped into her words.

Taking a quick breath, she pinned him with her eyes again. "But back to you and being the clown."

He scrambled to keep up with the direction of the conversation. "So we're not talking about foster care anymore."

"Nothing else to say. Back to you. You may be the clown in your family, but other people see more than that in you."

He set aside the piano leg. "Not so sure—"

"I see the way you are with Ms. Connie. You're over there at least once a week doing her bidding. Helping with a smile and for only a cookie or two. You're patient with Jared." She pointed to the pieces of her piano scattered over Millie's bedroom floor. "You've been over here every evening for a couple of hours and won't let me talk about payment. You're more than a clown, Sam. You're a good guy."

His eyes held her gaze for several beats then dropped down to her lips. Her tongue moistened her lips for a quick second. Beginning a slow lean toward her, he jerked back at his beeping phone alarm.

THE ALARM BURST the cocoon that had spun around the two of them. Merritt straightened her spine and blinked.

Sam quieted the alarm. "Man, some timing, huh?" Grinning, he glanced at her once more before standing and dusting off his jeans. "I'll vacuum this room before we start the stain and shellacking part of the process. Sanding's the messiest part. But at that point, you'll have to deal with the varnish fumes."

He picked up the used sandpapers and stuffed them into a garbage bag beside the door. "Sorry I gotta roll, but I'll be back tomorrow about the same time if that works."

"Sure." She accompanied him to the door.

"Thanks for the paninis. That's an upgrade from a regular ham and cheese sandwich. Really delicious."

"Yeah. I picked up on that when you ate two." Smiling, she opened the door, but he stood firm. Would he kiss her goodnight? The alarm had spoiled the mood of ten minutes earlier, but ...

He chuckled. "So you can be a clown too, huh? I'll remember that." Sam winked at her.

No witty comment formed in her brain to prolong the night. Would "please stay" work? Probably not. He'd set an alarm to leave.

Who does that? And why?

Ignoring the sinking feeling in her chest, she summoned her good manners. "Thank you for saving the piano. It's looking so much better already."

"No problem." He backed down the front steps. "Good night then, Merritt."

"Night."

CHECKING the analog clock on the wall, Sam smiled. Nine twenty-five, not exactly prime radio time for listeners who might be watching TV or getting children to bed. Perfect time, however, to shine on local bands with songs he'd dubbed into the system last week.

But playing local bands only a few times a week stretched his patience. How long before he owned his own station?

He stifled a growl.

Baby steps, Sam.

"Okay, ladies and gentlemen. That was 'With this Ring' by the Platters, one of the all-time great beach music songs. Now we're going to slide into some sweet tunes by local favorites.

"Carrie Butler has the voice of an angel, folks. She makes a twelve-string cry too. Her husband, Mack Johnson, accompanies on the violin or the sax or sometimes the steel guitar. Yep, he's that versatile. Take a listen and let me know what you think. Here we go."

The first few bars of "Sadie, Wait for Me" floated him back to the first time he'd heard Carrie and Mack play at a house concert west of Gastonia. His shoulders loosened as the familiar melody—

The door banged into the wall. Red-faced and wearing a faded Rolling Stones T-shirt over gym shorts, Doug, the station owner, burst into the on-air studio. "What are you doing?" Doug grabbed the door jamb and sucked in air for several beats. "So my buddy was right. You're playing other stuff. I've been sittin' in the parking lot, waitin' to hear for myself."

Sam's heart bounced into his throat, cutting off speech.

"This station plays beach music. All night. Automated

overnight. Not live. Why are you even here now?" Grimacing, Doug shook his head. "Who gave you the reins? Where do you come off playing strange songs nobody knows? People listen to this station, my station, for beach music."

"Is anybody listening now?" Reckless words escaped from Sam's mouth before rational thought could lock them down.

"What?" Doug's eyes bulged over flaming cheeks.

"Hold on a minute." Fingers trembling, Sam programmed three songs beginning with "Up on the Roof" without intros, just music.

In for a penny. In for a pound. Right, Granddad?

"With all due respect, sir, I'm not sure anyone is listening now. For weeks, I asked questions during the evening slot. On different topics. At different times. Not one person called in to answer. Not one. I thought—"

"You thought. Uh-huh. How 'bout this?" He hooked a thumb toward his chest. "I thought I'd hired someone who knew radio. Earl gave you a glowing report. I didn't think you'd give me a problem like with every wet-behind-the-ears wanna-be Wolfman Jack or Grandmaster Flash who have all the words but no substance, no technical ability, and want to be paid like they've got thirty years in the business, and if I don't, they jump over to the next station that'll give them air time."

Doug wheezed in a breath and leaned on the table. "And you're playing James Taylor right now?"

"It's 'Up on the Roof.'"

"During a beach music set, play the Drifters' 'Up on the Roof,' not James Taylor's."

"It's a solid version, sir."

"It's not the Drifters." Reaching deep into one of his pockets, Doug pulled out a bandanna and wiped his face. "And you're in no position to push back right now."

Sam ground his molars. This is not how his talk with the owner had gone in his mind for the past month. In his rehearsals, Sam wore a suit, carried proof of his financials in his satchel along with a list of new programming ideas.

But the way this impromptu night was going, he might not ever get another chance to talk with the man. Sam swallowed. "Do you want to sell?"

Breathing hard, Doug raised his head. "What?"

"Do you want to sell this station. To me."

"Are you being a smart aleck right now? Let me tell you, son, you're on shaky ground after your monkey business."

"I'm serious as I can be."

"Earl said you needed a job, so I gave you one. I thought you were down on your luck." Arching a brow, he stuffed the bandanna back into his pocket. "You think you can afford my station?"

"I have some savings. I'd like to talk about it."

Scratching the back of his head, Doug sighed. "You've got nerve, I'll give you that. Listen up. You leave the overnight playlist alone. Got it?"

"Yes, sir."

"The three songs you put in are just about up."

"Yes, sir." Sam switched the station to automation mode for the overnight shift.

"You know, I was this close," he pinched his thumb and forefinger together, "to firing you when I got here tonight."

Zeroing in on one word, Sam allowed hope to rise just a tad. "You said 'was,' sir. Have you changed your mind?"

"Well, you gave me something else to think about." He turned to leave and stopped at the door. He glanced back. "I'll think on it and let you know. Play beach music. Got it?"

"Yes, sir."

27

Tracing the blue swirls on the Italian marbled journal, Merritt let her mind wander for a minute to combat the disappointment from Sam's no-show this afternoon. Although they didn't have a firm commitment for a sanding schedule, they'd fallen into an unspoken pattern of his coming over to work on her piano most days, including a quick supper. Shooing the missing-Sam feeling away, she thumbed the pages of the journal and remembered Millie.

When Millie had discovered Merritt's poems, she'd given her this journal. Millie bought the journal during her semester in Florence but had never used it. She 'didn't want to mess it up,' she'd said. 'You use it. Put your words in there, not just the brushed-up, pretty ones. Use these pages to think with.'

After months of neglecting the journal, Millie took an ink pen and wrote, *I like you, Merritt*, scratched out *like*, and wrote *LOVE* on the first blank page. 'There,' she'd said, 'I already made a mistake on the first page. Write your poems.' Freed somehow, Merritt had begun that night.

Millie had wiped away tears while reading the poem Merritt wrote for her yet had never asked to see more—just simply checked in now and again to make sure she was writing. 'You've got a lot to say. God's allowed you a lot of fodder for powerful poems. Your words will help someone else. Use your adversity to bless others. Don't waste it.'

Flipping through the pages, Merritt scanned some of the early poems, full of teenage angst, but as she neared the more recent ones, the words became a thoughtful window into the inner hopes, feelings, and disappointments of a sensitive person. She highlighted phrases that showed a particularly interesting use of a verb or adjective, nodding with a mental pat on the back.

The last page with words carried images from the first day she'd seen Francine's green piano, visual as well as internal feelings and thoughts. And, of course, feelings about the duet with Sam. She allowed herself to relive those moments, watching their hands move over the keyboard together, feeling the touches as they swayed with the beat. Smiling, she jotted down more ideas.

Pondering these images, she played with new words to connect them. Her heart ticked faster as the poem took shape.

An incoming text sounded. Ugh. Usually, she silenced her phone when she wrote in her poem journal. *Whatever you want to bring for supper tomorrow night is fine with me, Dez.*

"Not a bad writing session, Merritt. Good job." Leaning into the velour bed rest behind her, she checked the text. Sam, not Destiny.

Calm down, heart. It's just a text.

Hey. I hope I didn't wake you.

She glanced at the time. Ten fifty-seven.

Not yet. Three minutes till lights out.

LOL. Gotcha.

Sorry I bagged on you this afternoon.

Work was a bear yesterday.

I was in a foul mood. Didn't want to spoil your attitude with mine.

No worries. But in the future, I can take bad attitudes. Lots of experience with them.

I'm intrigued. Too bad it's your bedtime or I'd call for more info.

I could sacrifice sleep if you need to talk.

Ha. Okay. I'll keep it short.

Give me a minute.

Before the time on her phone changed, it was ringing.

"Hey."

"Hey, back. Thanks for taking my call. I hated to apologize in a text, but I didn't want to wait till I saw you next either."

"Sam, you're fine. Sorry work was a pain. Wanna talk about it?"

MERRITT'S VOICE on the line washed over Sam, assuaging his regret at not seeing her today ... and the missing-her feeling too. The missing-her part knocked him off balance a bit. Her concern seeped in and beckoned him to rest in it, to explore what sharing more of his experiences with her would feel like.

Had their relationship progressed to the point of sharing dreams and disappointments ... fears? Wait. Relationship? He didn't have time for a relationship, especially not now when he was so close to beginning his dream.

Yet, she intrigued him. Yes, he admired her talent, her spunk, her tenacity, but she could be prickly and standoffish too. He couldn't determine if she'd lean toward him if he tried for a kiss or push him away. She kept him guessing, for sure.

Finally, he liked her big brown eyes and her expressive mouth which broke into smiles more often lately, but a relationship?

Still, what could it hurt to talk it over with her? Maybe if he shared with her something important, she'd reciprocate with a secret of her own.

"Sam?"

Her voice pulled him back to the conversation. "Yeah. About work. I'm working at WDVY. Have been for a while now." He took a breath. "Over the past few weeks, I tried an experiment. Instead of just doing what I was hired to do, I've been going into the station at night when it's automated and plugging in a few local bands."

"Cool."

"Not cool ... at least to the owner. He paid me a visit."

"Wow."

"Yeah. He reamed me pretty good. Floated the idea of firing me, but at that point, I'd already asked him to sell the station to me."

"Oh."

"Your conversation is scintillating, by the way."

She chuckled. "You remember your SAT vocab, huh?"

"I'm more than a pretty face."

"Confident too. You said, 'automated.' Like ... nobody's deejaying?"

"Right. No one's at the station overnight. It's cheaper to run automation than pay a human."

"So if I listen at night, it's all pre-programmed? Nobody's choosing music, talking to callers?"

"You got it."

"That's sad."

"That's business."

"And you want to buy a radio station?"

"Yeah." He held his breath, dreading the teasing to come. Would she tease him? *Please don't tease me about this dream.*

"That sounds like you. I remember your announcements in high school. You made even the lunch menu funny."

Releasing his breath loosened strained neck muscles, his head lolling on the pillows propped against his headboard. *Thank you. Thank you. Thank you.*

"But now you want to own a station, not just DJ?"

"I want to be able to dictate the programming, the music, and the talk shows too."

"Sounds like you've got ideas."

"My ideas have ideas."

"Care to share? Hey, what's the number on the dial?"

"Seven-sixty. AM."

The sound of a tuner creeping across a radio dial squeaked over the phone.

"You've got an AM radio?"

"It's Millie's clock radio. Don't knock it. It picks up a lot of stations. Wait. I found it, I think. 'Sixty Minute Man'?"

"Sounds right."

"What local bands are you introducing next time?"

"Are you kidding? There isn't a next time till I have my own station. I'm on probation for my job. Doug's keeping tabs. I can't mess up. I already lost one station. There's a limited number of stations around Charlotte."

"Maybe you could talk to him."

"Last time we talked, he showed me how close I was to visiting the unemployment office. I'm playing by his rules no matter how hard it is."

"I'm excited for you, Sam. Sounds like a great fit for you."

Pleasure ballooned in his chest at her words.

"I am too. Thanks." Fist gripping an ink pen, he rolled his neck to release more tension. Sharing hopes rated with jumping from a plane or coming face to face with a wild bear ...

"Thanks for telling me about your dream. I can't wait to hear more."

"Be careful what you wish for. I gotta lot to talk about." He chuckled. "I should be good to sand some more pieces tomorrow night."

"Thursday night. Game night. Destiny's brining supper."

"Gotcha. I'll try to come early to sand, so I can dominate in whatever game you pick."

"You can try. I'll let you get back to your plans. Good night, Sam."

He hung up and read a text that came in while he talked with Merritt.

Doug here. I'm ready to talk. How's Friday look for you?

28

Stretching his arms over his head, Sam strolled back into Merritt's den after cleaning up from a sanding session. Merritt and Destiny chatted in the kitchen while they set the table with plates and food. Jesse would be late if he could come at all tonight.

A book partially covered by the bean bag chair caught his attention. No title on the cover? He opened it and began reading. A journal. Merritt's journal. A privacy warning pricked his brain, but he couldn't stop reading the beautiful phrases.

Page after page, he lost himself in the images and stories written in poetic form. His focus blocked the chattering from the kitchen, the thwacking of the ceiling fan. His breath caught in his lungs as the words described a little girl's longing for—

"I doubt Merritt gave you permission to read her journal."

Sam startled. Jesse. He'd appeared in the room with the swiftness and silence of some kind of apparition.

With a quick movement of his hand, Sam smacked the journal closed. "Ah. No. I was going to pick it up off the floor. Just wondered what it was. It didn't have a title on the front."

"Trust me, man. That's her personal stuff. You need to—"

Nodding, he set the journal on the bean bag. "I get it."

"You shouldn't have read it."

"Yeah." Shuddering, Sam swiped his face with his palm. A few minutes to process those words and the shock of Jesse's presence might help settle him back to the present. "I thought it was a novel. I wondered what she was reading." He dragged his teeth over his bottom lip. "But it's hers."

"I know."

"You've read it? You know what's in there?" Tamping down jealousy, Sam studied the other man's face.

"I've known her since fifth grade. I haven't read her stuff, but I lived through some of what she writes about. Destiny told me she writes poems."

"Yeah. They're beautiful."

"Hey, boys, time to eat." Destiny poked her head into the room and smiled at Jesse.

A call to supper splintering the tension, Sam headed for the kitchen.

Jesse clapped Sam's shoulder as he passed. "You need to tell her. It's her personal stuff."

Sam narrowed his eyes. The warning cloaked as a suggestion gave him pause. Was there more than friendship between Merritt and Jesse? Had there ever been? "Right. I'd like to wait until it's just the two of us."

Dropping his hand, Jesse held his gaze. "All right. We'll talk in a few days." With a quirk of an eyebrow, he headed into the kitchen.

His game face in place, Sam joined the three old friends, ribbing each other with good-natured barbs. For his part in the friendly banter, he contributed a laugh or a quick "wow" every now and then, enough to keep questions about his mood at bay. Jesse telegraphed a cool censure each time his eyes lighted on Sam's.

I get it, man. You're protective of your friend. But you don't have to protect her from me. I'm not going to hurt her.

COASTING to a stop in her carport the next afternoon, Merritt enjoyed the familiar happy vibe that visited her every time she arrived home. She smiled. Her home. Old fears rose and snatched away the smile. How long would it remain so? Trey and Allison had been silent for a few weeks.

No news is good news? Maybe?

Sam had seemed subdued at Ms. Connie's, but he confirmed he'd come to finish the sanding tonight. Would he have enough time to stain a few pieces too? Fluttery feelings accompanied the images of a cherry-stained piano.

Happiness vibrated in her chest. Maybe she'd be teaching on her own piano by mid-September when her lessons began again. Her own piano.

Inside, the aroma of spices and onion welcomed her home. Unlocking the crock pot lid, she stirred the sloppy joe meat and then turned the setting to *warm*. She took out a plastic container of watermelon from the refrigerator as the doorbell sounded.

"It's just me." Sam glided into the kitchen. Smiling, his eyes flashed to the crock pot, the watermelon she held, the floor. Everywhere but her.

Interesting. *Still in a mood, huh, Sam? I understand.*

"Are you hungry now, or do you want to wait a while? We can have the sloppy joes whenever you're ready."

Biting the side of his cheek, he slid his hands down his jeans. "Let's wait a while."

"Fine with me. We can get straight to the piano then." She headed for the back room.

He caught her arm as she passed by him. "Wait. We need to talk."

Every bit of the happiness filling her chest since she got home scattered like a raindrop on a mud puddle. She'd heard those words before. She knew what they meant. He was done, moving on.

How could he leave her piano strewn in pieces on the floor, stripped naked, looking like sun-bleached driftwood on the coast? She pulled in a breath, counted to ten, and pushed it out. *Pull out the old mask, Merritt. Shut it down before he starts with a sad song about—*

"Merritt, listen." He wiggled her arm. "I—I need to apologize."

Starting with an apology? "You mean it's 'me, not you'? That kind of apology?"

He frowned. "What are you talking about?" He nudged her into the den, scanning the room for something. "It's not in here now."

"What?" Her head spinning, she concentrated on breathing.

"Last night. When I was here? While you and Destiny were getting dinner ready. Before I came to the kitchen."

"Sam, you're not making sense. Are you bailing on fixing the piano? Did your girlfriend—?

"Merritt, I don't have a girlfriend." He raked his hands through his hair. "Listen to me. I have to apologize for something I did last night before dinner."

Sam showed a different side tonight. No longer the clown or the brimming-with-cheeky-charm boy next door, this Sam doubted himself. His nervous energy bordered a bit on fear.

Heart pounding in her chest, she struggled to breathe normally. "Sam, what's wrong? You're scaring me."

"You don't need to be scared." He closed his eyes. "I'm worried about how you're going to feel—"

She thwacked his arm. "Tell me, for Heaven's sake. You're—"

"I read your journal last night. Some of your poems."

Hot and cold pinpricks stung up and down her body. She gulped air like a sprinter after a race. Opening her mouth, she shook her head. Her brain failed to cobble together a reply to his confession. Her poems? Sam had seen them, read them? She closed her eyes. This man in front of her had seen her innermost thoughts. Had read about—

Summoning strength to fake a calm, she banked her emotions and forced her breath to return to normal.

Put one foot in front of the other. Open the door for him to leave. You can keep it together until he's gone. "Tonight's not good to work on the piano. Sorry."

His face slacked. "Merritt, wait. Let's talk about this. Don't shut me out."

Gripping the doorknob like the reins on a bucking bull, she steadied her voice. "I need you to leave now."

"Come on, Merritt. I messed up. I know it. I'm so sorry."

Roaring in her ears, she turned to the door without a word. *Breathe in. Breathe out. He'll be gone in a few minutes.*

"Merritt, please. Yell at me. Tell me how mad you are. Tell me it was private. Tell me I didn't have the right to read it."

"You didn't have the right." She tossed her hair over her shoulder.

"I'm so sorry, but those poems are good. Really good."

Heat slammed through her body.

Chest heaving, she stomped back across the room, stopping inches from him, not caring about his personal space. "It's none of your business if they're good or not. They're mine. My experiences. My words. Mine. You didn't have the right to open that book. You should have closed it as soon as you saw what it was."

MERRITT'S EYES MESMERIZED SAM. They deepened from mocha brown to onyx with every word flying from her mouth. His gaze dropped to her lips, moving with words explaining her anger, her hurt. Her hurt.

He'd hurt her.

One minute he bore her accusations, the next he closed the distance between them, pressing his lips to hers. Keeping his hands by his sides, he kissed through her initial rigid stance to the gradual softening. Tentative fingertips lighted on his chest, then slid up around his neck. He circled his arms around her waist and pulled her closer to him, molding her to him. His senses filled with her floral scent, with her fingers threading through his hair, with her lips—

The force of her push staggered him backward.

Covering her mouth with the back of her hand, she accused him with her coal eyes. "Stop, Sam. I'm mad at you. I'm so mad." She sobbed but caught herself. "You don't play fair."

Dumbstruck, he sucked in air, snatched back to Merritt's anger, away from the kiss. "I crossed the line again. I'm sorry. You have every right to be mad." Biting his lip, he stepped forward. "Let me explain."

"No, Sam. Please. Go." Tears gathered in her eyes.

He needed to heed her wishes, but the hurt in her eyes brought him to his knees, his weak knees. That kiss.

"Merritt—"

"Sam, please." Holding her arms around herself, she pressed her lips together.

As much as he wanted to comfort her, an emotional collapse could be imminent. "All right. I'm going. But please don't shut me out. I didn't mean to hurt you."

Catching her lip between her teeth, she nodded.

"Please forgive me, Merritt."

Eyes glued to the floor, she remained silent.

Fear slithered into his chest. His gut clenched. What if she couldn't forgive him? Shaking his head, he refused to go there right now.

He turned at the threshold. "I'm so sorry."

MILLIE'S blue tweed cardigan hugging her, Merritt crawled onto her mattress, face planted into her pillow, and freed the tears straining to fall since Sam's confession. Muffled sobs filled the silence. Not since Millie's funeral had emotions wrecked her like his betrayal. Trey and Allison's theft faded to annoyance when compared to her feelings now.

Living on her own had lulled her into believing she'd never be wrecked by betrayal in her own house again. Complacency had ruined her sense of privacy. Time traveled backward, and she was ten years old again, trying to keep her small bag of stuff under the radar of grabby foster siblings.

With the tears subsiding, she dragged her heavy body onto her side, gathering her knees to her chest. She recounted the repercussions from tonight. Her piano lay in pieces. Jared expected a duet with Sam. Sam expected a duet with her.

No matter. She could strike their duet from the program. She could play Jared's duet. The piano? She'd find someone to help get it back together. She didn't need Sam. She'd figure it out herself. As usual.

Fresh tears escaped and dripped over her nose. Pulling up the corner of the cardigan, she scrubbed her face. Her throat constricted.

She didn't want to do it by herself. Hugging someone felt so good. Leaning into someone else ... How pitiful was she? She let him kiss her after he'd admitted betraying her. After he'd admitted reading her innermost thoughts.

She admitted to herself now that she'd been falling under his spell, enjoying his attention and time and help. Closing puffy eyes, she rolled to her back, tightening her arms around her waist.

Already, she missed Sam. No more sanding afternoons, or Thursday Night-Game Nights, or random visits to Ms. Connie's. No more Sam. Fatigue pressed against her body.

Forgive him.

No. He saw too much. He knows too much. There'd be no covering the stains of her past for him in the future, much less shining it up to make it presentable. He'd already seen the raw truth of her. She cringed and pulled the cardigan over her face.

The truth of your past does not define the truth of your present or future. Forgive him. I've forgiven you.

Her phone vibrated in her hand. Sam.

How are you?

Please stop.

Please talk to me.

Her fingers refused to perform the monumental task of texting. Palming the phone, she dropped her arm to the duvet, exhaustion ruling her body. The cell buzzed again. She turned onto her side to read the text.

I messed up. Doing a lot of that lately.

Please don't shut me out. Let me explain.

Let me make it up to you.

A tear slid out of her eye, dripped off the bridge of her nose. Her heart rate picked up speed. Could she let him?

Forgive him.

Pressing her lips together, she balked at the idea of forgiving him. But a Millie-ism popped into her weary mind: Sometimes you have to do first, then the feelings come.

Could she face him again, knowing what he'd read?

And then the kiss.

She winced. She'd kissed him like ... like he was her boyfriend. Like she wanted him to be.

Because she did.

This is hard.

I promise I will make it up to you.

There's more to it than you know.

Can we get together and talk?

I don't want to talk about my journal. I want things the way they were.

Groaning to herself, she tapped the darkened screen and texted one word.

Okay.

Thank you. I'll call you tomorrow.

She dropped the phone without replying, her head pounding between her temples. How would she face him?

Start with forgiveness.

29

Grasping the sweat-covered plastic cup at a local pizzeria, Merritt let the cold seep into her hand, hoping the icy temperature would freeze her emotions. Maybe the imminent conversation with Sam could be over in fifteen minutes, maybe twenty, if he began with small talk. Modulating her breath, she glanced to the back of the dining room.

At a round table near the kitchen, Destiny and Jesse offered their presence for moral support. They'd already ordered a large pizza she'd share with them after Sam said his piece. Destiny waved at her and smiled.

Thank You for true friends, God.

The chair across from her scraped against the floor.

Jerking her head back, she locked eyes with Sam, a blank expression replacing his usual grin.

"Thank you for meeting me here."

She nodded, fisting her hands in her lap.

Long, narrow fingers folding the corner of his placemat, he locked eyes with her. "I want to apologize for two things that happened last night. First, I apologize for kissing you. I've wanted to for a while, but last night wasn't the right time. I'm sorry."

Her breath caught. He'd wanted to for a while? "Thank you."

"I shouldn't have kissed you when you were so upset. I'm sorry it happened that way, but I'm hoping it'll happen again sometime when we both want it."

She shook her head.

He cocked his. "Why not? You didn't enjoy it?"

Refusing to admit the truth, she searched for a way to answer his question that wouldn't be lying or opening her up to more heartache. Leave it to Sam, of course, to begin—

"I believe you sighed and snuggled closer ..."

Heat exploding in her cheeks, she gasped. "I can't believe you."

A movement caught her eye at the back table. Jesse pushed his seat back, waiting for her signal to help.

Sam followed her gaze and turned back to her. "Hey, I'm sorry. Call your friends off. That's why we're meeting here in public, right? No repeats of last night?"

She aimed a wan smile in Jesse's direction, and he relaxed, sipping on his root beer.

Narrowing his eyes, Sam leaned against the back of his chair. He glanced over his shoulder and nodded to the other couple, then flicked his hazel gaze back to her. "Why no repeat?"

"It's not nice—"

"You'd be helping me because I really misread your response. What went wrong? I mean, I know the timing was wrong, but I thought we both enjoyed it."

Heat repeated its ascent over her cheeks. "You're really something."

"I've been told that. If you mean it as a compliment ..."

"I didn't. I'm not a casual dater." Remember that, Merritt, if he keeps talking about kissing. "Since I don't see us together in the long term, I don't see another kiss happening."

He folded his arms across his chest. "I didn't ask you to

marry me, but why don't you see us for the long term, as you say?"

"We'd never work. You have too much family."

Jaw dropping, he leaned across the table. "Too much family? That's a new one. What's the magic number? Would two siblings be too many?"

"Yes. I already told you. I'm looking for someone with no family."

He blustered. "I didn't think you meant it." Squeezing the back of his neck, he furrowed his brow. "An orphan? You're serious."

"Yes. I'm still serious."

"Orphans come with scars."

"That's hurtful."

"But true."

Lowering her chin, she challenged him. "Families come with opinions."

"All this sounds a might specific. Are you speaking from experience?"

She considered him. He'd already breached some of her secrets by reading her poems. She'd just explained why they wouldn't work. Why not explain herself? She could put the kibosh on anything else happening between them and save herself more heartache.

"I dated a guy all through senior year of college and then for several months afterward. He asked me to marry him. We were all set to begin the plans. I wore his ring for three weeks."

"What happened?"

"His mother."

Eyes hooded, she rotated the saltshaker. *Pretend you're telling about a series you binged. It's fiction, not your real life.*

"His father was the mayor back in his hometown with hopes of becoming a state senator and who knows what else. She had me investigated." Unable to stop herself, Merritt glanced at Sam.

Holding her gaze, he didn't flinch. *A point in your favor, Sam.*

"All of it, the reason I was in foster care, happened over twenty years ago now, but his mother was determined. She found out my whole sordid background and shared it with Caleb."

"Merritt."

"Once you know the names, it's easy. The story made front-page news for months." She swallowed to calm her shaky voice.

"Merritt, stop."

"His mother convinced Caleb he'd never be governor if he married me even though I was four years old when my mother shot my father for beating her again. To his credit, he didn't ask for the ring back, but I didn't want the reminder."

Clenching the cup, she sipped her water. "I suppose you're wondering if I saw it."

"Merritt, I'm not—" He reached for her hand. She slid both of hers back onto her lap.

"No. My mother, the murderess, as the papers described her—yeah, I looked it all up when I was fourteen—hid me in the closet when he got out of his truck yelling at her again. She protected me as well as she could. I didn't see anything, but I ..." She stopped to pull in a ragged breath. "I heard a lot. I still can't eat fried pork chops. That's what she was cooking for supper that night."

His eyes held steady on hers. *Good job, Sam. You're not afraid to hear hard things. I appreciate your effort.*

"I don't know what to say."

"You don't have to say anything. I want you to understand, if you can, why I say my type is an orphan."

SAM'S HEART crashed against his rib cage. He had no idea about Merritt's background beyond her foster child status when she was growing up. He couldn't imagine her life. His parents popped into his mind and garnered an overwhelming urge to call them and thank them for ... for everything.

"Merritt, I'm so sorry."

"I accept your apology." Twisting to the left, she removed her purse from the back of the chair.

"Wait. That's it?" Frowning, he wiped the beads of sweat from his upper lip. "You accept it, and you're leaving? No more questions? No explanation?"

"That's what you wanted. I'm giving it to you."

"I wanted to talk about it too. Now I understand more about why—"

She shook her head, wrapping her purse strap around her hand. "You don't understand much at all. Just because you read my journal—"

"I didn't read it. I read part of one poem."

A stillness settled on the table. "Which one?"

He licked his lips. "The one about a doll."

Closing her eyes, she hung her head, brown waterfall curls sliding over her shoulder and partially covering her face. "Destiny and Jesse are waiting for me."

"No." His hand shot across the table. He brought it back before Jesse could join them. "Wait. Please."

The waitress arrived with a pizza.

"That's not ours." Her posture rigid, she hugged her purse to her chest, ready for flight.

"Yes, it is. I ordered it before I sat down so we wouldn't be interrupted. I got several toppings. Pick off what you don't want."

Glancing at Destiny and Jesse, she shook her head.

"Please stay. I promise to be good."

She tightened her mouth. "Don't promise me anything."

Good night, she's tough.

Leaning back into his chair, he flattened his palms on the table. "Please stay. I'd like to talk a little longer, if you will."

30

Loaded with several toppings, the pizza steamed between them. The aroma of red sauce and cheese and oregano mingled together, roiling her stomach. As delicious as the pie looked, Merritt kept her hands in her lap. Nope. Not happening.

"Thank you, but I'm gonna pass right now."

"Yeah. I hear you." Sam pushed the pizza stand to the side of the table and leaned in. "You've shared a lot tonight. Thank you. I'm so sorry for what you've been through and for my actions that brought us to this point tonight."

She kept her eyes focused on her hands.

"Please look at me, Merritt."

She lifted her face, met his eyes.

"Your secrets are safe with me. I won't tell anyone about what you've told me. I won't bring it up again. Can we just sit here and talk about something else? The duet? Your piano?" Sam's thumb rubbed back and forth over the prongs of his fork. A worry wrinkle creased the space between his eyebrows.

Where was the normal Sam, the goofball, clown-around Sam? The one who made her laugh despite herself. She wanted to talk to him, but her secrets, her baggage, had turned him into this contrite Sam waiting for her to make everything right again. Things were different now. He knew all the bad stuff.

Some of it, at least.

What if she told him more? Dropping her chin to her chest, she considered a next step. Would one more story be the tipping point, the one that pushed him away for good, severed everything between them? Would one more story from her shameful past release him to find someone more appropriate than she was?

Swallowing against the bile swirling in her stomach, she clutched the red heart necklace. "Did you read the whole doll poem?"

His eyes locked with hers. "Most of it, but I'm so sorry—"

"Stop. I forgive you. I know you didn't mean to hurt me." She sucked in a breath and pushed it out again. "The fourth foster house I lived in had a girl about a year older than me. For Christmas that year, she got an American girl doll. They're beautiful dolls with beautiful clothes—"

"Yeah, our grandparents got one for Josie."

"I got an American girl book, not the whole series which each doll has. One book, plus some candy and underwear and socks. Of course, I was grateful for any presents, but Haley, the girl, hated sharing ... toys, the limelight, everything."

Merritt replayed Haley's taunts, 'Now it's my turn to play with my doll,' said whenever her mother came within earshot. "Her mother thought she was an angel sharing with her foster sister." Merritt wiped her hands along her thighs.

"After a few months, I'd had enough. Haley went to a sleepover one night. I pinched myself to stay awake until her parents fell asleep and took that doll to a little girl who lived about seven houses down the street. She rode our school bus, too, and had a houseful of brothers. I wrote a note with her name on it and left it on the front porch."

Remembering the scene brought goose bumps to her arms. The cold night air, the dogs barking as she ran past dark houses, a few driveway lamps lighting her way. She shivered and peeked for Sam's reaction. Still listening.

"Haley didn't look for the doll until Sunday afternoon, two days after the sleepover. She looked all over the house. She cried and cried and yelled at me, but I played stupid. In their defense, her parents assured her I couldn't have done anything with it, but her mother rifled all my things anyway." Pushing a lock of hair back in place, Merritt trailed her fingers to the curl at the end.

"The next weekend, we played salon, and she gave me a shearing with real scissors. The weekend after that, I was in a new house, looking like a little boy with my new haircut."

Sam shook his head. "Merritt, I ... I don't—"

"There's the inspiration behind that poem. Now you know the rest of the story."

He stared at the plate like it would have a script for him.

Trembling, she pushed away from the table. Her work here was done. *Now you can go back to your real life and leave the foster girl alone.*

"I'm going to say bye to those guys back there, then I'm going home. I'm not hungry."

As she rose, he glanced up.

"Bye, Sam."

THOUGHTS AND IMAGES swirled in Sam's mind. Warm pictures of his siblings laughing together and with their parents. He should say something to her, but what? Sorry couldn't help, couldn't erase the years of hurt and betrayal.

Merritt turned from Destiny and Jesse and headed for the front door without looking back his way. Glued to his seat, he didn't move.

"Would you like a box for that?" The waitress gestured toward the pizza.

"Yeah. Sure."

Four eyes from the back of the room bored into him.

You care for Merritt? Well, so do I. That's right. And somehow I'm going to fix this.

Unfortunately, the thought brought no comfort. A heavy feeling settled into his chest. Why did he feel he'd just failed a test?

As he transferred the pizza into the box, an idea formed in his brain. Bolstering courage and swallowing pride, he put leaving on hold and headed for the back table.

31

A malaise lingered into the next day, hovering and pressing on Merritt's shoulders, made worse by the muggy August heat. Hoping to work out the frustrations instead of wallowing, she beat the boxing bag for a while. Feeling strong after the solo boxing match, she researched piano restorers online but stopped short of calling one.

Instead, she chose two new songs to learn for her rotation at the Lamplighter. Preparing for the next birthday gathering, she made meatballs and simmered Millie's red sauce recipe on the stove.

Every time thoughts of Sam surfaced, she attacked another item on her to-do list, resulting in a productive morning. The to-do list shrank, but thoughts of Sam still lurked in her traitorous mind.

Putting away the last remnants of her late lunch of cheese and crackers, she startled at the sound of the doorbell.

The peephole showed a distorted version of Sam.

Her stomach clenched. She rocked back on her heels. Why was he here? They'd finished talking last night ... not what she wanted to do today.

He knocked on the door. Banged actually.

"Merritt, I know you're home. Your car's in the garage."

She rested her head against the door, whispering a prayer for strength. Maybe if she ignored him, he'd leave.

"I'm not leaving yet. I need to work on the piano. I don't leave a job undone, just so you know. I promised, and I deliver."

She rolled her head back and forth.

"The pizza was delicious, by the way."

Despite a command not to, her mouth tipped up.

"I shared with Destiny and Jesse. You probably already know that."

She didn't. She hadn't looked at her phone all morning. Or last night, either. She'd shut it off and climbed into a steaming hot bath, turning the faucet on with her foot every time the water cooled. She'd wallowed in solitude and silence last night. She'd hear from Destiny after her shift today probably.

"I think they're rooting for me. They know what a rock-solid guy I am, and they—"

She swung open the door.

"Now you're slinging it." Her eyes widened. The peephole had distorted his image somewhat, but the shadows under his eyes were real.

"Did you stay up all night?"

"I look that good, huh?" Raised eyebrows fished for a response.

He still looked good, but he didn't need her to confirm it.

"I got some shut-eye. Can I come in?"

Bristling, she squeezed the doorknob. "I think we said everything last night."

"You told your story. I didn't say much." His subdued words revealed a new layer to Sam, one that gave her pause. His cheek hid his dimple today.

"Yeah. I noticed that, but no worries. I understand."

"Sorry, but you don't understand because we didn't finish talking. You didn't give me much chance to say anything before you left."

"You were really quiet."

He pushed out a breath. "We're gonna have this talk on your porch?"

She didn't want to talk about last night with Sam on the porch or in the house or anywhere yet. Part of her wanted to pretend he'd never seen the journal so that she could smile and flirt with him, and he could flash his dimple and flirt back.

Part of her wanted to keep wallowing a bit longer.

She chewed her lip while the different parts of her warred with each other. Thankfully, her better self won the battle. Giving in, she stepped aside to let him enter.

"Thank you." He followed her into the den.

Sliding into a chair, she gestured for him to take the other one.

"You laid a lot of stuff on me last night, and I'd like the chance to reply."

"Laid a lot of stuff ... I explained about my life."

"Merritt, I'm sorry. My words are all wrong. I get that, but please let's talk some more. I want to understand."

"I'm not something to be understood. I'm not a lab project." Testy. That's what Millie would have called the way she was acting toward Sam. She summoned all the manners she'd learned from Millie and television programs and the etiquette books she'd scanned, trying to be better, trying to measure up to all the girls whose DNA carried genes for proper behavior. "Would you like something to drink?"

Snorting, he leaned forward. "I'm not here for a tea party. I'm here to talk through this wrinkle and get back to the piano."

She ducked her head. He genuinely wanted to finish the piano? He wasn't disgusted with her background?

"You're not here for closure?"

"I'm here for understanding. So we can move forward. So we can fix your piano. So we can explore whatever this," he motioned between them, "relationship's going to be."

Straightening her spine, she shifted in her chair.

"Don't shut me out, Merritt, please. I messed up. I should have told you last night that your past doesn't dictate your present or your future. You had a hard childhood. I get that as much as I can without living it, but look at you now. You own your own business, your house. People support you and care for you."

A tingling in her nose threatened tears. Why were harsh words easier to take than sweet, kind words? She raked her teeth over her top lip.

"I'm sorry I didn't say all that last night. I guess I had to process everything you told me."

That's fair. She'd ripped open a door to some heavy stuff and then left him at the table, dealing with the pizza and everything she'd said.

But he'd come back. He reached out for forgiveness and friendship. Who was the last person who had pursued her time and attention and forgiveness? Anybody?

"Okay."

Tracing circles over his knee, he studied her. "Is that you accepting my apology?"

She nodded.

Dipping his head, he let his shoulders drop. "Thank you." He cleared his throat. "You know, I was thinking. Maybe instead of looking for an orphan, you should look for someone who'd stick with you through thick and thin, as they say. Somebody who'd have your back no matter what." He kept his gaze locked on hers, waiting.

Caught under his spell, she couldn't react, couldn't push words from her corn-starched mouth. Would Sam be that kind of person?

"So, can we be friends again and maybe go on another ...?"

Thoughts scrambled with his question. She arched an eyebrow.

He grinned. "How 'bout we start with making your piano beautiful again, then take it from there?"

"Sounds like a doable plan."

"Thank you." He glanced at the bean bag chair to his right. "You know ... a buddy of mine used to have one of these in his bonus room." He moved over to the bag and dropped into it. "Just like I remembered. Not too bad." Stretching his legs out in front of him, he closed his eyes. "Not too bad at all."

AN ANNOYING SOUND persisted in Sam's ear, which didn't make sense. *Where are the sea gulls crying overhead? Where's the sound of waves crashing on the shore?* Emerald Isle always delivered relaxation and fun and good times. Delighted to be in his happy place, he pedaled his feet to dig deeper into the sandy beach.

"Sam, Sam. Your alarm is going off. Sam, wake up." A hand nudged his arm.

Wake up? Time for school? He moved to sit, but the sand shifted underneath him. He opened his eyes. Merritt. Merritt?

Chuckling, she knelt beside him on the floor. "Good morning, sleepy head. Only it's six o'clock at night. Your alarm. You need to be somewhere?"

Sam shook his head and blinked. Oh, man. "Um, so we're not at Emerald Isle, huh?"

"What? No. You're at my house."

Merritt's house. Her bean bag. Not a bad place to be if he could just get the fog out of his head.

"You fell asleep, and I didn't have the heart to wake you up."

He scrubbed a hand over his face. "Wow. Sorry. What time did you say?"

"Six."

"It's six? I was out for three hours?"

"Uh-huh. Are you hungry?"

"Man, I thought I'd finish the sanding today." Pushing himself out of the bean bag, he stood and stretched. "You said it's six? Whew. I'm trying to make sense of this. My head kinda feels out of it." He covered a yawn. "Sorry."

"Yes, it's a little after six now. Do you have time to eat something? I have spaghetti and meatballs, or I could scramble some eggs." A smile hovered around her mouth.

Joints popping, he rolled his neck. "Yeah. I think I am kinda hungry. If you're offering, I'll accept. Spaghetti sounds good. Any coffee, maybe?"

32

"This is going to be bright, huh?" Merritt flexed her fingers, questioning her color choice.

"It's going to look great. Be still." Destiny swiped a stroke of hot pink polish down the middle of Merritt's pinky nail. "I still can't believe he fell asleep on your bean bag."

Merritt looked forward to these bi-weekly visits for a quick pampering by her friend. Years ago, Destiny had resolved to break Merritt's nail-biting habit.

Her signature, short painted nails pleased her and gave her quality one-on-one time with her best friend. Sometimes she kept the same color. Other times, she chose a new one or agreed to a one suggested by a student. Violet had asked for the pink variety.

"Yeah. Then he ate almost half of the meatballs I'd made for the birthday dinner." Merritt smiled, however, instead of frowning. Remembering his enjoyment of the meal flashed another gush of pleasure warming her insides.

"I can't believe you let him in. I thought you were done with him."

True. Ordinarily, she would have been. But Sam wasn't ordinary.

"He was sincerely sorry for opening my journal. Plus, the domestic violence slash police story plus stealing-the-doll story didn't keep him away, so ..."

Destiny fixed Merritt's hand under the dryer and loaded color on the other thumb.

"He had to finish my piano, too, and Jared needs his duet partner."

"You're playing with him, too, right?"

"It's not unusual for me to play a duet with a student. And before you say anything, I know he's not my student, but he's helping one of mine."

"You got a lot going on with him." Destiny stole a quick glance at Merritt.

"Please share the point you're trying to make, Destiny. I'm a captive audience." Tugging her hand to free it, Merritt frowned at her friend, who gripped her fingers more tightly.

"Just looking out for my best friend. You like him."

True. She did like him. If she didn't, she wouldn't have let him in the door. There wouldn't have been a meeting at the pizza place. "He's a good guy. He's a helper."

"Yeah, I noticed that. He likes being needed. He likes helping people."

"Seems like you've got something else to say."

Destiny twisted the top onto the bottle. "He seems like a good guy. We shared his pizza the other night and talked. He's solid. But, Merritt," she brushed green bangs from her eyes, "he's not one of us."

"I know. I've met his family."

"He won't understand ... or at least it'll be hard."

"I get it. I'm fine. I'm spending time with a nice guy, okay?" Her tone said *back off* even as her heart agreed with Destiny. At the same time, Millie hadn't been one of them, yet she'd loved Merritt unconditionally, supported her, never judged her.

"Okay. I've said my piece. Hey, when you gonna let me give

you a trim?" She nodded to the curls draping past Merritt's shoulders. "It's been too long. Split ends need to go."

Merritt's stomach seized. It couldn't be time for a trim already. "Ahm."

"I'm talking trim, not cut. Your precious waterfall curls will never know the difference except for being more vibrant and bouncy."

"Next time. How about then?"

"Merritt, you have beautiful hair, whether it's halfway down your back or framing your chin. More importantly, you're beautiful on the inside, you know? It's taken me years to get that in my head about my own self, but it's the truth. For both of us."

Being careful with her hot pink-tipped fingers, Merritt pulled Destiny in for a bear hug. "I know it up here," she pointed to her temple, "but the truth gets lost sometimes way down here." She patted her heart. "Keep me straight, okay?"

"Will do. And your split ends in control too."

SAM PULLED into Merritt's driveway and parked to the side. She'd texted she'd be home around six. Cool. He could watch the next video showing the staining part of the process. They'd finished sanding and washing off the dust of every piece of her piano. The staining process wouldn't be too difficult.

So far, so good. Just go step by step, a little at a time, like eating an elephant, right? One bite, chew, and swallow.

An engine sounded beside him. Merritt waved as she glided her car past him and headed for her garage. The garage door lifted into place, revealing a well-organized space with something—What?

A punching bag hung in the far corner. He shut off the video and sauntered into the garage carrying the bag of stain and other supplies.

Opening the door for her, he leaned in with wide eyes. "Okay. Who's the boxer? You or Millie?"

Her tightened lips warned him that the punching bag must be off-limits.

"Sorry, but the door opened, and there it was. I didn't mean to overstep. Again. Didn't realize it was a secret."

Purse clutched to her chest, she joined him near the bag.. "It's not a secret. It's just—

"Not something you want to share. I get it. No more questions. Although ... it *is* intriguing."

She looked at him, a silent plea in her eyes.

He covered his heart with his free hand. "That's all I'm going to say."

Chewing on her cheek, she sighed. "Millie got it for me when I first came to stay with her. Anger, my go-to emotion back in the day, simmered and bubbled out more times than I like to admit. She tried everything—positive reinforcement, love, patience.

"She bought this bag used when a gym closed. We took lessons together. You should have seen her whacking it. She got pretty good too." Merritt trailed her fingers down the bag, lost in thought. "It's a great workout. In fact, I trade a boxing lesson for a piano lesson. The owner of Tryon Street Gym trains me once a week, and I teach his daughter piano."

"Cool trade. Maybe you can teach me some moves." He grinned at her. "Only if you want to, though. Hey, ready to stain your bad boy? I got the color you chose." Opening the bag, he extracted the can to show her. "We can probably stain most of the pieces today. I've got everything we need and nothing but time. How about you?"

She nodded.

Her quiet demeanor unsettled him. Did she regret telling him about Millie and the bag? "Hey." He touched her shoulder. "Your secrets. Your story. All of it's safe with me. Okay?"

Tears glistened in her dark eyes.

Nope. No, no. No crying today.

"Yeah, I think some boxing lessons for me are in order. When Josie starts to boss me around, I can bring out the ol' gloves and show her what's what."

The welcome sound of laughter burst out of her mouth. Bingo.

"You would never do that to Josie."

"Yeah, maybe not now, but back in the day ... we could really go at each other. When she was five and I was six ..."

Merritt led him from the garage. "No way. Not even then."

"Yes, way. What a little scrapper, my sister. I probably got bald spots I don't know about from where she pulled out chunks of these gorgeous locks." Raking a hand through his hair, he fluffed the strands to stand on end.

"You must have provoked her." Smiling, she hung her keys on the hook by the door and continued into the kitchen.

"Ouch. Here I am transforming your piano to an enviable piece, and you cut me to the quick with your character assessment."

Leaning against a counter, she crossed her arms in front of her. "Why are you here, Sam?"

The abrupt change in conversation gave him pause. He tipped his head to the side. "To restore your piano."

"Right. But why?"

"Because you need help. I can provide it." *Plus, you're interesting, talented, not to mention beautiful, and I want to keep hanging out with you. We'll share more of my feelings later, but too much too soon ...* "So let's get to it then."

MERRITT NODDED, weighing his words. Destiny seemed to be right. Sam saw her as a project, someone who needed something he could provide.

You're a good man, Sam, but I'm not a charity case. I appreciate your help. Once they got the piano finished, he'd be free to find his next damsel in distress.

33

For the past week and a half, Sam had faithfully layered a coat of shellac, waited a couple of days, lightly sanded the pieces, and then layered another coat. The dry August heat had helped quicken the process. Every time Merritt looked at the pieces, her heart somersaulted, visions of September lessons on her beautiful piano flashing in her mind.

Hesitating at the bedroom's threshold with Operation Piano Rescue happening, she offered a thank-you prayer. So far, Sam had kept his promise to transform this piano. After this last coat dried, he could begin reassembling.

She rapped on the door frame to announce her presence. "Ready for a snack?"

"Yeah. Perfect timing." Sam laid his brush on a piece of plastic wrap and tapped the shellac lid back in place. Arching his back and stretching, he smiled at her. "A break sounds great. If this layer dries as fast as the others, maybe we can start putting her back together this weekend."

Conflicting emotions swirled inside Merritt. She wanted a playable piano in her house, but she loved the time spent with Sam over the past few weeks, working together on this project.

Focusing on the positive and pushing the melancholy away, she led him to the kitchen for milk and cookies.

"These aren't homemade like Ms. Connie's, but they're the best store-bought around. Trust me."

"Oh, you're a connoisseur of ginger snaps?" He pumped liquid soap and washed his hands at the sink.

"Yeah, I am. They're my favorite cookie, and I know what I'm talking about."

"With an endorsement like that, let me at 'em." He grabbed one and popped it in his mouth.

"No." She laughed. "Dunk it first." Little pinky raised, she dunked a cookie into her glass. "See." Holding it above the milk until it stopped dripping, she bit off the soaked portion. "Hmm." With a glance at him, she froze, awareness jolting her body.

Sam stared at her lips, his second cookie forgotten. She stuffed the remaining moon-shaped cookie into her mouth and took a swig of the milk.

Swallowing, he reached for another cookie. "That's how it's done, huh?"

"Uh-huh. Yeah."

He dunked the cookie twice. "That scar near your mouth. You ever talk about it?"

So that's why he was staring. Good to know. "No big story. A foster brother chunked a piece of a broken toy, and, unfortunately, my face got in the way. Band-aids helped it heal."

No need to mention that the boy had thrown it at her out of frustration when he broke it. He lied to his parents, and they, furious because of the cost of the toy, had made pretty quick motions to have her re-settled. She'd been happy to be rid of the violent bully but missed the meals at that placement. The mother had been a great cook.

He studied her for a moment, and she forced herself not to squirm under his scrutiny. Tossing curls over her shoulder, she changed the subject. "The piano is coming together." Lame attempt, but a new topic nonetheless.

After several beats, Sam followed the new direction. "As I said, we're close to a finished product." He brushed crumbs from his hands. "Well, I should get going. If you want to open the vents in the bedroom now that we've finished the shellacking, wait till tomorrow. Dust shouldn't stick by then." He rose and headed for the front door.

"Will do." Something had passed back there, and Merritt wasn't sure what. She followed him with a knot growing in her chest.

Turning at the door, he caught her chin with her fingers, rubbing the scar with his thumb. "Merritt, you can be real with me, okay?"

She couldn't move. Her eyes searched his face for how to answer.

"You don't have to edit stories before you share them. I enjoy spending time with you, okay?"

She nodded.

His eyes flicked to hers, then dropped to her scar again.

Paralyzed, she tracked his face as it lowered to hers. He brushed a soft kiss on the scar, then jogged down the steps. At his car, he turned back. "Hey, when we get this piano back together, we'll bring Ms. Connie over here so she can see it. Sound good?"

Another time with Sam. Yes, please.

WATER BILL. Electricity bill. Coupon for the outlet center. Flier for a late-in-the-summer Bible school. Merritt dropped the mail in different piles on the kitchen bar. The last piece, a business envelope, caught her attention. Reading the return address label, she gasped. A law office? Electric charges pinged all over her insides.

She covered her face and flung up a desperate arrow prayer before dealing with the most likely bad news. Ripping open the envelope, she flinched at a paper cut on her thumb. *Ouch.* She pressed her thumb against her middle finger and smoothed out the letter with her other hand.

Heart pounding in her ears, she struggled to concentrate on the words. So much legal jargon. What did it mean? Trouble, for sure, if Trey and Allison had resorted to using an attorney. Was this retaliation for sending the letter confirming the will was valid?

She glanced at the clock on the wall. Destiny had a permanent wave set for this afternoon. Jesse said he'd be slammed the whole day. For a quick second, she wished Sam were here to settle her, tell her the world wasn't about to crash around her.

No, she needed to figure this out by herself. She couldn't run to Sam every time a problem reared.

God, what do I do?

Ches. Grabbing her purse, she pulled out her wallet. She slipped his card from the slot behind her library card. Exhaling, she counted to ten. Stop spiraling into what-ifs. Think positive thoughts and call Ches. He helped last time. Maybe he'd be helpful this time too.

Merritt's heart thumped in high gear as Ches read Trey's letter. On her third reading, the language became clearer, but she needed Ches's opinion and direction as to what her next step should be.

"He's alleging that you ingratiate yourself with senior citizens for profit. He points to your relationships with Millie, with Connie Frazier, with Francine Applewhite, and to your work at the assisted living center." Ches flipped the last page over.

A coldness swirled in her stomach and reached outward, filling her chest and skating toward her fingertips.

"This is a sad attempt at character assassination." Sliding the pages across Josie's kitchen table to Merritt, Ches flicked his hand. "These charges can be disproved. Feels desperate to me."

"Feels like a death knell to me."

"It isn't, Merritt." Josie leaned across the table, reaching for her hand.

The warmth felt good. Having these two for support felt good. "So, what do I do now?"

"You don't do anything but keep living your life. He has to prove these allegations. It's just a threat. He's trying to make you blink or fold." Leaning back, Ches clasped his hands behind his head. "He's a bully."

She should be adept at dealing with bullies by now. She'd had much practice until Millie came into her life, making everything easier, making her believe she'd never have to deal with bullies again.

A portrait of Sam and his siblings on the side table caught her eye, and she swallowed down the bitterness of jealousy. Fatigue bore on her shoulders. Why did everything seem so hard? Would she always have to fight for everything she wanted?

Enough wallowing.

Straightening, she folded the letter and slipped it back into the envelope. "Thanks so much for reading this and explaining it to me. I'll get out of your hair."

Josie squeezed her arm. "Wait. You don't have to leave. Come get frozen yogurt with us."

"I appreciate the offer—"

"Great. I'll text Sam—"

"No." Both heads swiveled toward her. "I mean. Thank you, but I have to get going."

"Are you sure? We could make it quick." Josie's hopeful eyes worked to convince her.

"I'm sure. Maybe some other time."

Josie's disappointed face almost compelled Merritt to change her mind, but she held firm.

"Let me walk you to your car then." Josie threaded her arm

through Merritt's and escorted her out the front door, Winston trotting along behind them.

Merritt retrieved her arm and reached for her car, concentrating on the handle.

Arms folded at her waist, Josie cupped her elbows. "You know, Merritt. I hope you won't let Trey get in your head. Anyone who knows you knows you're a wonderful person."

Considering Josie's words, Merritt pushed back a bit. "That's sweet, but you haven't known me very long, Josie. You couldn't be a character reference, you know."

"I remember you in high school. I know you now. Ms. Connie sang your praises the other Sunday at church, talking about what a great piano teacher you are. How encouraging you are to all your students, especially the tough ones. I video-called with my mother the other day; she remembers how having you live with her transformed Millie."

Merritt contemplated those words. "She was already a cool person when I met her."

"And having you gave her a new purpose, a new direction. You enhanced her life. You bless people all the time. And Sam ..."

"He's been helping me a lot with the piano." Sliding into her car, Merritt tossed her purse on the passenger seat.

"Right, he's been spending a lot of time with you." Josie grinned. "I think he likes you."

A few words from Sam's sister sent her heart galloping again. "He's a helper for sure."

"Sam?" Josie made a face. "Okay, maybe. When he wants to help."

"That's his personality. Helping people."

Josie cocked her head. "You think so? I guess I think of him first as an annoying brother, but you're right. He has a helping side." She arched an eyebrow. "Did he tell you he's never refinished a piano before?"

"What?" She made a face. "I thought he knew what he was doing."

"Everything he knows comes from YouTube videos."

"You're kidding."

"Uh-uh." Josie grinned. "That's pure Sam right there, jumping in before he has a concrete plan. Must really want to help you ... 'cause he likes you."

"Mmm." Making a non-committal noise, she buckled her seatbelt.

"Let's plan a time for frozen yogurt or coffee or something. Soon, okay?"

Merritt smiled and waved, wondering if a play date with Josie would ever happen. The pang in her heart confirmed she wanted it to.

34

Running his finger around the neck of his button-down, Sam glanced again to the back of the restaurant where Merritt played piano. Still no luck catching her eye. Maybe later he'd say hello.

"Stop messing with your collar, Sam. You're not choking." Josie surveyed the table, beaming at her brothers and newly-minted fiancé, Ches. "All of you look handsome tonight. Thank you for humoring me and dressing up. This is a fancy restaurant and a dressy occasion. I appreciate your effort to look the part."

"Tell me what you think after you wear a tie for a few hours. Then you'll find out what these lassos around your neck can do." Wincing, Sam wiggled his neck.

"We're glad to make you happy, Joey, and you look beautiful." Heath raised his glass. "Ben, why don't you make a toast to the happy couple?"

"Good idea." Lifting his glass, Ben smiled at the couple. "Josie and Ches, we're thankful God brought you together. Some of the things He brought you through were a little dicey, but look where you are now. Here's to celebrating many more special times with you. Congratulations and best wishes for a long and blessed life."

"Oh, Ben—"

"Uh-uh. No, crying tonight, Josie. Listen, she's playing our song." Clasping her hand with the diamond, Ches slid his other arm around Josie's shoulders. The beginning measures of "What a Wonderful World" floated over the other diners.

"How did you do that? You haven't been back there to request our song."

"I know some people." Ches kissed her temple and motioned to the empty glass goblet in front of her. "You didn't like your chocolate mousse, huh?"

Licking her spoon, she smiled. "Not a bit. Thank you for letting me eat most of yours." She gazed into his eyes until her brothers started clearing their throats in unison. "I get it, wise guys. Chill out." She turned her attention to Merritt at the piano. "You know, she's really good."

"Yeah, she's crazy talented." Every head swiveled to Sam. He ran his finger under his collar again.

"Crazy talented, huh? Want to tell us about her, little brother?" Popping the last piece of his pie crust into his mouth, Heath grinned.

Great. Four little words had doomed him to probably four weeks of teasing from the family.

"I just got a fabulous idea. I'll be right back." Pushing her chair back, Josie headed toward Merritt, leaving Sam to face his brothers' inquisition.

He ignored the good-natured questions and kept his sights on his sister weaving around the dining tables. What was her fabulous idea?

MERRITT FORCED her attention on her fingers to keep from staring at the Daniels family laughing at the big round table near the front window. Every now and then, their laughter broke above the ambient noise of the restaurant. She transitioned from

"Love is a Many-Splendored Thing" to "Daydream Believer." Something upbeat and fun ... just the ticket for the last song before her break.

As she held the last chord, she raised her gaze to find Josie a few steps from the piano. Her stomach rocked. Back at the table, Sam watched his sister with wide eyes full of interest and ... what? Maybe chagrin? Because she was coming her way?

"Hello, Merritt. I didn't realize you play here. We've been enjoying your music all night.'

Merritt stood to roll her shoulders. "Thank you. I play a few times a month."

"And thank you for playing our favorite song, 'Wonderful World.' We're here celebrating my engagement."

"Best wishes."

"Thank you." Josie positioned her hands on the curved top of the baby grand. "You're so talented. I'd love for you to play at our wedding if you do that sort of thing."

Surprise mingled with a dash of intrigue. Another paying gig that could garner more paying gigs from wedding guests. Her heart stuttered at another thought. Would Sam take a plus-one?

"Merritt?"

"Oh, sorry. Yes, I do play weddings." She reached for the stack of business cards on top of the piano. "Take one of these, then you'll have all my information. When's your date?"

Making a face, Josie shrugged. "We've just gotten engaged, but I've always liked May."

"Right. Well, May can get busy with recitals and end-of-the-year concerts."

"Of course." Josie tipped her head to the side, a smile playing around her mouth. "Maybe we could get together soon and chat about song choices. We'll check our calendars, too, and nail down a date."

"Sounds good." *Where to meet?* "Do you know the coffee shop on Pearl Street?"

"That's a great place, but I have a better idea. Would you mind coming to my house? I'll check my calendar and text you."

"That'll work."

Josie offered her hand. "I'll look forward to it."

"Are you two plotting to take over the world?" Sam appeared at his sister's side. "Hey, Merritt."

Up close, he took her breath away in his jacket and tie, loosened and revealing the unbuttoned top button.

"We'll never tell." Josie winked at her. Being in cahoots with Josie. Nice.

"Hey, give me a hug, Joey. I've got to roll." He pulled her close. "Congratulations and all that."

"It's best wishes—" Merritt and Josie chimed simultaneously and then laughed.

"What?" Sam gawked at both of them.

"Offer *best wishes* for the female and *congratulations* for the male." Before she could stop herself, Merritt shared the rule she'd memorized years ago. *Way to sound like an old-fashioned schoolmarm.*

"What difference does it make? I'm happy for you all the same."

"If you want to use correct manners, bro ..." Laughing, Josie rubbed his cheek with her palm.

"Ah, okay." Shrugging away from his sister, Sam turned to Merritt. "Your playing was great tonight, Merritt. We enjoyed it."

"Let me get back to the table. I'll text the date to you as soon as we decide. Okay?" Josie waved and headed back across the restaurant to Ches, who stood, smiling at her.

Merritt's heart pinged at the love in Ches's eyes. Maybe one day ...

"I'll be over this week to finish putting the piano back together. Maybe Monday?" He stuck his hands in his pockets. "Just in time for your parties."

"Great."

"And then you'll be playing on your own piano again."

"Wonderful." Except, would that be the end of seeing Sam?

He glanced over his shoulder and groaned. "My family is tracking every move we make, trying to read lips, maybe." Positioning himself squarely in front of her, he widened his stance. "No privacy with those guys."

Was it a desire for privacy, or was he embarrassed for his family to see him talking with her? No, Sam was usually honest. He owned up to reading her journal when he didn't have to. Maybe he actually did just want privacy from his family's eyes.

"I gotta go, but maybe we can celebrate the unveiling?"

Yes. "Sounds good." She'd already begun thinking of a sing-along party, but if Sam meant a celebration for just the two of them ... Yes, please.

"I'LL HOLD the third and fourth Saturdays in May until you confirm with your venue." Merritt penciled in the two dates in her planner. In less than an hour, she and Josie had created an interesting list of contemporary and classic love songs as well as religious selections. "Just let me know as soon as you can."

"Pastor Dunleavy said both those dates are open at the church. We're having the reception at Ches's uncle's farm west of Charlotte. I'm leaning toward the fourth, but I'll confirm—"

The front door banged open. "Man. Smells good in here, Jo Jo." Heath sauntered in from the foyer, followed by Sam.

Garlic and onions and tomatoes had simmered long before their meeting had begun, making the kitchen smell like a trip to Italy.

Nodding hello to Merritt, Sam reached into the glass cookie jar and snatched two cookies, ignoring Heath's outstretched hand. "You two got everything worked out?"

"Not quite, but we've got a pretty cool playlist for the wedding." Josie gathered her notes.

Heath grabbed two for himself. "A firm date yet?"

"I'll let you know."

Sam eyed the cake on the counter. "Italian Cream, eh? Ben'll grin all the way to the coast."

"And maybe the memory of delicious food and captivating conversation will bring him back here sooner rather than later." Rising from the kitchen table, Josie gestured to her brothers. "When you set the table, guys, set an extra one. Merritt, please stay for dinner. I meant to mention it before now."

Two colored pens slipped through her fingers. Merritt caught a quick glance between Sam and his sister before bending to retrieve them. A slack jaw suggested the invitation surprised Sam. Maybe even dismayed him a bit. No worries, Sam.

"Thanks so much for the invite, but I can't tonight."

"Convince her, Sam. The crock pot's full of spaghetti sauce. We have plenty."

A bit of hesitation confirmed his discomfort with the offer. "Sure. The more the merrier."

"I appreciate the invitation, and the sauce smells wonderful, but, really, I have plans." With Destiny or Jesse or Ms. Connie or somebody.

"Rats. Well, we'll give you a rain check. I'll make sure you use it too." Josie's genuine smile settled Merritt's quivering insides.

"Thank you. Let me know when you have the real date and if you remember any favorite songs you want to add to our list." Merritt turned to the foyer. "'Bye."

"I'll walk you out." Sam tossed a handful of napkins on the table. "There you go, Heath buddy."

A churning in her insides cranked up again. "You don't—"

"I'm upping my game as a gentleman. Can't you tell?" The dimple accompanied his grin.

Merritt chuckled despite herself. "Is that right?"

He leaned against her car with his arms folded in front of him. "You sure you can't get out of your plans? Tonight's a going-away shindig for Ben. He's taking a temporary job on Hatteras

Island, so it's kind of a special dinner. Josie must like you a lot. She surprised me with the invite, to be frank."

Hackles rising, Merritt adjusted her purse strap on her shoulder. "Because I'm not—"

"Nothing to do with you. Josie's taking this temporary move kinda hard. Probably why she didn't ask you till now. She keeps pressing for a return date, but he can't give it. It's fluid based on a new hire down there."

"Oh." Warmth swirled in her chest. "Got it. She's missing him already." What would it feel like to have someone miss her before she left?

"Yep. That's it." Sliding his hands in his pockets, he scuffed his toe on the driveway. "Well."

They stood still and silent for a moment. "Well," he repeated.

"Yeah, I need to get going." But she didn't want to.

"Right." He leaned to grab her door handle and paused, his face inches from hers. "Have a good evening."

She held her breath, memorizing the gold flecks in eyes that looked more green than blue today, then slipped into the car. "You too." Grateful for the seat beneath her, she tossed her planner and purse to the passenger side. Shaking fingers made turning the key more difficult than usual.

Looking forward to replaying the up-close view of his hazel eyes later, she steered the car toward Millie's.

35

Butterflies fought for space in Merritt's midsection as she checked over the refreshment table spread for the unveiling party. Everything was in place and ready. She'd baked black and white cookies, lady finger cookies, and cheese straws. An eighth-note ceramic dish cradled specially-ordered black and white M&M's.

Violet's mother had fashioned chocolate keyboard lollipops for favors. Blackberry punch the guests could make into floats with a scoop of vanilla ice cream rounded off the menu.

Paper products decorated with musical staves prompted a smile. "Give me a theme, and I can host a party. Thanks, Millie. You'd be proud, and you'd love today, for sure."

She'd invited students and family members to come for refreshments, play a favorite song on the newly refurbished piano, and browse through sheet music for new selections. She pressed a hand against her chest, her heart racing.

"I can't wait to show you off today. You are so beautiful." She trailed her fingers along the edge of the piano, wood gleaming in the afternoon sunlight.

Recently tuned, her piano waited regally to make music throughout the day. Tommy, her piano tuner, had expressed his delight in working on the instrument. 'You got yourself a fine piano here. Gorgeous sound. Tell Sam he did a bang-up job on restoring it.'

Nodding at the memory, Merritt spoke out loud again. "Yes, he did."

A slow smile inched its way across her face at a secret she and Sam shared. On the back of the piano, all the way at the bottom right corner, he'd left a quarter-sized smudge of avocado green paint. "A nod to its history." Sam had explained. "History's important."

Her heart twisted at the thought of Sam. He'd miss the afternoon party because of work, but he'd be able to make the birthday party tonight.

"With bells on." He'd joked.

Happiness threatened to pop out of her chest whenever she looked at the piano or thought about today's celebrations. Commemorating September and October birthdays, today would, no doubt, go down as one of her favorites in her history.

Thank You, thank You, thank You, God, for this day.

Bells chimed throughout the house. She checked her watch. Two-oh-five.

"Unveiling party, here we come."

Quickstepping it, she grinned all the way to the door.

STILL REVELING in the oohs and ahs and compliments from the afternoon party, Merritt reached her arms behind her back to stretch her shoulder blades. The last student left about five-thirty, giving her an hour to recharge for the evening festivities.

"Two parties in one day. Takes a toll on a body, huh?" Destiny entered the kitchen, leaving Ms. Connie playing hymns on the piano.

"I can handle two parties. No problem." Merritt poured salsa into a brightly colored bowl. A Mexican menu, she'd prepared chicken and beef fajitas with all the fixings at Ms. Connie's request. "Set this on the table for me, please." She handed the bowl to her friend and stirred the peppers and onions simmering on a back burner.

"These black and white cookies are to die for." Destiny grabbed two from the serving plate.

"The recipe is—"

"You know baking stresses me out."

"Which makes me sad. If you keep eating cookies, you won't want any birthday cake."

"Not happening. You've met my sweet tooth, right?"

A knock sounded. They headed to the den in time to see the front door opening with Sam smiling his way into the room with an armful of flowers. "Happy birthday ... whose birthday are we celebrating tonight?"

"Mine." Ms. Connie giggled and clapped.

He handed her a bouquet. "Happy birthday!"

"Who else is on the celebration hot seat?"

Destiny smirked. "Me."

Chuckling, he handed her a bouquet. "Happy birthday to you too."

Grunting out a laugh, she grinned and stuck her nose into the blooms.

"And the last bouquet for the one who started all this party mayhem, Ms. Millie. Will you accept this bouquet in her memory, Merritt?"

Heart pinching, she bit her lip and nodded. He'd remembered Millie's birthday. She clutched the bouquet instead of hugging him like she wanted to. Maybe later.

"Let's eat, everybody."

THE GRAND PIANO-SHAPED birthday cake brought cheers from the party-goers and pleas for second slices from Jesse and Sam.

Merritt made a mental note to add that detail to her social media review for the local baker.

After passing out a few song sheets, she sat at the piano. "Okay. Let me know what you want to sing, and maybe I know it."

Ms. Connie called out, "'Magic Moments!'"

"I can play it, but you'll have to lead out singing it." Merritt began the intro, and Ms. Connie scooted forward on her chair.

A half-hour of show tunes, patriotic songs, and hymns passed before Sam suggested, "Name That Tune."

"Great idea, but I'm done. My fingers need a break. Someone else play."

"Sam, it's your game. You play." Ms. Connie clapped her hands, ready to guess the tune.

"Ooh, I don't know many songs by heart, so you'll have to promise not to look up here at the music." Sam slid onto the piano stool.

Another half-hour passed with shouts of song titles and laughter before Ms. Connie pleaded her bedtime.

"Yeah, I need my beauty sleep too. Let's get you home, Ms. Connie." Destiny rose and helped Ms. Connie stand. "I'm going downtown tomorrow, so I can drop off the bags for Eva."

"Perfect. Thanks, everybody, for bringing the foster kids personal care items. Next time, we'll collect winter weather accessories."

Everyone left carrying leftover treats from both parties.

Sam hesitated in the middle of the den. The butterflies from earlier in the day revisited her midsection. How would Sam end the night?

"You look tired."

The butterflies skedaddled.

"Oh, thanks."

"How about this? You look beautifully tired." Sam raised his eyebrows.

She made a face. "Better. Maybe."

"You had a huge day."

"Because of you. Thank you again for seeing the potential in that green piano. You had a vision, and you carried it out.

"My pleasure. I'm good like that." Sam shifted his feet. "Look. I'm gonna get outta here and let you get some rest."

Her heart sank. She missed him already.

"Seriously, Sam. Today happened because of you. I don't know how to repay—"

Pressing a finger to her mouth, he shook his head. "Tonight was a blast. Let's have more of these, okay?"

Way down deep, flutters whirled and stole her breath. More time with Sam? She wanted it so badly, but—

He brushed a quick kiss on her lips and headed for the door. The house, crammed with laughter and life all day, took on a bit of a melancholy ambiance.

God, help me, please. Am I setting myself up for heartache?

Taillights disappeared around the street corner.

I want more of these times too.

36

Unusual nerves jangled Merritt's composure in the minutes leading up to the piano program. The main reason, the only reason ... Sam. He came here to help Jared, but he'd also see her 'doing her thang' as he so laughingly had described it. This event always held a special place in her heart.

Please, Sam, understand how important it is to me.

He'd been faithful to finish her piano. He'd been faithful to practice the duet with Jared, finding time for the teen when he could have been sleeping or working on his own projects. He'd been faithful and helpful and kind. He'd wedged his way into her life and heart with his determination and commitment, silly humor, and smiles.

Oh, boy.

"We have one more resident to bring in here." The director of Crossroads whispered to Merritt at the back of the activities room as she checked her clipboard. "Then whenever you're ready." She smiled. "I'll make sure the ice cream is set up when you begin playing your song. It's the last one on the program, right?"

"Yes. We'll run about thirty minutes, like usual. Don't want to wear out our welcome."

"There's no danger of that. You're loved here. You know we record the programs so the residents can watch again if they want to."

"I'm glad they like us."

A nurse rolled a wheelchair in with the last resident, and the director left to help make room for more guests. Merritt scanned the room. Most of her students had moved to the front row of chairs near the piano. Parents sat or stood in the back, with residents taking their places in between.

The door opened and Josie entered. Waving, she grabbed a spot near the parents. Merritt's heart squeezed. *She comes to support you helping someone else? What kind of family do you have, Sam?* She glanced around the room until she found him.

He and Jared conferred near the side entrance. Glancing up, Sam caught her stare and gave her a thumbs up.

The positive affirmation helped settle her nerves. Spotting a cardinal perching on a bird feeder on the other side of the window, she breathed in air and held it.

"Ready to roll?" Sam's voice jolted her.

Air swooshed out of her lungs. "I thought you were talking with Jared."

"Five minutes ago. You ready?" He smiled. "It's going to be great. Let's go jam."

And just like that, Merritt was ready, eager to begin. Taking her elbow, he led her to the front for her welcoming speech.

The program stirred excited applause for every student, even the beginners. Sam and Jared anchored the first half of the recital, and their piece was a hit. Three people stood up for an ovation. Jared's smile as he bowed paid her dividends.

Sadie played "Somewhere Over the Rainbow" from memory, and Violet's "Let It Go" had even some of the men singing along on the chorus. When it was time for their duet, Sam stood and wiggled his eyebrows at her. *Comedian.*

On the piano bench, Sam leaned into her shoulder. "Don't mess this up for me, got it?" Then he winked.

"See if you can keep up. Ready?"

"I was born ready." He flexed his hands.

She nodded off the count, and they began. Within a few measures, she relaxed, swaying in time with him. Smiling at his long fingers moving rhythmically over the keys, she lost herself in the music.

Too soon, they came to the song's end and held the last note until the agreed-upon signal. The heat of her thigh next to his had threatened his concentration, but he'd persevered through the distraction, hitting the correct notes at the right time.

As they swayed to the music, her shoulder nudged against his, punctuating the tempo ... another positive to their mini-concert. How long till they could play another duet? Maybe he should suggest it earlier rather than later.

They stood to wave to the cheering crowd. In a quick moment of chivalry, Sam grabbed Merritt's hand and brushed a kiss on top of it. Stopping near her ear as he straightened, he whispered, "Thank you. That was fun."

Rising color in her cheeks stoked Sam's wide grin.

She pressed her lips together and faced the crowd, still clapping for them.

"Kiss her on the mouth next time," a wheelchair-bound romantic yelled.

The crowd whooped its agreement as a nurse moved toward the octogenarian and patted his shoulder.

Blushing again, Merritt rallied to her task. "Thank you for letting us perform for you today. I also want to thank our special guest, Sam Daniels, for playing duets with Jared and with me. I hope you liked the selections, but it's also fun for beginner players," she paused and smiled at the youngest students, "to see adults and young adults enjoying the piano. You're learning a skill you can use for the rest of your life. Now,

I have one more piece for you, and then," she paused again, "ice cream!"

The little ones cheered along with the residents of Crossroads.

Clearly, Merritt loved what she did and enjoyed sharing it with these people who loved her back.

At the piano again, she positioned her hands over the keys. Adjusting her spine, she began the piece. Several measures passed, but no title popped into Sam's head. He took out his phone and began recording the performance. He remembered it from the Lamplighter but still couldn't place the name. The music moved him exactly as it had the first time he heard it.

A melancholy, a longing … the emotions swirled in his chest. He craned his neck for a better view. Why didn't he sit somewhere so that he could see her face while she played? The song ended, and the crowd showed its approval.

Rising, he noticed a paper on the chair beside him. A discarded program. He scanned the order of players and smiled at his name in print. Then he came to the last line: Merritt Hastings. "Mourning Dove Lament" by Merritt Hastings.

His breath caught. Mystery solved. She'd composed the haunting melody herself. No wonder he'd never heard of it. Many people lined up at the back table for ice cream, while several surrounded Merritt with hugs and congratulations. Heart thumping at this revelation, his mind dinged with possibilities for her music, with people who might be able to help her move forward with it.

Eager to talk with her, he studied the fans surrounding their teacher. *Come on, everybody. Scramble to the ice cream table. I need to talk with Merritt.*

PEEKING over Sadie's crown of braids, Merritt caught Sam's stare. She grinned at him. A full-heart kind of afternoon, the students played well, and the residents had been fully engaged. Jared fist-bumped her on the way to his ice cream, and Sam had come. And, of course, Sam being Sam, he'd ended their duet with a dramatic flourish. Sparks still tingled where his lips had touched her hand.

"I'm glad you had so much fun, Sadie. Are you ready for some ice cream?"

"Yes, ma'am!" Sadie skipped over to the table and chose a bowl.

Sam stepped up to her. "Well, finally. I thought I'd have to make an appointment to talk with you. All your fans wanted a few minutes with the star."

Raising eyebrows, she grinned. "Jealous? They liked you too."

"Your last piece was something. You played it at the Lamplighter when we were there for the engagement party, right?"

Her heart did a little stutter. He'd recognized it and remembered it. "That's right." A wave of self-consciousness blanketed her. Why did she keep that piece on the program once Sam was a sure thing to play the duets? Did some part of her want him to know she wrote music? Did some part of her want to share that intimate knowledge with him?

"It's a great piece."

Protective of her music, she considered him, wary of his line of conversation. "Thank you."

"And you wrote it." He tapped her name of the program. "Do you have other pieces?"

"Yes—"

"That's fantastic. You play. You arrange. You write music. You could—"

"Teach. Like I'm doing now."

"Yeah, but that piece is ... it's beautiful. You could—"

"Teach. That's what I want to do, Sam."

He shook his head. "I don't think so."

An incredulous look passed over her face.

"I mean, yeah. You're great with these students. You energized Jared. He's jazzed to play another duet, can you believe it? And he's learning the harmonica you gave him."

"Thank you."

"Your students clearly love you, but—"

She folded her arms in front of her. "But nothing, Sam. I have a good, solid life doing what I'm doing now."

"Uh-uh. I think you want more."

Gripping a nearby chair for support, she grimaced. "What? Why do you think that?"

He waved the program in front of her. "Because of this. Why'd you put your name in the program as the composer if you didn't want people to know?"

"Because it matched the rest of the program. Symmetry."

"Symmetry?"

"That and no one here cares about the composers." She bit the side of her cheek. *Breathe. Breathe in and out. Drat, Sam. I don't want to talk about this. You're ruining this good day.*

Quit, Sam. Give her some breathing room. "Hey, I'm sorry. I'm pushing too hard. I'm just excited about your talent," He paused. "But this is the time to celebrate your students. And you too. Oh, and don't forget the ice cream. Come on. Let's go get some, okay?"

She nodded, but she'd pulled back, retreating behind an invisible wall. Every time he chiseled away a piece, his own stupidity helped erect another one.

Oliver, one of the youngest students, appeared in front of them. "Ms. Hastings, they've got sprinkles."

"Wow. It must be a party."

"That lady over there says she can't wait for us to come back. I need a new song."

"We'll start working on one next week. Sound good?"

The little boy grinned and scooped up another spoonful of sprinkle-covered ice cream.

Sam locked eyes with Merritt. "You've made a lot of people happy here today. Good job."

With a polite smile in place, she moved toward the ice cream table.

He caught her hand. "Wait. Seriously. This is a great day, and I'm sorry I rained on it by pushing. I wasn't thinking."

Making eye contact again, she gave him a genuine smile this time. "Thank you. I appreciate that."

"You're welcome. Now, let's enjoy this ice cream before it's all gone. The residents are giving your students a run for their money on this stuff. Look at that loaded bowl over there." He pointed to one of the men by the chess table holding a dish with at least three scoops.

"No worries. They always have plenty."

Relief lightened his heart. She'd forgiven his impetuousness again. *We'll celebrate today, but more people need to hear your talent, Merritt.* Brain spinning with ideas and names of contacts, he chose the caramel sauce and covered his scoop of chocolate ice cream. "Good music and good food make a great party."

Her smile lit him up. *I'm going to work for more of those, Miss Merritt.*

37

Ms. Connie passed Merritt the basket of homemade rolls. "Have another one. I baked all the calories out." The sweet woman insisted on celebrating the piano and the Crossroads program and fall and anything else she could think of with Merritt and Sam. She'd refused Sam's offer of going out to eat to celebrate.

"I love cooking for two of my favorite people. I hardly get to see you now the lessons are back at Merritt's house."

Sam accepted the basket and grabbed another roll. "Well, I'm happy to eat here. You're one of the best cooks I know, and I know a lot."

"Oh, Sam. You're making me blush. Now tell me how everything's going with you."

Sam chuckled and buttered the roll. "Good news. Doug's going to sell the station."

"Wonderful."

"Bad news. He hasn't settled on a hard price or timeline for the transaction. He told me one thing, then came back with a couple of contingencies." He sighed and twirled his water glass.

"Sounds a little sketchy." Merritt laid her fork on her plate. "Does he actually want to sell?"

"I wasn't sure at first, but whenever he talks about moving to Myrtle Beach, he gets this big grin on his face. We were heading to a deal, but everything changed when he got a real estate agent on the advice of his wife. He wants a bigger down payment now too."

"Which agency did he choose?" A knot twisted in Merritt's stomach.

"Omega Properties. Why?"

"Just curious." She'd seen that name at the bottom of emails from Trey.

"I'm trying to learn this patience thing, Ms. Connie. But let me tell you, it's hard. I'm champing at the bit to get started with my own station, my own programming."

"It'll come." Ms. Connie dabbed at the corner of her mouth.

"You think so?"

"You're a hard worker, Sam, and smart. Not to mention all the people in your corner, praying for you."

"She's right, Sam. Be positive." Merritt ignored the bit of heaviness in her chest. She gave her attention, instead, to the homey atmosphere she'd missed since teaching back at her own house.

The refurbished piano blessed her every day, but it also kept her from daily visits with Ms. Connie and piano repair sessions with Sam. The texts and game nights were fun, but more time with him ... she pulled herself back into the table talk.

Sam's enthusiasm about his program ideas sparked his eyes and summoned his dimple. If excitement could run a radio station ...

Clapping for his plans, Ms. Connie added humor, common sense, and God to the conversation.

A good mix.

A FLITTING, wavy idea had fluttered through Merritt's mind on occasion in the past few weeks, continuing to grow and plague her until it would not release her. Ignoring it didn't help. Praying hadn't given her peace. Surrendering, she'd reached out to Trey and now sat at the coffee shop on Pearl Street waiting for him to show, her red heart between her fingers.

The bell at the door dinged signaling a customer. Trey.

A smug smile on his face, he sauntered toward her table and sat. "Well, I can't say I'm surprised you called because I'm not. I knew you'd come around when you realized what you were up against. Allison sends her regards, by the way."

Breathe. She clenched her fists in her lap. "Hello to you too, Trey. And I doubt very seriously you know what I'm coming around to."

"Is that right? You're here to beg me to call off my dogs, so to speak. You don't want your history dragged back up in all the papers, and you're ready to leave the premises."

Two young mothers walked by carrying mugs and saucers, a cloying smell of cinnamon churning her stomach. The enormity of her plan doubled her over the table. "Excuse me. I'll be right back."

She made it into the bathroom just in time to lose her dry toast. Could she go through with this? She leaned against the stall partition. Breathe.

God, I thought this was the plan. I finally felt peace last night, but now ... I need some strength here. Somehow Trey knows how to push all my buttons.

Hovering over the sink, she rinsed her mouth and splashed water over her face. The image in the mirror needed a pep talk. Bad.

"You can do this. Millie's memories will be with you no matter what. Trey's a jerk. Don't succumb to his taunts." Stirring the contents of her purse, she found a piece of peppermint gum and chewed for a moment. The peppermint settled her stomach, the extra minute, her nerves. The clear vision of her task set before her.

Let's go do it, girl.

Seated back at the table, she laid out her plan, her offer. "Here's the deal, Trey. You know I own Millie's house by rights. Her last will is as valid as your driver's license."

He opened his mouth, but she quieted him with a raised palm.

"You know I could sue you for all the contents you stole from my house. Your letter was a pathetic attempt to scare me into bending to your will."

Narrowing his eyes, he bent over the table. "Now wait a minute—"

"I'm not finished." Regrouping, she licked her lips. "You know I'd win any case you care to bring against me. The will is valid, and two of the three people who witnessed it are alive and will attest to the fact Millie was of sound mind when she wrote it." She smiled. "Forgive me, but I love knowing these facts."

Recoiling, he pushed away from the table. "I don't have to listen to—"

"Yes, you do if you want Millie's house."

He froze. "What?"

"That's right. You can't win it in court, but I'll sell it to you. I have some conditions, though."

"You're in no position—"

Lighthearted with a new strength, she chuckled. "You still don't understand. I have the upper hand for all the reasons I've laid out." Shifting in her chair, she pushed aside her coffee cup. "Here're my conditions. I'll sell you the house at fair market value minus closing costs and your fees."

"Well, now—"

"Stop. I'm not finished. I believe you have a client with a radio station with a fair deal on the table, but you've advised him against taking it."

He frowned.

"You will advise your client to take that deal also with no closing costs and no fees."

His snicker sounded forced. "Why would I do all this you're asking and get no payment for my real estate services?"

"I'm saving you a considerable amount in court costs and lawyer fees."

He pulled at the loose skin under his chin. "I'll think about it."

"You'll let me know by the end of this week."

"You've got nerve. That Daniels guy." He curled his lip. "Some dude letting his girlfriend cut deals for him."

"He knows nothing about this deal. I'm doing a favor for a friend. One more thing. There's no negotiation here. You've heard my offer. It won't change. If you don't take it, I will sell the house myself or live in it, whatever I choose, after I beat you in court if you're reckless enough to pursue it. Is that clear?"

"You think you—"

"No. I know I have the law on my side and peace in my heart. Something I don't think you're familiar with." Standing, she grabbed her cup. "I'll be waiting to hear from you by Friday afternoon at five."

Filling her lungs with long draughts of cool air outside did nothing to calm the trembling in her hands. The bit about peace in her heart, true to a point, was mostly bravado. Leaving him sputtering at the table, however, did lift the corners of her mouth.

I think you'd be proud of me today, Millie. It felt good explaining the plan to Trey and cutting him off. Right, not good manners, but still. *You always wanted me to stand up for myself.* She sighed. *I just wish I could keep the house too.*

She wiped away a tear, and another one took its place.

Sam bounded up the steps and banged on Merritt's front door. "Hey, Merritt. It's me." He knocked again for good measure. This was a great day, the beginning of his dream. His grin bordered on pain it stretched so much.

The door swung open in mid-knock. "Hey—" The next words disappeared on his tongue, and he stepped back, withholding the hug he'd been primed to give. Red rimmed her eyelids, the lashes spiky.

"Hey."

"Merritt, what's wrong?"

"Everything's fine. Thinking of Millie, that's all. Come in. You sounded excited on the phone." Backing up, she let him enter.

"Yeah, but are you really all right?"

"I'm fine. I just cracked open some homemade coffee chocolate chip ice cream. Want some?"

Her smile seemed genuine. He'd tread lightly and maybe she wouldn't go to pieces on him.

"I'd love some." Studying her for any breaks in her armor, he ran his fingertips along the oak table that had recently replaced the card table. "Nice addition here. It's got an extension, too, right?"

"Yes. Seats ten with that added." She scooped the mocha-colored treat studded with chocolate chips into a bowl and passed it to him. "It's perfect. So what's your news?"

"Doug accepted the offer. He called and said 'let's do it.' He wants to move to Myrtle Beach asap, so he wants the deal finished. No contingencies." Loading his spoon, he took a breath to settle himself. He'd planned to swoop her up and hug her to celebrate, but the ice cream, the table between them, her mood ... not exactly conducive to hugs.

"That's great news, Sam."

"Yeah. I'm pumped. I wanted to tell you in person."

Sensing eggshells under his feet, so to speak, Sam steered the conversation to antics at the station and his ideas for future programming. She listened and laughed at appropriate times, but her ice cream melted in her dish.

"All right then. I'm gonna get out of your hair. I need to get a few things done at work."

Standing immediately, she voiced no protest to his leaving.

He shrugged on his jacket at the door. "You up for doing something maybe next weekend?"

"I think so."

"Man, girl. You know how to wreck a guy's ego. How 'bout some enthusiasm?"

She chuckled. "I'd love to do something next weekend, Sam."

He cupped her cheek, exploring the skin below her ear lobe with his fingers. "Much better." He closed the gap between them, brushing his lips over hers. "I'll call you to plan it, okay?"

A slight lean into hand, she nodded before backing away to let him leave.

As he jogged to his car, he added one more item to his to-do list.

38

Sam tugged at his collar band hoping for easier breathing. Was the tie overkill? Maybe, but today was important, and he wanted to dress the part. Signing to own a radio station. His own station. His station to plan the programming and music he chose. A shiver tripped up his spine.

A long way from announcing the lunch menu at high school.

He mentally high-fived himself. Fingers shaking, he clutched the ink pen tighter, ready to write his name on the dotted line.

Decked out in a Hawaiian shirt, Doug sat across from him in the real estate agency office, ready for his move to Myrtle Beach. He clicked his pen in a steady rhythm. "So you're gonna own a station. I have to say, I never saw this day coming two or three months ago. When I made that surprise visit, I meant to lay you out for messing with my music."

"And fire me too."

Doug chuckled. "True. But here we are, and I'm happy for you, buddy."

"Thank you."

The door to the office opened, and Trey entered carrying stacks of papers. "All right. I've got the copies." He put a stack in front of Doug, one in front of Sam, and another in front of an empty chair at the end of the conference table.

It chafed a bit for Trey to get the sale, but Doug didn't ask for advice. Somehow, however, Doug had worked out a sweet deal with the rat. *Sign the papers and be done with him. Plan a celebration with Merritt.*

"So, where do I sign?"

"Hold your horses. We're still waiting for one more person."

Sam frowned. *Didn't Doug own the station by himself?* A glance at the top of the lease confirmed it. Well, then—

The door opened again, and Merritt entered, greeting the room but avoiding eye contact with anyone.

What?

"Glad you could make it, Merritt." Sarcasm dripped from Trey's words.

Sam's hand closed into a fist.

"Traffic." She sat in the empty chair with the other stack of papers.

"Since we're all here now, let's get started." Trey chose a pen from glass case in the middle of the table.

"Um. Wait. Why're you here, Merritt?"

With a hasty peek, she acknowledged him, but quickly transferred her attention to Trey. His heart, jazzed by Merritt's entrance, tightened now. Something was definitely off.

EVEN IN A PROFESSIONAL SETTING, Trey's attitude made Merritt grind her teeth. *Focus on Sam, not Trey. Be positive, not negative.*

Trey cleared his throat. "Let's get started. I believe we all know each other except Doug and Merritt. Doug, Merritt is the girl I told you about."

They nodded to each other.

"Now, here are the documents for the radio station." He

touched the piles in front of Sam and Doug. "And, Merritt, you have your set of papers for the house, and I have mine."

"Wait a minute. Hold up. What's going on? Merritt?" Sam's eyes telegraphed confusion.

She inhaled and smiled at him. Seeing his face when he'd shared about finally getting his radio station confirmed this was the correct path. The peace she'd longed for came next. Happiness—that she could do this for someone who'd helped her so much—settled into her chest now.

God, help me sign these papers.

"We have what is known as a three-party sale. Conducting everything together in one meeting is time efficient and makes for a trustworthy deal." Trey quirked an eyebrow at Merritt. "Doug sells you the station, Sam. Merritt sells me the house."

"What?' Sam burst from his chair, sending it flying backward into the wall. "Merritt, no."

"Yes, Sam." She bent over the papers, her heart necklace swinging free of her blouse. "Are these pages the only ones for me to sign?"

Trey moved to her side. "Yes, and I sign there." He pointed to the orange flag beside the blank for signatures.

"Merritt, I'm not going to let you do this." Fists clenched at his sides, Sam breathed like a prize fighter after ten rounds.

"It's not up to you, Sam." She signed her name on the first line.

"I won't sign mine." Shaking his head, he crossed his arms in front of him.

Doug sat straight in his chair. "Woah, woah, woah. You're not backing out on me now, son. My car's packed and sitting in the parking lot, headed for the beach."

Sam's throat worked.

"Let's everyone calm down." Merritt flattened her palms against the tabletop. "I've worked it all out, Sam. It's a good deal."

"She's a girl boss when it comes to negotiation," Trey admitted the truth with a smirk.

Merritt reached across the table. "Sam." She smiled. "I'm good. Allison agreed and convinced Trey to let me stay in the house through the beginning of January. I'll celebrate the holidays one last time in Millie's house, plus I'll have time to look for something else." The expected pinch in her chest didn't happen. *Thank You, God.*

"Come on, son. I've signed mine. The waves are calling. Hey, that should be a song. Oh, wait. It's 'Summertime's Calling Me' by ... anybody know?" Doug waved his hand toward the group.

Ignoring Doug, his eyes searching the floor, Sam worked his jaw.

"The Catalinas. Man, come on. I know beach music ain't your favorite, but a DJ in North Carolina should know that answer."

Disregarding the mockery, Sam strained across the table. "No. This can't be the way this happens. I can't be the reason you lose your house." Red staining his cheeks, Sam searched her face.

She loved him for it. She loved him. She sucked in a breath.

I love him.

No wonder signing away her house didn't cripple her. Warm tingles swirled through her chest.

With lips tipped at the corners, she pushed the pen toward Sam's hand. "I'm not losing it. I'm selling it. Please sign it, Sam."

Fingers twitching beside the pen, he held her gaze for several beats.

She covered his hand with hers and squeezed. "It's all good."

Transferring his gaze to the document, he swallowed and signed his name.

"Great! Time to get rolling." Rising from his chair, Doug reached to shake Trey's hand. "Oh, I almost forgot." He turned to Merritt. "My buddy in Nashville loves your music. He wants to hear more."

Her mouth falling open, the hair on the back of her neck stood stiff.

Wide eyes flew to Sam's.

"What's he talking about, Sam?"

WHIPLASH.

Is this what whiplash feels like? Oh, Merritt, this isn't the way you were supposed to find out. Sam's heart roared in his ears, impeding thoughts.

"Sam. What is he talking about?"

"Your music. Your arrangements. Sam showed me your stuff, and I sent it to a couple of my buddies in Nashville. One just got back to me. He's interested. I'll text Sam his info so you can get in touch." Doug saluted the room. "It's been real. See you cats on the flip side."

Confusion. Hurt. Anger. Those emotions and others warred on Merritt's face. He reached across the table. Closing off from the room, she withdrew to the back of her chair.

"Sounds like a heavy conversation is coming up, but my colleague has a lease signing in here in," Trey glanced at his watch. "Fifteen minutes. Merritt, January fourteenth. Your move-out date. That's it. No grace period."

Sam shoved his hands in his pockets to avoid hitting something, the wall or Trey's face.

Wordlessly, she gathered her things and walked away from him.

"Merritt, wait." He followed her through the front office and outside. He caught her shoulder. "Let's talk. Please."

She shrugged off his hand. "I need some time. By myself."

"I need to explain first. Let's talk."

Hugging her purse to her chest, she focused on the pavement. "You've ripped me open, Sam. Laid me bare. I feel naked to the world. There. I've talked."

Sam forced that image from his mind and focused on trying to fix the hurt he'd caused.

"Listen, we need to talk somewhere else ... not ... not in a parking lot. Please, let's go back—"

She whirled toward him. "We can't go back, Sam. The house is sold, and you ... you ... let me go." She jerked her elbow out of his hand. "I need to think all this through."

"Yeah, your house is sold. Why, Merritt?" He shook his head. "Why'd you do it? I didn't ask—"

"Right. It was a gift, Sam. A gift." Turning toward her car, she stomped away, leaving him standing alone.

"When can we talk about this?"

"I'll let you know." She climbed into her Honda and drove away from him, never looking back.

This morning he'd thought today would be one of the best days of his life. The first day of his radio dream coming true. Waking at five o'clock to pitch black, he'd scribbled notes for an hour before running six miles to drain off adrenaline.

With the one-hundred-and-eighty-degree swing from euphoria to horror, his body sagged under the weight of his enormous mistake.

How could a day start with so much promise and end with so much wrong?

Hey, God. I need some big-time help here. Please.

39

Stuffing the half-finished cowl in the crochet basket, Merritt tapped her phone to check the texts that had vibrated through moments earlier. Two unread texts. One from Josie and one from her brother.

Her finger hovered over Sam's text. Yesterday morning, she would have opened it as soon as it hit her phone, but yesterday she didn't know he'd given her music to Doug and other phantom people in Nashville. Her practical side reminded her she shared her music at the Lamplighter and at Crossroads too. The emotional side argued no one at either place would want to do anything with her music other than listen to it.

The more people who heard her music, however, the bigger chance someone would begin digging into her background again. Would bring out the skeletons and dirty laundry again for rumor and judgment.

She exhaled and tapped Josie's text.

Hey. Thanksgiving is soon.

We'd love for you to join us.

It's usually a big crowd, just FYI.

Thanksgiving with the Daniels clan. Back in the summer, Josie's invitation would have sent her over the moon, not that she could have accepted. Not with her usual holiday guests invited from year to year.

Now it simply reminded her of the awkwardness and disappointment and irritation with Sam's betrayal. She'd focus on her own harvest bash instead. At her own house.

For the last time.

Thanks so much, but I'm hosting.

A pang piqued her heart. Declining a real invitation after years of planning her own ... Nope. Quit wallowing.

I should have asked you weeks ago!

No. I always host.

Enjoy your holiday!

Thanks. You too.

We're going to Hatteras to see Ben the day afterward. Fun!

Happy Thanksgiving!

So. Sam would be out of town Thanksgiving weekend. A missing-him flutter filled her core.

Stop it. You pushed him away yesterday. You don't get to miss Sam. Her practical side dug in her heels.

I don't care. I still miss him, and I'll miss him more if he's all the way on Hatteras Island. Her emotional side refused to be bullied.

Ignoring the chaos in her head, she opened his text.

Just checking in.

I hope you're doing okay.

I'm fine.

Before pressing SEND, she paused and added a few more words.

Thank you. I hope you are too.

Another apology appeared from Sam.

I accept your apologies. I just need space.

Lots going on now.

Let me help.

Good night, Sam.

Enjoy Hatteras.

She tossed the phone to the side and slid her fingers into the ball of wool. The yarn comforted her heavy spirit like usual, proving again Millie's wisdom in teaching her to crochet.

Her mind zigzagged from Sam to the list on her to-do plate. Finding a place to live, and moving, then figuring out lessons again. But before all that ... planning for Thanksgiving. A break from thinking about Sam and the strangers who'd listened to her music would be welcome and helpful.

Grabbing a pen and her planner, she turned to a blank page and jotted down the menu for next Thursday. Her shoulder muscles released as she jotted down dishes and made a corresponding grocery list.

Planning ... a peaceful but boring activity on a Friday night.

A FEW DAYS LATER, unable to quell her curiosity, Merritt flicked on Millie's clock radio already set to Sam's station. The top-of-the-hour news finished with the local weather, shared by a young voice she didn't recognize. Not Sam's. A slight downshift occurred in her chest. She lowered the volume during the commercials and scrolled on her laptop through local listings of houses for sale.

Commercials gave way to music she remembered from college. The trip down memory lane through melody brought a smile. Humming, she highlighted three houses in her price range and location. She'd hoped for more choices but would take what she could get.

A text buzzed her phone. Sam.

Just checking in. Hope you're doing well.

I am. Thank you.

Can we talk sometime soon?

Okay. But still slammed with students and the holiday.

Gotcha. I'll wait.

You're worth it.

Three words from Sam, and a tingle pricked her nose. Really, Sam? You think I'm worth something? She read the text again. Tears blurred the message on the screen but not in her heart.

Sam, you're worth it too.

THANKSGIVING WEEK PASSED in a blur of shopping, cooking, and preparing the house. Whenever *for the last time* tried to high jack her holiday mood, she slapped it out of her mind. Sam sent a Happy Thanksgiving text and a bouquet of fall flowers. 'For the table,' he'd texted. She'd texted a thank you.

The gesture chipped away at her heart, and the flowers elicited a happy sigh from her every time her eyes lit on them. They reminded her of the ones he'd sent when he found her in a sad mood days before the signing.

On Black Friday, she toured two houses that were fine but ... just meh. Paint would always help, but the little square boxes had no character, not like ...

No. The deal was done. No going back. She'd know her new house when she saw it.

On Saturday, Destiny accompanied her to a house on Lavender Lane just a block farther from the elementary school. Two mature oak trees flanked the walkway of a craftsman-style bungalow.

"That'll be a lot of raking come next October." Kicking at leaves on the walkway, Destiny finger-combed orange-tinged bangs from her eyes. "Just my two cents."

"But they're beautiful and majestic." Merritt threaded her arm through her friend's. "Come on. Keep an open mind." She'd try to heed the warning herself, but her heart beat a bit faster as she stepped up the walkway.

"My mind stays open. I thought you knew that."

The front door swung wide. A young woman greeted them. "Right on time. Don't you just love the front porch and the swing? Come in. I can't wait for you to see this little jewel."

Rose Marie, the real estate agent, gestured toward the waiting family room and handed both of them papers with house specs. "Now, the current owners did a few upgrades before they had to relocate. It's no secret the house has been on the market for a while. Things slow down in the fall a bit, but the owners are ready to sell. No pressure, though. Let's take a look around. Follow me to the bedrooms."

Destiny mouthed, *but no pressure,* and Merritt elbowed her in her side.

Stop. She's nice, Merritt mouthed back.

"All righty. This one is the master." Rose Marie clipped into the bedroom on the right of the hall. "The double windows showcase the beautiful, private backyard. You've probably noticed hardwood floors throughout the house. The owners ripped up the old carpet and refinished the floors themselves. They were great DIYers. A good-sized closet over here, and here is the bathroom. Now, I know you like tubs."

Uh-oh.

"This bathroom has a beautiful spa shower instead, but the guest bath has a tub. Look at the beautiful tile."

Her heart dipped a little at the disappointing news, but at least the house had a tub. Maybe she could make it work.

Rose Marie led them to the other bedroom before heading back to the kitchen. "Here we have the *room de résistance*. Ha ha! Forgive my French, but I'm so excited about this kitchen." She leaned on the island in the middle of the L-shaped floor plan. "All these appliances are new, and notice the cabinet space." She spread her arm like Vanna White. "Here we have a breakfast nook looking out at the backyard also."

Merritt's breath caught. The breakfast nook brought images of the bay window off Millie's kitchen. *Stop it. Be excited.* "Nice."

"This is an interesting countertop." Destiny pulled her toward the island.

"Yes. It's poured concrete stained to look like stone. Very durable."

Destiny opened a side door.

"Oh, oh. Before you go in there ..."

Too late. Destiny stopped in the tiny room and laughed. Merritt followed behind her. "Oh, wow."

The wall opposite the washer and dryer hookups blazed with yellows and oranges streaking from a smiling sun face.

"Yes, well. The owners enjoyed a sense of humor and didn't have time to paint this room a neutral color before moving. We took that into consideration with the asking price. Why don't I let you walk around alone and then come back with any questions you may have."

They descended the steps onto the back patio. "You could put a deck here if you wanted to. Jesse's good like that. Sam could help."

Merritt ignored the reference to Sam. "Did you see the asking price? Twenty-five hundred over my budget."

"Twenty-five hundred." Destiny shrugged. "If you like it, you could probably make it work. Or negotiate. Look what you did with Trey."

A few bald spots marked the backyard. It could use some gardening TLC. But, honestly, so could Millie's yard.

"You know. You don't have to do anything too fast." Destiny draped her arm over Merritt's shoulders. "My offer still stands. Move in with me. Take your time."

"Thank you. Ms. Connie offered her house again too, but I'd have to put my piano in storage." She wrinkled her nose. "I can't do that."

Wonder what Sam would think about this house? It didn't matter, but it'd be nice to have another opinion, some more words of advice. She bit her lip. "I kinda like it, Dez."

"You're a big girl. Do it if you want. Wanna pray about it?"

"Please."

Destiny closed her eyes. "God, Merritt needs a new house, and she likes this one. Please give her wisdom to proceed or stop, whatever is Your will. Thank you."

Chuckling, Merritt hugged her friend. "I love your prayers. Thank you." She let out a breath. "I'll wait till Monday and then maybe make an offer. If they accept, fine. If they don't, I'll keep looking."

THAT NIGHT A TEXT buzzed her phone. Sam. He'd sent a selfie with a helmet on. She widened the picture to see the figures in the background. Big kites.

Hey. Have a good Thanksgiving?

Yes. You?

Great. I'm still stuffed.

Can you guess what I was doing in the picture?

No, but you should wear a helmet more often.

Funny. We went hang gliding yesterday.

Much fun.

Sounds like it.

I think I bought a house today.

You think?

I'm offering on Monday. We'll see.

Great news!

Several beats passed before he sent another text.

Could I come see it?

Did she want him to? Yes, but also no. She'd be opening herself up to another possible heartache. Could she do it again?

Postpone a definite answer.

They have to accept my offer first.

On Monday morning driving home from her standing appointment at the Crossroads, Merritt switched on the radio to Sam's station again. After the second commercial, Sam's voice came on loud and strong. "We're back with our Get to Know Your Neighbor segment, and our guest today is Mr. Leon Daughtry, a Pearl Harbor survivor.

"Before the break, Mr. Leon, you were telling us about waking up on that Sunday morning to sirens and machine guns and just plain chaos. Were you hurt that day?"

"Not really, son. Not like some of the other people. A lot of the other people. I just got some burns on my arms. Nothing to it."

"Would you like to share how you felt that morning?"

"Terrified. Like any human being would. Confused. I woke up out of a sound sleep to all this craziness. We just had to start doing what we were trained to do while all H. E. Double hockey sticks broke loose around us."

"Yes, sir. I can't imagine. Don't want to."

"No, you don't."

"Have you been back to Hawaii?"

"Yes, my wife and I, God rest her soul, traveled back several times. It's a place everybody ought to go once. Let me tell you."

"Sir, it's been an honor to have you this afternoon. Thank you for your service and your sacrifice and for being with us today. Thank you so much for sharing about your interesting life, Mr. Leon.

"Remember, folks. Submit names of people you'd love to hear

on the radio. Someone who's interesting or working hard or making this world a better place—in other words, a Next Door Star. Call us," Sam rattled off the station's number, "or send it through the tab on our website. Mr. Leon, here's a treat for you. You mentioned your favorite song, and we've got it." The strains of "Don't Sit Under the Apple Tree" came over the radio.

Merritt rushed inside as soon as she arrived home and grabbed her laptop. Scrolling to the station's website, she blinked at the updated layout. Though the home page explained the site was still under construction, Sam had clearly been busy since the signing. The Next Door Stars tab had two links with it. One read "Lossie Howell, skydiver at seventy-five," and another "Connie Clark, a Wee Warbler."

He'd interviewed Ms. Connie.

Three more Coming Soon Tabs suggested checking back to discover the new programs in development. Evidence of Sam's dream coming to fruition marked the colorful site.

Choosing to focus on happiness for him, she pushed away lingering doubts about the house and tapped on the real estate agent's number in her phone.

40

After days of either ignored texts or one-word replies, Sam determined a new strategy for rebuilding a relationship with Merritt. Opening Destiny's shop door, he stopped short. His stomach sank to his feet. Jesse sat in a barber chair, with Destiny trimming his hair.

"Really? She cuts your hair? You wear a ponytail."

"Split ends, man." Jesse grinned, shrugging his shoulders under the animal print cape.

Pushing out a breath, Sam slid into the next-door chair. "Okay. I get it. I'm fine with both of you being here." He leaned his forearms on his thighs. "I'm sure you know the story by now."

Both nodded.

"I messed up. Big time."

"Again." Both spoke at the same time, then burst out laughing.

"I'm here for advice."

"And you think we'll give you some?" Destiny raked a blue comb through a hank of Jesse's hair, evaluating the ends.

"I think you'll know what I should do. How to fix it. Whether you'll tell me is another matter."

"We've got her back." Nudging Jesse's head to the right, Destiny studied the length.

"I know you do. I didn't mean to hurt her. I wanted to help her."

"We know."

"Are you two going to answer in tandem all night?"

"We might."

All three laughed this time.

Sam clasped his hands between his knees. "I've apologized. She said she accepted. She still won't agree to see me again yet. She replies to some texts. Ignores others."

"Give her some time." Destiny rested both hands on Jesse's shoulders, one thumb nestled against his neck.

"It's been weeks."

"A couple."

"It feels like longer."

"Sam, think about her life. Every time problems happened, she got sent down the line to a different house, a different family. Until, of course, a different problem developed, and the process repeated itself. She never learned to deal with problems, face them, work them out. Until Millie. Millie stuck with her, helped her learn to face hard stuff."

Nodding his head, Sam leaned closer. "Okay."

"With you, she's reverted to her old ways of coping. She hasn't completely cut you off and moved on, though. She tried, but you keep coming back. That's a good thing."

"It is?"

"Yes," Destiny met his gaze head-on. "Because she likes you."

A slow smile began.

"But she feels betrayed by you."

His smile died. Sighing, Sam rubbed his temples.

Jesse tossed his head. "That's good. Thanks." He unsnapped the cape and pitched it into a nearby basket.

"Are you sure? I could give you a really cute style." Destiny brushed her hand across the fresh-cut ends of his black hair. "But I like it long."

Jesse caught her hand and smiled at her.

A new development in this relationship, maybe?

Coughing, Sam shifted in his chair. "Can you help a guy out?"

Jesse stood, brushing loose hairs from his jeans. "I gotta get going. I'm just about done with a sixty-seven Mustang engine. I'll be putting it back in the shell soon." He reached for Sam's hand and shook it. "You're a good man, Sam. You just keep messing up. Quit doing that."

Pithy advice, but valid.

Leaning down, Jesse brushed Destiny's lips with his own. "See ya later."

Grinning, Destiny slipped into the seat Jesse had vacated and watched him leave. Glancing back at Sam, her eyes dared him to comment.

He took the dare. "Just so you know, I saw that coming."

She tilted her head, the diamond stud in her nose twinkling. "But you didn't see what would come if you shared Merritt's music."

"Fair point." He tightened his mouth. "Can you help me or not?"

"How do you want me to help you? She's texting you." She sighed. "I'm telling you. She needs time."

"Help me understand. I get that reading her private journal wasn't cool, but she'd shared her arrangements with Jared and with me. She performs at the Lamplighter and at Crossroads."

"Those are other people's songs, not hers."

"She plays her own music at both places too. I recorded her at Crossroads, the same song I heard at the Lamplighter."

"Yeah, she sticks them in the rotation from time to time, but it's her choice to share, not someone else's."

"Right. You're right. I overstepped. I should have given her time, asked her again. Then repeated. But I thought it'd be cool to surprise her with a contract or at least the possibility of one. I thought if people in the business told her ..."

"You thought about a lot of things, but you didn't think about her."

Hanging his head, he squeezed the back of his neck.

"What you don't understand is her relationship with music."

He lifted his eyes. "What do you mean?"

"If you Google her family—"

"I've never done that."

"Restraint. Good for you. Anyway, you'll find most of what I'm about to tell you."

Indecisions warred in his gut. "Wait. If this is—"

"You want to understand her, right?"

He nodded.

"She loves music, gets a ton of joy from it, and she's talented. But so was her dad."

"Wait. Don't tell me anything—"

"I told her you were coming today. She gave her blessing."

Jealousy, disappointment, and relief bumped up beside a tiny bit of hurt in his chest. *When can we talk, Merritt? I'm trying to be patient, but—*

He swallowed the negative feelings. *Focus on Merritt and fixing her hurt, not me.* "She's not mad I'm here?"

"She won't admit it, but I think she's a little glad. She gave the okay, anyway."

"Gotcha. So her dad liked music."

"From the accounts I read, he was a musician. From Merritt's talks with people who knew him, he was a frustrated one. He always chased the neon lights, wanted more. When Merritt came to live with Millie, she played a few instruments, the flutophone, the harmonica. Little ones she could carry with her from house to house. Millie saw her musical talent and gave her piano lessons. Merritt loved them."

"All that sounds good."

"Then she found out about her dad. She quit all the

instruments and lessons. She didn't want to be like him. You can probably guess the rest."

"Millie."

Destiny nodded. "Millie kept after her. Not really pushing, but encouraging. Gradually, Merritt came back to music. Yes, she performs, but look where ... in the back of a restaurant, not in a piano bar. In a retirement home, not on stage. She's sharing with others what makes her happy in a way she chooses."

"Yeah. I see that." He scrubbed his jaw. "So, what do I do?"

"Give her space."

"I ha—"

"More than a couple of weeks. Try a little patience, Sam."

Patience, his old nemesis.

Pushing out of the barber chair, Destiny took hold of the broom leaning near the mirror. She swept the black bits of Jesse's hair sprinkled on the floor into a pile. "Prayer never hurts either."

"Right. I figure you pray for Merritt. I could use them too."

Wiggling her fingers, Merritt studied the red tips chosen for the season.

"Give the poor guy a chance to explain. You're shutting him out without hearing his side of it." Destiny tightened the bottle of polish and set it aside.

"You've done a turnaround. You warned me about him, remember? 'He's not like us,' you said. Remember?"

"I remember, but I always liked him. How could you not? I just didn't know if he deserved you."

Tears burned in the back of Merritt's throat and stung her nose. "And now you think he does?"

"His eyes follow you like a hound dog follows a scent. He's always smiling when he looks at you. He pushes you to be your best too." Destiny hesitated. "Like Millie did."

Merritt flattened her lips in a tight line.

"Don't get mad. Think about it. She made you go to college when you wanted to stay home with her. After every weekend visit home, she had to make you go back. She nagged and nagged until you auditioned for Luca. You have a college degree and a standing gig at the Lamplighter because Millie kept pushing you out of your safe little nest."

True. It was all true. Merritt hadn't liked any of it at the time, but the blessings she enjoyed now came partly because Millie had prodded her along the hard road.

'Doing hard things will yield marvelous blessings on the other side.'

Yes, Millie. I remember all the times you told me that.

"I'm taking your silence as proof you know I'm speaking truth. I won't make you agree with me out loud because I also know how you hate being wrong."

Covering her face, Merritt laughed at her friend. "Well, let's change the subject then."

"Watch the polish. It's not quite dry yet." Inspecting the nails, Destiny placed Merritt's hand back under the dryer. "And one more thing while I'm on a roll. You like him too. If you didn't, you wouldn't be this torn up about it. You like him, and it scares you."

Merritt's eyes flew to Destiny's, then dropped to the table. Her friend could always read her like a set of shampoo directions.

"That's it, isn't it? I knew there had to be more than just being mad about your music. You got over his reading your poems. Other people have got up in your business and ticked you off before, and you just kicked them to the curb. But that's it. You don't want to cut him off because he's important to you." Destiny gasped. "You're in love with him."

At that, Merritt burst into tears. Destiny moved to her side of the table and pulled her into a fierce hug.

Her face pressed against Destiny's chest, Merritt mumbled,

"What am I gonna do, Dez? I'm scared to death. He's got all those brothers and Josie."

"You've faced scary stuff before. This is a good scary thing, Mer."

Merritt breathed in the potions and sprays clinging to Destiny's smock, grateful for this true friend. "You're speaking truth to me just like Millie did."

"That's what I'm here for. And also the manicures and trims. You desperately need a trim, you know?"

Backing out of the embrace, Merritt swatted Destiny's hands. "Get your paws off my curls. They're fine." Her heart, however, felt left out in a downpour unprotected, banged up, a little sore. Sam had two strikes against him. Could she open herself to the possibility of a complete strikeout?

41

As the last student walked to her mom's car, Merritt waved, then headed straight for her laptop. She tapped her ruby-tipped fingers as she waited for it to power up. Destiny had texted at the end of the first lesson this afternoon, but she hadn't been able to respond yet. She reread her texts.

Have you listened to Sam's station today?

Of course not. She had a booked afternoon.

If you missed it, listen on the website.

Switching on the radio, she relaxed to strains of a Latin instrumental piece. Ah, Taco Tuesday. Sam had recently added a classical/instrumental set during the dinner hours. From six o'clock to eight, he chose a different country's music to highlight. Thursday was Americano-themed, and Friday night featured Italian music for pizza night.

Other nights he changed it up, but background music played for those two hours. "Adds a little somethin'-somethin' to the evening meal," he'd said.

Destiny had sneaked on the radio station last Thursday Night-Game Night, so they played Pictionary to the sounds of Nanci Griffith and John Prine and Emmylou Harris, plus others for the folk music night.

She texted Destiny back.

Listen to what?

While she waited for a reply, she clicked on the station's website. Wow. He'd added several pages since the last time she visited. She clicked on the What's Cookin' Tonight tab. He'd posted a Taco Casserole recipe and the playlist for tonight's music. Menus and song titles linked to corresponding pictures of dishes.

Is this what Destiny wanted her to see? Probably not. Destiny rarely cooked when perfectly good restaurants served perfectly delicious food. She clicked on the website menu and saw it.

Finding Forever Families

He had a foster care component? Her stomach seized. Is this good or bad? No, it had to be good, but ...

A text came through. Destiny.

He did a quick segment with a kid in foster care. Gave links to more at the website.

I just saw the link. Haven't listened. How is it?

She hated to ask. She didn't want to know, but she had to.

Please let it be good, not something cheesy or pitiful or...

Listen to it. It's good.

Okay. Good. Dez likes it.

Her neck muscles loosened a bit. She clicked on the first of two interview links. The thumbnail accompanying the recording showed the back of a little boy's head with huge earphones. In the background, Sam waved at the camera from the other side of the studio.

"Hey, listeners. As I said last time, we'll be talking with foster kids from time to time here on WDVY. We want you to get to know these valuable kids who are looking for forever homes. Today we have Truman. Say, hey, Truman."

"Hey."

"Truman is eight years old, and he loves to play soccer. What do you love about soccer, Truman?"

"Kicking goals and snacks."

Sam laughed.

Her heart squeezed in her chest. She missed that sound.

"Right, I hear ya, man. What's your favorite snack?"

"Oreo cookies in the little packs. Everybody gets a whole pack, and we can eat all the cookies."

"Hey, that sounds good. I may have to start playing soccer, too, if they give out Oreos."

"We don't get them all the time. Sometimes we get Cheez-its. They're good too. And we get orange slices at games."

"Soccer sure does offer a lot. Do you like football, Truman?"

"Yes, especially the Steelers."

"The Steelers? What in the world? What about our hometown team, the Panthers?"

"They're good, too, but I like the Steelers."

"All right, man. You do you. Well, our time's coming to an end right now, Truman. Anything else you want our listeners to know about you?"

"Yes. I can empty the dishwasher except for knives. Maybe next year I can do that. I can make my bed if somebody helps me and dust too."

"Wow, buddy. How about windows? Just kidding. That's quite a commendation list. I'm sure any family would be blessed to have you. I've really enjoyed our time together."

"I enjoyed it too. Thank you."

The interview ended with Sam giving statistics about how many children were in foster care in North Carolina and how listeners could help by visiting the website for more information.

Sure enough, he'd included a page for Foster Care of Mecklenburg County and an application form to start the fostering process. Her breath caught in her throat. Dez was right. It was a good interview. Sam made sure it had humor, and little Truman added the heart, for sure. No cheese. No pity. Just a little boy being honest.

She should call Sam.

As Sam backed down his family's driveway, his phone began ringing. A quick glance jazzed his heart rate. Merritt. He braked and answered before the second ring finished. "Hey."

"Hey. Do you have a quick minute?" Her voice sounded breathy. Did she want to talk about everything, maybe try to get back to where they'd been?

Please, God, don't let me mess up this time.

"I got a quick one and several long ones too. What's up?" He continued backing and began a slow drive to the station, taking his time with the conversation.

"I just listened to your interview with Truman."

He gripped the steering wheel. This is why she called. She hated the interview, the segment, the idea of putting the children up for people to see. "Oh, yeah. I wanted to talk with you—"

"It was really great, Sam."

What?

Relief surging through his body, he wheeled into—a bank parking lot to concentrate on her words. His heart pounded in his chest. Jerking the car to halt, he breathed in through his nose, out through his mouth. "You're serious?"

"I am. It had the perfect mix of humor and heart. Truman's a natural."

She liked it. *Thank You, God. Help me to be ... just help me.* Hoping she'd talk for several minutes, he put the car in park and killed the engine.

"He's a cool little man. I just wanted it to be authentic. I thought, let the kid talk for a few minutes. People will respond to him, want to know more, and go to the website for more information."

"Your website looks great too, by the way."

"Thanks to Jared."

"Jared?"

"He's a computer whiz like most kids his age. I told him what I was hoping for, and he started fiddling around with my ideas. He's smart. He loves the harmonica, too, and wants to add it to his piece for the next Crossroads event."

She chuckled. "Am I going to rue the day I ever got him that thing?"

"He's getting real good. You'll be impressed."

"The menus and music thing looks interesting too."

"That's a work in progress. Josie's been shooting me some of her recipes. Hey, I'd love to feature your meatballs. They were delicious."

"Okay. Thank you. It's an exciting time for you."

"It keeps me hopping, for sure. I'm heading back to the station now to schedule other stuff."

"Well, I won't keep you."

He cringed. "No. I didn't mean—" Why had he mentioned heading to the station? *Lame move, bud.*

"I need to go too. Good job, Sam. Thank you for ... for—"

"You don't need to thank me. I'm trying to transform this station into a community asset like I always wanted." He swallowed and lowered his voice. "You made it possible. I want to make you proud."

"Sam—"

"In fact, if you ever want to come down to the station sometime, I'm putting my thumbprint on the building too."

Silence.

Okay. Maybe he was coming on strong, but she shocked his boots off, calling him. He cleared his throat. "Like I was saying, we're making some cool changes at the station and on air too."

"Sounds good, Sam. Congratulations. Take care. Bye."

"Later." Tossing the phone into the passenger seat, he rested his forehead on the steering wheel. *But how much later, Merritt?*

Why did she call him? Why didn't she just text him? Now she missed him all over again. *Not good. Not good.* Tossing her phone on her bed, she bent at her waist, flattening her hands against the floor to stretch.

Listening to the interview had started it. Actually, talking to him had cemented him in her mind. She just wanted to thank him, to encourage him.

Okay, fine. She wanted to talk with him. Truman had ignited a pang of jealousy over his conversation with Sam, and she wanted one of her own.

Pitiful.

Also stubborn. He clearly wanted to talk too.

Her phone rang. *Sam, I can't*—Destiny. She ignored the tiny dip of disappointment in her chest.

"Hey, Dez."

"What'd you think? I thought you'd have listened by now and called me."

"I did listen."

"And didn't call me?"

"I called Sam."

A whoosh of air sounded in her ear. "Wow. Didn't see that coming. How's he doing?"

"He's fine. I told him good job."

"It really was good, wasn't it? I mean, so many times, those interviews come off trying to make you cry, making the poor kid look pitiful. Sam did a great job. I listened to both, did you?"

"Not yet. I listened to Truman's."

"Oh, that kid! He was perfect, and Sam played it perfectly, just nonchalantly. Just talking with a little man. I loved it. But let's back up." Destiny paused. "You called Sam. And nobody made you. You just called him. To talk. To pat him on the back?"

Merritt closed her eyes and took Destiny's questions. "Yeah, I did. So what? We need to encourage any kind of positivity directed toward foster care."

"Uh-huh. I'm proud of you. You're getting over yourself."

"What? I called to congratulate him on a job well done. Not a big deal."

"It's a huge deal for those of us who know your stubborn streak up close and personally."

Merritt snorted. "Shockingly, I'm glad you called. We need to figure out Christmas."

"And my whiplash. Sam to Christmas in two seconds flat? Okay. We don't have to talk about Sam anymore, but you probably need to think about him."

No problem there. "Christmas? How many so far?"

"Right. Jesse and his dad. One of my clients who's due in January isn't traveling to family, so I asked her and her husband."

"Cool. With the two people from church, we have eight for Christmas day. We're still on for Christmas Eve, right?"

"Of course. Spaghetti and watching *Elf.* If Jesse keeps being good, maybe we'll watch *The Christmas Story* for him."

Grimacing, Merritt jotted a list of guests. "Ugh. That movie. Okay. We have the guest list. Now the menu." Flipping the page, she wrote the dishes on one side and the grocery list on the other of her notepad.

Keeping focused on her tasks would keep her mind off Sam.

Yes, of course it would.

42

Merritt flipped through the *Betty Crocker's Guide to Easy Entertaining* Jesse had given her earlier in the afternoon. Published in nineteen fifty-nine, it was a throwback to fancier times when people enjoyed dinner parties throughout the year, not just at holidays.

"This book has recipes, but it also has suggestions for treating guests well and being a good houseguest. Did you know houseguests should offer to change the bed linens before leaving? If there's time, it says." She turned another page. "What a great book. I love it. Thank you again."

Jesse wrapped the navy and red scarf Merritt had crocheted for him around his neck. "You're welcome. I picked it up in the little antique store down the street from my garage. I know you like recipes and entertaining. Didn't realize it had more etiquette stuff too."

"Etiquette stuff. Just what our girl likes to learn about, huh, Mer?" Destiny stuffed her legs under her, hiding her Christmas sock-clad feet.

"Not that she needs to learn more. She's got the best manners of anyone I know."

"Hey, thanks a lot." Laughing, Destiny threw a balled-up piece of Christmas wrapping at Jesse, who swatted it back at her.

"I meant mechanics and bikers."

"Now you're throwing those guys under the bus."

Jesse raised his hands in surrender. "I meant just the ones I hang out with. Let me go make some popcorn. It's almost time for *A Christmas Story*, right?"

Both girls groaned.

"You secretly love it. I know." Jesse hummed "Jingle Bells" all the way to the kitchen.

"So, have you heard from Sam?" Lowering her voice, Destiny fashioned red and green curling ribbon in her hair like a British fascinator.

"Wow. You don't waste any time, do you?"

"Do you want to talk about this in front of Jesse? He'll be back in five minutes with the popcorn."

"Who says I want to talk about it?"

Destiny cocked an eyebrow.

Tracing the worn cover of the entertaining book, Merritt shook her head. "I haven't heard from him."

"No surprise there, I guess. He's giving you your space. Why don't you text him? Just wish him a Merry Christmas at least."

Truth be told, she wanted to have some contact with him today. Weeks ago, when she thought about Christmas, she'd daydreamed he might be sitting here with Destiny and Jesse, commenting on Christmas movies, on all the cookies she'd baked.

Wonder if he liked *A Christmas Story*?

"You know you want to. Give yourself another present. Call him."

Scowling at Destiny, she picked up her phone and sent the text.

STARING at the fire crackling in the fireplace, Sam stretched out on the couch. Winston snored near the hearth.

"Getting hungry yet?" Josie asked from his dad's recliner.

Ches leaned against the front of it from his place on the floor. "Please don't make me think of food yet. Everything was delicious, Josie."

"Thanks." She combed her fingers through Ches's hair. "Ben should be getting close to Hatteras by now."

"We should hear from him soon. Kudos to you for making him go back. Or should I say, letting him go back early." Heath piped in from his place on the couch perpendicular to Sam's.

"I can't wait to hear how the reunion with Ginny goes. Maybe he'll bring her here for a visit. Hey, maybe she'll be his plus one for the wedding." Josie sighed, looking over at Sam.

He sent a silent warning to his little sister. *Do not ask me about Merritt, Jo. Especially in front of Heath and Ches.* "Maybe I'll make half a turkey sandwich." He padded toward the kitchen, and a text vibrated his phone.

Opening the refrigerator with one hand, he checked the text. Merritt. He caught his breath. He'd been trying not to hope to hear from her.

Thank You, God.

Merry Christmas

Merry Christmas

He fisted his fingers to keep them from typing more. *Be cool, buddy. Let her keep driving this texting bus.* Setting the sandwich fixings on the counter, he opened the Tupperware bowl of turkey and waited for the phone to vibrate.

The text came through as he folded over the slice of bread.

I hope Santa was good to you.

I didn't get one thing on my list, for sure, but a text is better than nothing.

I got some socks and some new shirts, a couple of gift cards.

No coal?

Chuckling, he bit his sandwich. Funny girl.

Proud to say I've never found coal in my stocking. Good holiday for you?

Yes. We're about to watch A Christmas Story.

You're a fan of that movie?

No. But Jesse is. Dez and I humor him by watching.

So they're together for the day. At one point, he'd hoped he would have been with her today, but no. He'd wanted to send her something. Instead he laid low, giving her space. How much longer, though, would he have to wait?

Leaning against the counter, he considered his next move. It was his turn to text. Could he ask a new question?

Did you get a favorite gift?

He finished the sandwich waiting for an answer. Opening a tin of glazed pecans, he heard the text.

Probably an entertaining and etiquette book.

Oh? You must collect them. I've seen others on your bookshelves.

Ugh. Did that seem creepy? Did looking at her bookshelves

violate her privacy? This girl. He tossed a few glazed pecans in his mouth and chomped. Solace.

True. It's cool reading them, especially the old ones. Well, enjoy the rest of Christmas. Bye.

And just like that she was gone. Sulking, he scooped more nuts into his palm. An ache tapped at a tiny place in his chest.

"Hey, don't eat all those pecans, Sam. I know that's what you're doing."

Jiggling the nuts in his hand, Sam teased back. "You need to move out of here before you completely turn in to Mom, Joey."

"Bring them in here so we can have some too." Heath yawned away his nap. "Hurry up. The movie's starting."

All right, Miss Merritt. You're teaching me to exercise my patience. How many more lessons do you have for me?

Pushing off the counter, Sam grabbed the tin and headed toward his family.

43

January fourteenth dawned bright and frigid. The sun resembled a summer sun but warmed like the winter one it was. *Thank You for this sunshine, Lord.* Maybe the bright rays would keep a cheerful bent on the day.

Moving day.

Arms folded tightly against her mid-section, she breathed slow breaths. Her night had been fitful with quick dreams of Millie laughing and opening presents. She found the necklace at her throat. Oh, Millie. *I feel like I'm leaving you and the house too.*

The piano caught her eye. Her beautiful piano. Francine had given it up, but the gift didn't diminish her husband's love or erase all the music she and her children played on it.

A quick knock and Destiny burst through the door, one hand cradling two coffee cups against her chest. "Coffee in the house. Come and get it before I drink both." She laughed and encircled Merritt with a fierce hug.

Next to her ear, she whispered, "Millie is not this house. Millie is what she taught you, how she loved you. Millie is with you in all your memories. You're going to be great. You chose this. This didn't happen to you."

A sob escaped, but Destiny hugged more tightly. "I got you a double shot. I thought you'd need it. By the looks of you, I was right."

Pushing back from her friend, Merritt stepped out of the hug. "Thanks a lot." She smoothed back her hair, pulled into a ponytail this morning. "We're moving furniture, not doing a photo shoot."

"Here's to a smooth morning."

They toasted their paper cups.

Another quick knock and Jesse entered, followed by Sam.

Merritt gasped, all nerve endings firing.

"We needed extra help and a truck." Jesse had the grace to look a bit sheepish.

Sam lifted his arms. "I've got two and a truck for the day." Dipping his head, he kept his eyes on Merritt.

"Many hands make light work, right?" Destiny offered her two cents.

"The coffee maker's already packed—" Hoping for composure, Merritt gestured to the stacks of boxes.

"We left our cups in the truck. What goes first?" Sam rubbed his hands together, surveying the room.

So far so good. *She didn't throw me out or hightail it into the kitchen to get away from me.*

Sam's shoulders slipped down a notch. Various scenarios had replayed in his mind since Jesse asked him to help with the move, citing the need for more hands. Shocked and grateful for the invite, Sam had agreed, banking on the warming of Merritt's attitude toward him.

Plus, a prayer or three had definitely helped with the thawing.

Play it cool and follow her lead. No extra questions, just strong arms to help.

Both hands wrapped around the large coffee cup, Merritt

clutched it to the front of her green sweater. "Thank you for coming. I'm glad Jesse brought you."

She was glad he was here? A lightness spread through his chest, replacing the weight camping there for weeks. "You're welcome. Happy to help. Oh, Josie wanted me to thank you again for being able to switch the wedding date."

"Of course. I'm sure you're excited your parents are coming home early." She smiled a cool, professional, kind of stilted smile.

Still. A smile. He'd take it.

"Yeah. Their return was always fluid, so Josie picked a date with a cushion built in. Now that they've bought their tickets for March, Josie and Ches don't want to wait. The church was free in March. Ches's aunt and uncle are having the reception on their farm, so no problem there. It's not a really big shindig, and March isn't exactly a busy time for weddings, so vendors were willing and able to change."

"I don't think Josie worries too much about all the wedding fluff. She just wants to marry Ches." At that moment, her eyes changed, going soft like warm molasses. Her fingers found her heart necklace under the neck of her sweater.

Lost in those positive changes, he soaked up her nearness. He worked his jaw, searching for a response. "True."

Jesse cleared his throat. "Hey, what goes first?"

She stepped back, throwing off the momentary softness and donning her armor again. "You guys choose. It all has to go." Sipping her coffee, she maneuvered around the boxes in the den and headed for the kitchen.

Relief shared space with something near to happiness in his chest. Toying with her necklace always meant some kind of emotion for Merritt. He'd take heart in the small but positive shift in their relationship. Maybe the New Year would hold good things for them.

Smiling, he nodded to the piano. "Let's start with that gorgeous piece."

Hours later, Merritt closed her eyes, but her mind refused to take the hint to relax. Images from the day played on repeat. Sam smiling, talking about the wedding. Sam lifting the piano, cautioning Jesse to be careful with the masterpiece. Sam eating the pizza she bought as a thank you for the group, licking his lips and smiling. Sam always smiling.

Opening her eyes, she surveyed her new bedroom. The streetlamp highlighted furniture through the gauzy curtains. Mental note: buy blackout shades for the bedroom.

Her first night in her new place. Her new house. Heart thumping like she'd just watched a thriller movie, she rolled onto her stomach, hoping the change might slow it down.

It's good. It's all good.

Everything was in order. Most of the boxes had been emptied, and items now rested on shelves or in cabinets newly covered with pretty contact paper, thanks to Destiny staying late to organize.

A neighbor had already been by to greet her and bring a plate of cookies. A good sign, right?

Stubborn and relentless, her mind returned to Sam. With the wedding just weeks away, it was a good thing he helped move. The dreaded first encounter with him was history now. She could enjoy the wedding without anticipating an awkward first conversation.

Destiny kept advocating for him. She put the idea in Jesse's ear to invite him to help move. The shock of seeing him in Millie's house had lasted a brief moment, replaced by breath-stealing joy. Random texts and listening to him on the radio were poor substitutes for the real thing. *Sam.*

She grabbed her phone and texted him before her brain could talk her fingers out of typing the words.

Thank you again for helping today.

That's enough. No need to add more. Short and sweet. Closing her eyes to wait for sleep or maybe a text, she let the phone down on the bed beside her. Before the phone left her fingers, a text came through.

No problem. Glad to help.

You got a great house. Homey.

Homey?

Yeah. Looks like a happy house to me.

I hope so. Feels strange tonight.

First nights anywhere can be rough. Once you have a Thursday night game night, piano lessons … It'll start to feel like home.

Sam. Advocating for patience. She smiled.

Good advice. Thank you.

Good night, Sam.

Sleep well. Night, Merritt.

As the screen faded to black, butterflies stirred a homesick feeling in her mid-section. Sleep well? Hardly. An idea struck. A nice, hot bath, even if she did have to visit the guest room for it. Gathering her pajamas, she headed down the hall toward the waiting tub and magnolia-scented bath salts. Just the ticket for tired muscles and unrelenting thoughts about dimples and hazel eyes.

44

Rinsing her coffee mug, Merritt jumped at a banging on her front door. She stacked her breakfast dishes into the dishwasher and headed for the sound.

"Hey, wake up. It's me."

Destiny, checking on her. Merritt's heart twisted. Her best friend had remembered the date.

"What's got you up this early on a Saturday?"

"A gorgeous morning and you. Come on. Get your duds on. We're going for a walk at the park."

"I'm fine. You don't have to babysit me or do something as drastic as hiking to help me get through the day. I had my Italian dark roast in memory of Millie and wrote in my journal. I'm good."

"I'm not babysitting. I'm including you in my morning."

Merritt tapped her phone. "It's forty-five degrees outside."

"Perfect for a brisk walk to clear your head."

"Who are you?" Merritt glanced at her friend's feet. "Walking shoes? When did you get those? You hate sports. What's up?"

Destiny threaded her arm through Merritt's and headed toward the closet. "People can change, you know. I got these on clearance after Christmas. Jesse and I walk a few times a week." She smiled a sheepish grin. "It's kind of fun."

"Why don't I make more coffee, and we sit here and talk. I'll share my delicious orange and pistachio biscottis."

"No." Destiny dragged a pair of running shoes out of the closet. "You need to get out of here. You've been moping around for weeks. You need fresh air in your lungs."

"Okay. That's it. What have you done with the real Destiny? This is, for sure, not one of her plans." Tugging on the laces, Merritt tied her shoes.

"We started walking with Jesse's dad, but now he walks around the high school track with a group of retirees. Jesse and I like the park." She grinned. "Come on. It'll be fun and good for you too."

An hour and a half later, they rested on a bench positioned beside a creek. Birds whistled songs to friends, and water splashed away from them on its way downstream. Pungent moss and decaying leaves added to the ambiance.

"Hey. Did you hear that? A woodpecker." Merritt glanced behind her, hoping to spot the bird.

"I'm impressed. You can identify birds."

"Because he's literally pecking on wood. I don't know his call. I know a duck's call and an owl's. That's about it."

"All those years in Girl Scouts."

"Not."

Shining from high overhead, the sun raised the temperature near to warm. Merritt pulled off her tassel cap and unzipped her parka. "That's better."

Unwinding her scarf, Destiny focused on rocks planted on the other side of the creek. "So ... Have you thought any more about your poems and your songs and ..."

Merritt's head snapped toward Destiny, who continued studying the far bank. "Random." Stroking the pompom on top of her cap, Merritt blew out a breath. "I've tried not to think about them."

"You'll just ignore the whole business then."

"There's nothing to ignore. Nothing's going to happen."

"Have you read through the jail pamphlet yet?"

Merritt's eyes popped wide open. "What is this? Dump-on-me day? You saw the pamphlet?"

"I packed your junk drawer, remember? Plus, I'd seen it months ago. I just never mentioned it. You had a lot going on."

"You snooped in my stuff?"

"I was looking for a chip clip. You're avoiding the questions. Maybe you should think about going to see her."

"When did you get your therapist's license or your own talk show?"

"I've known you for a long time, Mer. I know when something's getting at you. You're missing Millie. You like Sam, but you don't know what to do with him. Music people like your poems ... maybe you should go see her."

"No, thanks. I don't need to see her." Hating the way her voice shook, she shrugged out of her parka.

"I get that you're angry with her."

"Yeah. I am mad at her. I think I have a right to be. She's ignored me for more than twenty years."

"Right. So sharing your poems, your music shouldn't be a problem."

Merritt frowned. "What do you mean?"

"If you're mad at her, then you wouldn't care if people hear the songs and find out about your background, about her. If you're mad at her, then stop protecting her."

"I'm not. I'm protecting me."

"You had nothing to do with why your mom went to jail."

"It's still my story."

"Yeah, and writing about it helps you process it. Maybe your story can help somebody else."

Merritt groaned, keeping her focus on the water lapping at her feet. A hazy memory fluttered in her mind. A porch swing. Her mother. Grapes. Her mother held a grape in one hand and a paring knife in the other, slicing open the grape and fishing out seeds before handing the halves to her.

A pang constricted her heart. That memory hadn't surfaced in years.

A scene like that meant something, right? She'd been loved, right?

STILL STEWING a bit hours later about the blindside from her so-called best friend, Merritt paced from the den to the back bedroom.

"Why do I have to lay myself bare to help somebody else?" She planted her hands on her hips, enjoying the adrenaline pumping in her veins from yelling in her own house.

I did it for you first.

She gritted her teeth and clamped her eyelids together. Why were Sunday School lessons coming to light now?

"I know that, God, and I'm so grateful. Truly. But this is hard."

So was the cross.

Part of her ire deflated. "Yes. Yes, I believe that." She turned around at the end of the hallway and marched back toward the kitchen. "I just don't want to reach out to her. I don't want people to read my stuff and then Google what happened."

Stubborn. Don't be selfish.

Jerking the junk drawer open, she fished out the pamphlet, flounced to the den, and dropped it on a stack of sheet music. "There. That's it. That's all for today."

It's a start.

Crossing her arms in front of herself, she stomped to her bedroom and slammed the door.

Enough for today.

45

February arrived with a patch of hyacinths breaking through the mulch in the front beds of Merritt's new house, signaling the hope of spring. Other patches sprouted under the two oak trees. Visible from the street as well as her windows, the brave early flowers brought a cheery welcome of purple to her yard. Waiting for Jared to arrive for his lesson, she enjoyed the beauty of the colorful stalks swaying in the breeze.

Her students were acclimating to the new place for their lessons, ever resilient with all the changes since last May. She was too. With touches of Millie in every room, the dwelling felt homelike more quickly than she'd imagined.

Lost in her thoughts, she started when Jared appeared, jogging up the walkway. He tipped his fingers to her as she waved through the window.

Opening the door, she teased him. "Glad you could make it."

"Sorry. The band director caught me after last period. He wants me to think about band for next year. Wants me to sit in with some of his jam sessions, he calls them." Jared grunted. "Somebody ratted me out. Told him I play the piano and the harmonica."

"Ratted you out? Sounds like maybe he did you a favor. I

played in the band. It's a well-kept secret that band members are cool, you know."

Laughter fell out of his mouth like a piano dropping from a sixth-floor window.

Her jaw sagged open. "Ahm, it's true. I'll get you a list of cool, famous people who played in their high school bands."

"I'll look forward to it." A raised eyebrow accompanied his words.

Snark? Weren't they past that attitude yet?

The doorbell thundered through the house. She shuddered. That gong sound announcing visitors had to go.

Who could it be in the late afternoon? Girl Scout cookie time? Booster Club for spring sports?

"I'll be right back. Choose the song you want to play first."

Nearing the door, she practiced saying, "Please come back later." She swung open the door, and hot pinpoints zinged through her body.

A guitar case propped beside him, Sam waited on the porch. No Girl Scout cookies today. Her face went slack.

"You didn't know I was coming?"

She folded her arms in front of her. "Should I have?"

"Isn't Jared's lesson today?"

"Yes, it—"

"Hey, Sam." Jared joined her at the door.

Sam cocked his head. "You haven't mentioned me, have you, Jared? You said be here about twenty till."

"He was late." Squeezing the doorknob, Merritt fixed a composed look on her face.

"Then I forgot because we were talking about band. She's trying to get me to believe being in the marching band is cool. Says it's a well-kept secret."

A glance at Merritt telegraphed a message. *Do not ruin this—*

"I can't believe you let the cat out of the bag, Ms. Hastings. I guess that means ..." Sam glanced at her for help.

"I'll have the list of cool celebrities next week. Right now, start talking about why Sam's here, Jared."

RUBBING the side of his nose, Sam caught Jared's gaze and shook his head. *Not a good look for me, man.*

"Sam's here because I want to play something else at Crossroads next week. I asked him to play the guitar with me, and I'll play the harmonica too. *That* will be cool."

A struggle showed plain as day on Merritt's face. *Will you quash the dreams of a fourteen-year-old and hang on to control, or will you let go of the reins and let Jared captain his own ship this time?* If so, she'd be letting Sam back into her life with more than just random texts.

Yes, he admitted to the mixed metaphors and clichés in his assessment, but they worked in his mind.

"I thought you wanted to play 'All of Me.' That's what you've been practicing for weeks."

"Yeah, but I thought those people might know 'Hey, Jude' better. They might like it more. Since it's for their Valentine's party ..." He shrugged.

Merritt's lips parted.

Yeah, I know how you feel. He's growing up, thinking about other people, not just himself.

"'Hey, Jude' is a great song too, and we've been practicing."

"Yes, but the program ..."

"We don't have to be in the program. You can just introduce us." Jared's eyes lit with excitement.

Merritt turned to Sam. "I didn't know you play the guitar."

He lifted a shoulder. "I can play chords and strum along to slow songs." *Come on, Merritt. Let him play what he wants. I'll be good. I promise.*

Backing into the den, she capitulated. "I guess you want to play now."

Jared leaped to his backpack, pulling out the harmonica holder and snapping it into place around his neck. "Sweet. This will be epic."

Merritt met Sam's gaze, a tiny smile on her mouth.

"Epic, huh."

It'll be something.

LIFTING the whistling teapot off the stove eight days later, Merritt held the blue Italian mug with the embossed lemons and poured in the steaming water. Peppermint tea, a solid choice for winding down after the Crossroads program and spending almost two hours with Sam nearby. Sighing into the wingback chair, she dunked the teabag repeatedly to release the pungent flavors. Smiling over her mug, she reviewed Sam's duet in her mind.

She had to hand it to Jared. They'd done a great job, and the crowd loved it. During the reception time, two men had retrieved harmonicas from their rooms and shared their skills with Jared. He had plans to go back next week for a dueling harmonica session. Excited about music. Exactly what she'd wanted.

Resting her slippered feet on the needlepoint stool Ms. Connie had insisted made her extra room too crowded, she studied the bouquet of flowers gracing her end table. She grabbed her phone, texting Sam.

Thank you again for the beautiful flowers.

When he'd presented them to her at the program, he said they were for planning another great event for the Crossroads folks, but all the flowers were red with white baby's breath. Red carnations. Red tulips. Red roses too. She bit her lip, but the grin escaped. A beautiful arrangement with lots of red roses.

No harm in pretending they might be for Valentine's Day, too, right? She sipped her tea and admired the bouquet while waiting for a text.

Come on, Sam. Text me back.

You're welcome. You deserved something special.

Everyone had a great time.

Your duet was a hit.

You two could probably pick up a night at The lamplighter.

Nope. That's your gig. Don't want to horn in on your space.

Still glowing from the afternoon's success, she didn't want to end the texting yet. She wanted a few more minutes with Sam.

Your Saturday Night Shine program is cool.

I'm glad you're getting to highlight local bands like you wanted.

Thanks. You listen to the show?

I've heard it a few times.

Did she reveal too much? Would he get the wrong idea? What was the wrong idea? She liked Sam. Yeah, he messed up, but he'd helped her more times than hurt her.

Get it together, Merritt.

FINGERS HOVERING OVER HIS PHONE, Sam studied the keyboard. She listened to the Saturday night show? A good sign, right? Had to be. How to proceed with this one, though. *Hold back for a bit more, buddy.* He flexed his fingers and took a breath.

Do you have a favorite local band?

That one with the husband and wife. I forget their names. You play them a lot.

Which means you must listen a lot. His heart swelled thinking of her listening.

Probably Carrie Butler and Mack Johnson.

I do play them a lot.

He'd play them more if Merritt liked them.

Yes. That's them. They're really good.

They play a lot around Charlotte.

He wiped his hand on his jeans. In for a penny ...

If you want to see them live, I could probably connect you with some tickets. I know a guy.

He sent a laughing emoji with the text too. Was the emoji too much? Wait. Did it sound like he was getting her tickets to go with someone else? All his confidence evaporated with this woman.

Or maybe we could go together.

Maybe.

Not *Great!* Or *sounds good*, but he'd take *Maybe.*

Okay. Pull back. Give her some room. Is the wedding a safe topic?

The wedding's getting close.

I guess you'll be at the rehearsal and dinner afterward?

Yes.

See you soon then.

His fingers itched to keep texting. He wanted to call, but she probably needed to chill. Give her some space. Maybe leave her wanting more?

Till the rehearsal, Merritt.

HER PHONE SILENT, Merritt set it aside as her frame of mind took a bit of a nosedive. Sam quit texting just like that. Probably for the better. But still. She gazed at her red flowers. Flowers he gave her for a job well done. He'd asked her about going to see Carrie and Mack together.

Valentine's flowers?

Did she want them to be? Her heart picked up speed at the thought.

Maybe.

Yes, but his family.

They're great.

Argh.

A pamphlet weighing down a stack of sheet music caught her eye and derailed her thoughts about Sam.

HANDBOOK FOR FAMILY AND FRIENDS

She could keep playing the question game about what might happen in the future, or she could be proactive in her own life.

Powering up her laptop, she found the Anson County Jail website and filled out the visitation request form. She hit *send* before she could change her mind.

Body shaking, she headed for the garage and a date with the boxing bag.

46

Her heart strangling her throat, Merritt locked her purse and phone in her car. She pressed the car key into her palm, hoping she could focus on the pinch in her hand rather than her runaway thoughts.

Breathe. You're meeting your mother, not a monster. Just breathe.

She shuddered.

Meeting my mother. After all these years.

What would she look like? What would she sound like?

Her mother's voice had shushed in her minimal memories years ago. Would she recognize her voice now? What would she think of Merritt? What would they talk about? Prison life? Music? The last twenty-something years?

She leaned against the car hood. Why hadn't she asked Destiny to come? She opened the car again and texted her.

I'm at the prison. Just FYI.

Please pray. It's hard to breathe.

Locking the car, she rested her forehead against the window

and pulled her necklace from under her sweater. *God, I need Your help here. That's all I know to pray.*

Sucking in a lungful of air, she held it till she reached the prison door.

TWENTY MINUTES LATER, after undergoing security, watching a dog sniff for drugs, and seeing a couple of women denied entry because of apparel issues, she waited with other visitors behind a red line. Her heart had slowed to just racing.

A prison guard motioned to follow him and marched down the hallway. She jerked into motion, her stomach whirling with each step.

At a closed door, he turned to the group. "Okay. We're ready to enter the visitation room, and the residents are seated at the tables. As a reminder, I'll be with you the whole time. You'll get a ten- then a five-minute warning toward the end. When we walk in, find your loved one and have a seat. Enjoy your visit." He opened the door and gestured for the group to enter.

Ice threatened to smother her lungs.

Hanging back, Merritt let the other, more eager, visitors go before her. As she stepped into the gray room, she balked. Twelve square tables in rows of three filled the room. Inmates seated in plastic chairs at the tables stood as their visitor approached them. Catching the guard's eye, she cobbled words together.

"I ... I thought we'd have to talk on a phone ... with glass between us." Wasn't that how all the cop shows depicted jail visits? What if her mother wanted to hug her? What if she reached across the table to hold her hand?

What if I left right now?

Ringing in her ears intensified. She glanced back toward the hallway.

"First time, huh? It's minimum security here. You sit at tables with the residents." He searched her face. "You okay?"

"I'm fine." If she spoke it out loud, would the words become true? She glanced into the room. Visitors hugged inmates at all the tables except one. Near the back, a lone woman dressed in orange tracked every movement, then locked eyes in a fierce stare.

That's her. That's Momma.

Antiseptic smells combined with perfumes and lotions churned her stomach. Curling her fists into her palms, she swallowed, keeping her gaze on the petite woman waiting for her.

I need some help here, God.

A sweat drop slid from her right arm pit down her side. Too late to reconsider the fifty-percent wool sweater she wore today. She tugged at the crewneck. *I dressed for February, not—*

The guard nudged her toward the back table and her mother. With feet like the cinderblocks making up the gray walls, Merritt approached the table. Sinking into the hard plastic chair, she wiped her palms along her khakis.

Tears stung Merritt's eyes, but she kept them fastened in place. Scenes from the last time she saw Kathy Hastings flooded her mind, but she shook them out. She wanted to focus on the real woman across from her.

"Hello, Merritt." Her voice, soft and hesitant, sounded like a memory, a good memory ... a safe one too.

The banked tears spilled and dripped in a steady stream down Merritt's cheeks. Kathy bit her bottom lip, tears wetting her cheeks too. Perching on the chair opposite Merritt, she gripped the edge of the table.

Ready to flee?

"We're a pair, huh?" Kathy sucked in a breath. "I mean," she wiped her cheeks with open palms. "I mean all these tears."

"It's not all the tears."

Pressing her lips together, Kathy slowly nodded. "No truer words have ever been spoken."

An awkward silence clouded the table. Clasping her hands in her lap, Kathy slid back in her chair. Her throat worked. "I apologize for what happened that night and for what happened to you because of that night."

Merritt bit the inside of her cheek. Pressing her arms tight around her waist, she searched for appropriate words. *I accept* would be appropriate, but was she ready? Forgive her so quickly, so easily?

She'd refused herself the luxury of imaging how the visit would go. She had no plan, no script to follow.

Of their own accord, words creaked from her mouth. "I needed you."

A spasm passed over Kathy's face. Breaking eye contact, she focused on the table. She pursed her lips to let out a stream of air. "For a long time, I wasn't in any shape to ... to be a mother. Then you had Millie."

"How do you know about Millie?"

Kathy chanced a quick peek at Merritt. "She wrote me about you ... about high school, where you went to college, what you studied, details of your graduation, how you acquired piano students." She folded her hands together on the table.

"Millie continued to write you after I stopped? When you never wrote me back, she kept writing you?"

"Yes."

Merritt firmed her mouth. "Why didn't you write me back?"

"I don't know. I didn't know what to say." She shrugged, her thumbs rubbing back and forth along the side of her pointer finger. "I thought it'd be for the better. I thought you should forget about that ... that time and live your best life."

"How about just answering the questions I asked you? Tell me how you were doing?"

"I thought I was doing what was best for you, Merritt. I didn't have a handbook." She licked her lips, then sucked in a breath with widened eyes. "It's ... been about a year, right?"

Merritt firmed her mouth, allowing a tiny nod.

"I ... I, ah, was very sad when Millie passed. I wanted to send a sympathy card."

"Why didn't you?"

"It seemed like it was too late. I'd never reached out before. I didn't want to confuse you more or make you sadder. My Bible study group was praying for you. Tiffany told me—"

"Who's Tiffany?"

Kathy took a breath. "Tiffany is part of a monthly prison ministry, but she's been more ... a close friend for years."

"She sees you every month?"

"Sometimes twice or three times a month."

A hurt feeling took root and began climbing up her chest.

"She's the one who convinced me to allow this visit." Kathy watched her daughter through hooded eyes.

"I couldn't trust my own judgment. The first time I read your letter," a grin split above her chin before she could capture it. "I squealed. The guard came running. When I had a chance to think it through, let my sane side rule, I knew it probably couldn't happen. I decided just to put it in my stack of letters like your others." She peeked at Merritt.

"You know. Fall back into old habits, but Tiffany knew something was up when she visited and badgered me until I confessed what was going on." Kathy swallowed. "I'm glad she kept at me."

"Why now?"

"You're an adult now. I thought I owed you a face-to-face meeting."

Merritt's heart rate kicked higher again. It was her turn to speak again, and again words failed her. What did she want to say? Was she happy she came? What result did she want?

Kathy's thumbs worked overtime on her forefingers. Her hands were tiny. She'd probably have trouble reaching an octave on the piano. Greenish brown stains dotted her—

Intercepting her line of vision, Kathy flexed her hands. "These are plant stains. I work in the garden and greenhouse every day. My hands are clean, but the stains are there for the duration, I think." She laughed a soft, tiny laugh.

An involuntary movement hitched up one corner of Merritt's mouth. A deliberate one tamped it back down.

"Merry—"

Merritt's eyes whipped to Kathy's. Her mother had been the only one to call her Merry. Not even Millie or Destiny used that nickname. An overwhelming urge to hug her mother warred with the desire to run.

Kathy cleared her throat. "Merritt, there's so much I want to say to you, but you're here for a reason. I'm sure you have questions. Why don't you talk for a while?"

Questions? You bet I do, but where to start?

Her mind blanked except for images from that last night with her mother, hiding in the closet, her mother crying, the smell of burnt pork chops, the police trudging through every room, a policeman picking her up—

"Merritt, are you okay? Do you need some water?"

The soft questions yanked her back to the present. *No, I'm not fine. I'm visiting my mother. In prison.* "I'm fine."

A guard glided by their table on his circuit through the groups. Humming with low voices, the room vibrated with the sounds and sights of happy visits. Laughs and smiles and clasped hands—

"Are you still writing poems?"

Bouncing back to her own table, Merritt's eyes widened.

"Millie mentioned your journal. I'm glad you had that outlet. She gave your writing rave reviews." Kathy smiled. "I'm sure I'd agree with her."

"Someone thinks they might work as songs."

Kathy's eyes lit. "Wouldn't that be something? I mean, if you want that, of course."

Grooves stacked in rows on Merritt's brow. "You'd be okay with that?"

Kathy gasped. "Why wouldn't I be?"

Shaking her head, Merritt lowered her gaze. "Some of the poems are about you. About that time."

Her face relaxing, Kathy nodded. "I've put that behind me." Leaning forward, she whispered. "My actions took a man's life. My actions separated me from you for twenty-five years. My actions changed the course of my life. I've begged God for forgiveness, received it, and now I'm walking in grace."

When Merritt didn't respond, Kathy continued. "Do you understand me?"

"I think so."

"Our story is one of redemption, Merritt. Do I wish things had happened differently that night? Of course. Do I wish I could have raised you instead of leaving you to the foster system? Absolutely, but I'm grateful for people like Millie who stood in the gap for me. I have to look at the positives of our story instead of all the bad stuff. We live in a fallen world, but there's good in it too."

She smiled. "I'm so proud of the woman you've become. I'm proud of your talent. If you have a chance to share it with the world, go for it."

Merritt's laugh freed fresh tears. "I doubt it'd be with the world."

"Don't sell yourself short. Be positive. You don't know what could happen."

Just like Millie, always cheering her on no matter what.

"I'm afraid."

Another guard called, "Ten minutes."

Startled, Merritt straightened in her chair, looking for the door.

"Wait." Kathy slid her palm toward her. "We've got ten more minutes. Afraid to let the story out?" She shrugged. "It's already out."

"That I'll be like ... like—"

Understanding flooded her mother's gaze. "No. You're not him, Merritt. I see contentment in your eyes. He never was content ... with anything." She searched her face. "We're getting close to the end of visitation." She licked her lips and took a short breath. "Any other questions?"

The end already? Yes, she had more questions. Twenty-five years' worth of questions.

Her heart pumped hard in her chest. Kathy's eyes drank her in, but Merritt lowered her eyes under the intensity.

So many questions, but where to start? What's your favorite color? What music do you like? Why did you marry him?

"Five minutes." The guard's voice bumped Merritt out of her chair.

Kathy joined her in standing. "It was so good to see you, to talk to you, Merritt. Just let me know if I can help you anymore. I'll be glad to answer other questions. I promise to answer your letters now. If you write."

Heart thundering so that she could feel the beat in her ears, Merritt spoke before she could stop the words. "Can I come back?"

Sucking in a breath, Kathy fisted her hands at her sides. "Any time you want."

Merritt lunged for her, grabbed her in a swift hug, and quickstepped it to the door. Not exactly ready for a hug back, she didn't want to see her mother's face after the hug. She didn't want a long goodbye.

But she wasn't ready to say exactly what she did want either.

MERRITT'S BODY followed the line of visitors down the gray corridor and into the original waiting area. Her mind whirled with scenes and words from the visit. She waited to pick up her key, then followed others to the outside. Nerve endings vibrated on high alert. Her breath came in long pulls as if she'd just rung the bell at the top of a rock-climbing wall.

Searching for her car in the parking lot, she blinked. Jesse and Destiny leaned against her hood. Racing to her friends, she released the banked tears and sobbed in Destiny's arms.

"Oh, Merritt. How was it? Was it that bad?" Destiny squeezed her through the storm. "You don't have to answer. Just cry it out. It's okay."

Destiny smoothed her hand from Merritt's temple down through the waterfall curls, cooing softly in her ear. "We've got you. You're fine."

"When you're ready, Jesse's going to ride his motorcycle, and I'm driving you back. Aren't we the best? I read your text, and we hopped on his hog and BAM. Here we are." Her hand repeated the soothing motion.

Jesse chuckled. "It's just a bike, not a hog. Maybe I can buy a Harley-Davidson one day."

"Hog. Bike. Semantics." Destiny shrugged.

A muffled snort sounded against Destiny's shoulder. Merritt came up for air. "You crazy people. I'm fine. You didn't have to come rescue me." Straightening from her friend, Merritt wiped her hands over her cheeks, under her chin.

"We're not rescuing you. I wanted to ride his hog."

"Stop saying 'hog,' woman." Jesse pushed off the hood.

With that, breathy hitches morphed into shaky giggles. Relief and gratefulness and fatigue surged through her body, ramping the giggles into giddy laughs.

Picking up signals, Destiny threw a steadying arm around Merritt's shoulders. "Hey, what say we get on down the road?"

Grateful for friends who had her back, for not having to drive in her fragile state, and for not needing to say one more word, Merritt let Destiny lead her to the passenger side of the car. Sinking into the bucket seat, she closed her eyes, the last image of her mother seared into her brain.

She'd take a while to process the morning, but she could see herself coming back. Her heart kicked up a notch at the thought.

Yes, I'll be back. Not sure when. But I'll come back.

47

After coming in like a lion, March had settled into a calm, warm month, perfect for a spring wedding. Backing under the shade of a crepe myrtle tree, Merritt parked her car and surveyed the reception venue. Owned by Ches's aunt and uncle, Heidi and Jack, the farm sparkled with a festive atmosphere.

A huge white tent in the backyard teemed with people looking for their places at round tables. Touched at having been invited to the reception, Merritt declined to ride in the wedding party shuttle, preferring to be able to leave at her leisure. Maybe she'd write her mother about the decorations.

She and Sam had been texting and calling more regularly the last couple of weeks. They were becoming close again—but close to what? How would the night go with all his family being here? All his siblings, plus Ben's girlfriend, Ginny, and his parents, who probably still suffered from jet lag.

Deleting the question from her mind, she focused instead on reviewing with relief the beautiful ceremony with no sour notes coming from her end of the duties. The church had dazzled with yellow roses and tulips adorning just a few vases and one small candelabra behind the altar.

Surprised by the small number of attendants, Merritt understood the saying, *less is more*. The wedding had a simple but tasteful air. Making her way under the tent, she found her name and corresponding table number affixed to a CD. Josie and Ches's favorite CD mix. A thoughtful and personal favor to remember the night. She tucked it into her clutch and spied her table near what appeared to be the wedding party's table.

Introducing herself to the two couples already seated, she gazed at the pond in the distance. What a lovely place. No wonder Josie wanted to have their reception here.

The rehearsal dinner had hinted at a simple affair having taken place at Ches's favorite restaurant, the Red Door Tavern. Not much to look at from the outside, but the serving staff clearly loved Ches. The various kinds of sliders piled onto trays were delicious and fun.

She nodded silently to herself. That's what a wedding should be, filled with all the people and places important to the couple.

A pang of melancholy threatened to bloom. *No, Merritt. No sad thoughts tonight—*

"Hey. You found the farm, I see." Breathtaking in his tux, Sam slid into the chair beside her. "What do you think? Great, huh?"

"It's beautiful."

"That sounds like a movie cue for me to gaze at you and say, 'Yes. It is.'" Sam grinned.

"Can't come up with your own line, huh?" But did he think she looked nice tonight?

"Good one. I'll think of something brilliant and tell you while we dance later. Save one for me, okay?" He fiddled with the collar of his shirt. "I gotta sit up there." He motioned to the head table. "But I'd rather be back here with you."

He clasped her hand. "Seriously, I'll see you in a few and claim a dance or maybe more if you can keep up with Mr. Bojangles here."

Happiness poured out of him and spilled onto her.

Leaving her laughing, Sam joined the best man and his brothers near the wedding cake. A dance with Sam. Could be nice. Thank goodness Millie taught her beach music steps, swing, and even waltzing. She should be able to keep up with Mr. Bojangles.

FINALLY, all the speeches, the bride and groom's first dance, and all the other wedding formalities had taken place, and now Sam anticipated the fun portion of the evening. The strains of the first dancing song wafted through the speakers, and the DJ urged people to take to the floor.

Ugh. Beach music.

The DJ chose a crowd favorite, of course, to stir guests to their dancing feet. "Give Me Just a Little More Time," an oldie but always a goodie. But maybe it was appropriate for their relationship. He stepped toward Merritt.

Offering his hand, "I'm guessing you know how to dance to beach music if you went to a North Carolina college. Am I right?"

"Actually, Millie taught me so that I could keep up at college. Yes, I know how."

"Great. Let's go. Not an original choice for the beginning set, if you ask me, but beach music does get the crowd on its feet."

He spun her onto the dance floor, smiling when she turned exactly right. "Nice. You got rhythm. Here we go."

Keeping up with him for the first verse, she met him toe to toe. Pleasantly surprised, he complimented her kick, ball, change step. "You know how to do this, all right. Can you do the duck walk?"

She grinned.

"Cool beans. I'll give the signal, okay?"

At the beginning of the next set, both bent their knees,

waddling like a duck. He laughed and spun her under his arm. "Nice."

She threw in a sailor side shuffle.

"Now you're just showing off. Millie must've been good." He led her on a pass-through and back. "How about sugar footin'?"

She grimaced but didn't miss a step. "Not my favorite, but I'll try."

With his nodding prompt, they began the variation, but her knees hit his and threw them off beat. He grabbed her shoulders to steady her.

"Oops. Sorry. I told you." She shrugged.

They stopped cold on the dance floor, gazing into each other's eyes. He smoothed a curling tendril of hair from her temple and dropped his gaze to her lips. Dancing was fun, but kissing ... He leaned toward her, but the music changed to an up-tempo "Sixty-Minute Man." A couple jostled from his left, and the moment evaporated.

"With your dance moves, we gotta keep going." He spun her around and twirled her back to the middle of the floor.

After a fifteen-minute set of beach music, Merritt begged for a time out and refreshment.

"Sit for a minute. I'll get something for you." He brought her to her table and then took a detour toward the DJ. "Hey, man. We're digging this music, but what else you got up your sleeve, and please don't say, "Shout" or "Jump"? I really need a slow song. Help me out?"

The DJ smiled. "I gotcha, man. Get back to your lady. 'Thinking Out Loud' is coming up. Will that do?"

"That works."

He grabbed a glass of ginger ale from one of the waiters and headed back to Merritt. Heath stood next to her, laughing. *No, sir, bro.*

"Ginger ale." He handed the glass to her. "Nice time, eh, Heath?"

"Marvelous. I was just about to ask Merritt—"

The beginning measures of the first slow song sang over the crowd. "Sorry. She promised me a dance." He whisked her away from his brother and onto the dance floor.

"Ah, we already danced, remember?" She had a teasing set to her mouth.

"But not like this." Pulling her toward him, he pressed his hand against the small of her back. He slid one step closer to her. She remained close, swaying with the beat and following every signal he gave her. A waft of something sweet and floral heightened his senses. He bent his head to breathe in more of the heady scent. She leaned in closer to him.

Nice. Very nice.

MERRITT FOLLOWED Sam perfectly on the dance floor with just the touch of his hand on her back. One of Millie's male friends had shown her how to slow dance the real way, not just stepping around and around in a circle. A skilled dancer, Sam followed the rhythm and created an interesting pattern on the dance floor too. Snuggling closer felt natural and warm and perfect.

His aftershave held just the right amount of spice and outdoors. Inhaling the scent, she allowed herself a quick moment of pretending ... pretending this was their first dance at their wedding. That he'd promised to love and honor and cherish her forever.

At some point in the song, Sam had brought her right hand over to his chest. Heat singed her wrist through his jacket. His signals stopped, so they stood together, swaying to the beat. His scent and his arms made the perfect cocoon.

Nestling against him, she rested her forehead along the curve of his neck. Contentment and joy bloomed in her heart along with a heat of her own. He nuzzled a kiss at her temple, his five o'clock shadow grazing her cheekbone. Desire like she'd never felt, more than having her own home—and certainly not with Derek—burned way down deep.

And it terrified her.

TWO THOUGHTS CONSUMED Sam's mind—dancing like this for the rest of his life and getting her somewhere so he could kiss her like he wanted to. Away from the prying eyes of his lame brothers. Away from all the traditions that hadn't happened yet, the cutting of the cake, throwing the bouquet and the garter. All the stuff he'd have to participate in before they could get more time alone.

She snuggled against his neck. He slid his hand up her spine and jolted when he found the scooped back of her dress. He traced the top edge with his fingertips and felt her shiver. So as not to break the spell, he slid his hand back down her spine, drawing her closer without speaking.

The last notes lingered in the air for a few seconds before the jarring sound of "Shout" echoed across the dance floor. They jerked apart, but Sam kept his arm on her back.

She glanced up, a dazed expression on her face combined with something else. She muttered, "Thank you," and headed back to her table.

"Hey, Sam. Mom wants another family picture," Heath called from the middle of the dance floor, hooked his arm around Sam's shoulder, then pulled him to the side of the tent.

Sam glanced toward Merritt's table, letting go a relieved sigh. She was talking to her table mates. Good.

Stay there, and I'll be right back. We got to talk.

Josie fluffed the veil hanging down her back. "Where's Merritt? You were supposed to bring her with you. Go get her."

Hustling to the table, he found an empty chair. Gone. She was gone, along with her purse and shawl. Maybe the bathroom?

"No, she told us goodnight when she left." One of the table mates offered slim help. "You might be able to catch her."

He jogged to the parking area by the barn, but taillights already lit up the path to the road. Clamping his mouth shut against a word that would scorch Ms. Connie, he kicked a clump of grass with his shiny black shoe.

Bailing on his sister's wedding wasn't an option, but ...

We're gonna talk some more, Merritt. Somewhere. Somehow. We will have another conversation.

48

The soft notes of a popular beach music tune filled the studio. Sam grinned despite himself. Operation Beach Music Blast had been going since early this morning. Since one o'clock this morning, to be exact. Would his plan work?

Please let this plan work.

He checked over the schedule for the day. Jared's buddy, Brent, was penciled in for the afternoon shift. Great. An eager beaver, Brent learned quickly and had some interesting ideas for new programs too. A solid find and not too expensive either.

The station phone rang. Not able to afford a call screener, Sam did the job himself. "WDVY where music and community still matter. What's on your mind today?"

"Calling about your playlist. Specifically, 'With This Ring.'"

Sam smiled. "Hey, I can put you on the radio if you want. Tape you now and play it after this song."

"I don't care. I just want to know what's going on."

Pressing the record button, he began the on-air conversation. "Hey, caller. Who do I have on the line?"

"Frank from Rock Hill."

"What's up, Frank?"

"Something's up with your playlist. You've played 'With This Ring' about a hundred times today."

Twelve times, actually. Once every hour.

"It's a great song, don't you think?"

"It's fine, but I don't need to hear it every time I turn around."

"Well, Frank, today's your lucky day. We were doing a little experiment here at the station today. You're the first person to call questioning our program. I've got a prize basket with some local goodies in it along with two tickets to Charlotte Out Loud, a local food and music festival happening next weekend. How does that sound?"

Frank chuckled. "Good, I guess. I just wanted you to pick another song."

"We will certainly change the playlist now you've noticed what we're doing. Thanks, man. What's your favorite radio station?"

"WDVY, where music and ... and ..."

"Where music and community still matter, Frank. It still matters."

Smiling, Sam adjusted songs on his program screen, changing the order from playing 'With This Ring' at the top of the hour to the top and the half-hour too.

All right, listeners. The next move is yours.

WAITING for her microwave to warm the last piece of the spinach quiche from Sunday, Merritt tapped Destiny's number on her phone.

"What's up? Your text said to call when I finished lessons." Merritt sipped her sparkling water.

"Yeah. I guess you haven't been listening to the station?"

"No. I've been teaching this afternoon. I listened a couple of times this morning, though."

"Well, tune in now. You need to hear what's going on."

The microwave dinged. Still a bit cool in the middle, the quiche needed a few more seconds of heat.

"Why? What's Sam doing now?"

"Just listen." Destiny hung up without a goodbye.

The nerve.

Merritt switched on the radio and took out the steaming quiche. Glancing at the kitchen clock brought from Millie's, she sliced the corner of the triangle with a fork and blew on it to cool the bite. Just in time for Menu and Music.

Sam's voice sounded strong after the commercial, reminding listeners to check the air conditioning units before the late spring rush. Not a bad idea since she hadn't used the a/c yet. "... get to Music and Menu portion of tonight's programming schedule, but first, here's a little song that's becoming really popular around here. Have you heard it before? Here we go."

"With This Ring" brought forth a smile as she swallowed another morsel. Millie taught her how to dance with this one, along with a few other beach music favorites. *Why is he playing beach music now? Unless seafood is on the menu for tonight.* She chuckled at her own weak joke.

Tapping her toe to the beat, she finished the quiche. Should she have a salad too? Not really feeling it. Maybe some grapes?

Sam cut into the last measures of the song. "Hey, folks. I've got Marci on the line here. What were you saying, Marci?"

"I was telling you you're driving me insane playing that song over and over. I like beach music as much as anybody else but play a different one already."

"So, Marci, when did you notice the song was getting on your nerves?"

"About four o'clock, I noticed that you'd played it twice since three o'clock, and you played it again. I thought it must be a mistake. I mentioned it to the cashier next to me, and she said you've played it all day. It didn't bother her because it's one of her favorites. It used to be one of mine, too, before you wore it out."

Sam chuckled over the line. "Oh, Marci. I'm sorry I've ruined it for you. But since you made the effort to call in and complain, we've got a prize package waiting for you. How does a gift certificate to Queen City Day Spa, some locally-made goat milk soap, and a jar of local honey sound?"

"Like a dream. I'm not really complaining. I just wanted to know what was going on."

"You're curious. I like that, Marci. What's your favorite radio station?"

Merritt turned down the station and called Destiny back. Her heart thumped a strange rhythm. *Sam's playing "With This Ring" on repeat?*

"Okay. I listened to it. He's playing beach music, which is a surprise, and giving away cool prizes."

"He's playing 'With This Ring' like a broken record, or a broken radio station. Have you talked with him?"

"Not since Saturday night at the wedding."

"Girl, call him."

"I don't know what to say."

"I think he's talking to you with that song. With this ring ... I promise I'll always l—"

"Okay. Okay. I know the lyrics."

"But do you—"

"I need to call him. Bye."

THE CLOCK on Sam's dashboard read six-fifteen. What if this plan didn't work? What if she didn't listen to the radio today? What if—

His phone buzzed in the cup holder. Merritt. Ice captured his insides.

Clearing his throat, he accepted the call. "Hey. What's up?"

"Hey, Sam."

Her voice sounded breathy and low. A good sign because she'd listened and wanted to talk about that song? Or a bad sign because she'd listened and worked out her anger on the punching bag.

Oh, this woman.

"Everything good?"

"I listened to the station tonight. I thought it'd be classical or instrumental like usual. But it wasn't."

"Nope."

"You played 'With This Ring.'"

He squeezed the steering wheel. "Yep."

"The caller said she'd heard it several times already today."

"Uh-huh. Twenty times to be exact."

"Twenty?" The squeak in her voice summoned his grin.

"That's right."

"I didn't think you liked beach music."

"I like it fine. It has its place. I like this song's particular message."

"Oh."

"Are you decent?"

"Yes, of course. For Heaven's sake."

"Can I come in?"

"Now? Aren't you at the station?"

"I'm in your driveway."

The line went dead. A good sign?

The front door opened. She rested one hand on the storm door.

In for a penny ...

Exiting his car, he stuffed his phone in his back pocket. "Hey again."

She opened the storm door and stepped back. "You made it over here quick."

"The part you heard was taped." He moved into the den,

noting the furniture she'd added since the move. "Jared's buddy, Brent, is flying solo for a few hours. He's learning fast."

"Good. I'm glad you have help." Confusion, wariness, and a couple of other emotions took turns on her face.

"Want to sit in here," he motioned to the wingback chairs, "or in the kitchen?"

"I want to talk about ... about ..."

A slow grin sprawled across his face activating the dimple in his cheek. "Good. I do too. Let's sit at the table."

"Have you eaten?"

"Not here for dinner, Merritt. I just want to focus."

He pulled a chair out for her and then sat on the opposite side.

"Here's the deal. I'm showing my cards, so to speak. That song has a message for you." He reached behind him, and her eyes rounded. He laid his phone on the table, and she let go a breath. "No, I don't have a ring for you. Yet. But I'm here to say I hope we'll get to that point."

Her lips parted.

"Merritt, I'm going to mess up. Look how many times I've messed up since I've known you. That doesn't mean I'm doing it on purpose. I don't want to hurt you or make you mad. But I'm going to mess up again. Just ask Josie or anybody who knows me."

A tiny smile played around her mouth.

"I'm sorry I shared your music with Doug and he sent it to Nashville. I hoped you just needed a little nudge. I thought I'd completely ruined my chance with you until that slow dance Saturday night." He paused. "I think you liked it too."

She dropped her gaze.

"Merritt, don't shut me out like that. We need to talk."

Turning his palm up, he slid his hand toward her. She placed hers on top.

"I played that song all day long, hoping you'd hear and let me talk about it. I couldn't think of another way."

"It worked."

He laughed. "Yeah, and all my listeners I've been trying so hard to win think I'm crazy and we're doing some crazy stunt before going back to all beach music all the time." He pretended to shudder. "Anyway, I think we've had some pretty fantastic dates—"

"Some? I count two."

He slapped his chest. "You slay me, woman." He pointed the index finger with his free hand. "Blueberry picking." Two fingers. "The restaurant. Playing the duet at Crossroads." Three fingers. "The time I brought you a coffee milkshake." Four fingers. "Thursday Night-Game night." Five fingers. "Sanding—"

"Okay. Okay. I didn't realize." She laughed. "Those are some interesting dates, absolutely."

"Pretty sure you've never picked blueberries on a date before." He reached for her hand again.

"Pretty sure a sweet little old lady never set me up on a date like that either."

"Point taken." With his fingertips, he drew circles on her palm. "I'd like to have some more interesting dates like that. I hope you do too." Releasing her hand, he leaned back, giving her space. "You're strong and talented and hardworking and smart and beautiful, Merritt. I want to make promises to you for a long time, but the ball's in your court now. We've known each other for about a year—"

"Eleven months."

He chuckled. "Eleven months?"

"Since last May when I was playing the church's piano."

"Wow. Eleven months." He nodded. "Okay. So here we are. You know I'm being serious. I want to date you, but I'm not going to push you into anything. I realize my huge handicap with my wacky family that just got bigger by one. And by the looks of it, Ben could be headed down the same path before too long." He hung his head. "I come with lots of baggage."

She laughed. "Yes."

"Yes, I come with baggage?"

"Yes, I'll go out with you. And, yes, you come with lots of baggage, but it's not your family."

Frowning, he reached for her hand again. "What?"

"Your family's great. You tend to stick your nose in ..."

"I'll work on that. Maybe you can help me."

"A tough assignment, but I can try." She bit her lip, but a smile lit up her whole face.

"That looks like a happy smile." The same emotion surged from his own gut.

"It is. Really happy."

"Whew. That's good." He wiped his hands on his jeans. "Oh, I should call Brent. Cancel the rest of the 'With This Ring' slots. I don't need to lose all my listeners."

49

"I promise you won't get in trouble, Brent. I promise you won't lose your job." Merritt crossed her fingers behind her back, knowing that action didn't cancel out the almost-lie she just promised the teenage DJ. She didn't think Sam would fire him, but she shouldn't promise protection like that. "You'll be doing your job like you're supposed to. I'm just asking you to play one song until I text you to play another one."

"Sam and Ms. Hastings are kinda like boyfriend and girlfriend. They got something going on." Jared shrugged. "You know Sam's cool."

"Yeah, he's cool, but this station's his baby. I don't wanna mess with it. And I don't want to go back to busing tables. I love this job." Chewing on a cuticle, Brent ping-ponged his gaze between his friend and the piano teacher.

"Sam knows you love it. He's told me how you're a good worker and bring so much to the table. He won't fire you, Brent." Merritt licked her lips. "How about this? How about playing the song and then calling Sam to say you need his help switching the song? That's true. I want you to play the song until he arrives. He'll help you by coming to the station. I'll text you from the parking lot when he gets there, and then you can play 'The Perfect Space.'"

"I don't know, man." Brent rubbed his brow.

"Ms. Hastings teaches Elise."

His hand halting, Brent peered at her through scraggly bangs. "You know Elise?"

"I've taught Elise Jacobs since she was eight years old. She comes to my house every week. Yes, I know her."

"Oh. Well. Um."

"He wants to ask her to the prom, but time's running out. Most people already have dates if they're going."

Would Elise Jacobs hold the key to setting this crazy plan in motion? Prom was only three weeks away. If she said yes, could Elise find a dress?

Not my problem.

"Brent, I promise to do anything and everything to help you woo Elise if you help me with Sam."

"Woo?"

"Get Elise's attention, I mean. In a good way. Do we have a deal?" She offered her hand, and the teen dropped his limp hand into hers.

We'll begin with how to give a proper handshake. "Wonderful. I'll let you know when the plan goes into action."

If her plan worked, Sam should be pulling up to the station any minute. *Sam.* For the past few weeks, they'd seen each other almost every day, eating at fun places all over the city or at her house or with his family. They'd played duets, shared dreams, and thought up new programming to try.

She'd entertained the possibility of maybe sharing her music with more people at some point. Her mother had helped her think through sharing her music too.

And now, today could be the beginning of a new chapter for them.

Thank you, Elise, for your part in these shenanigans. The sophomore had been excited to accept an invitation to the senior prom. Whether the prom date led to anything more depended on Brent and Elise. With his prom date secure, Brent kept his end of the bargain.

Breathing in for four counts, holding for four, and then breathing out for five, Merritt willed her insides to relax, to calm, to enjoy the peace she was supposed to have as a believer.

Please help this go well. Please, God.

Sunshine glinted off a car pulling into the station's parking lot. *Sam.* Any peace she'd achieved flew out her window. She texted Brent to return to regular broadcasting with a special song from a North Carolina band.

His car jerked to a stop, and Sam jumped out, slamming his door behind him. Maybe she'd misgauged his irritation.

God, I need a lot of help here ... clearly.

Hopping out of her car, she shouted before he disappeared into the building. "Hey."

"With This Ring" blared on the outside speaker.

He stopped and turned toward the sound of her voice, tilting his head. He glanced back at the station but stepped her way. "Hey."

Hugging her arms around her middle, she forced a smile on her face. "Got a minute?"

"Sure, but I need to help Brent—"

"Yeah, I know about Brent. He's doing a great job."

"Huh?" Motioning for her to walk with him, he glanced toward the door again. "Let me fix the problem, and then—"

She clasped his upper arm, pulling him to stop. "It's my problem." She shook her head. "No, that's not what I meant." Taking a breath, she began again, words tumbling over each other. "Brent is helping me. I asked him to repeat 'With This

Ring' until I texted him to stop." She held onto his arm for support. "Kinda like bait, I guess. To get you here."

"With This Ring" faded to a different selection.

"Listen. He's playing something new." She cocked her ear to the speaker hanging at the corner of the building.

Confusion gave way to understanding, slacking his features.

"That's the Avett Brothers."

"Uh-huh. A local band that's popular everywhere now." Her other hand settled on his chest. "'The Perfect Space' is a beautiful song. I know it's written from the male perspective, but I identify with it too—wanting people in my life I can trust and somewhere to feel natural and safe—"

"Right. And someone to 'love me,'" he locked eyes with her and swallowed. "For the man I've become," He glanced at her fingers fiddling with one of the buttons on his shirt. "'Not the man I was.' I love this song."

"I do too. I'm not the foster girl. She'll always be part of me, but I've become more—"

"I like to think we've both evolved."

"Me too." She blew out a long breath. "You've spent a lot of time apologizing to me, but—" Letting go of him, she rubbed her forearms. "I should have thanked you—"

Sam stepped closer to her, grinning.

"Wait. No. Not for sending my music out. That's still not cool. No, for wanting the best for me. Millie always wanted the best for me too."

Sam opened his mouth, but she held up a hand to silence him.

"I also should thank you for liking my music enough to take an interest in it." Her breathing came in short puffs. "And I should apologize for dragging my feet with forgiving you. I wallowed in hurt and self-righteousness instead of letting it go. My reason is this—" she motioned between them "—terrifies me. You terrify me."

"If it helps, you terrify me too." Reaching for her hand, he shook his head. "Man, I can't believe we're doing this here." He glanced at his building. "I've been praying for a real conversation with you, but not quite like this. I wanted something special ... like you." Sighing, he relented. "For what it's worth, I don't want to terrify you."

"It's not your fault. You come from a solid family—people who love you, have your back."

"So do you, Merritt."

She grimaced. "You have a real family, not one you hodgepodged together."

"Kinda harsh, don't you think?" He cupped her cheek. "Do you love Destiny less because she isn't a blood relative? Do you think Ms. Connie would have helped you more if you'd been her own granddaughter? Sounds like Millie—"

"Okay. I hear you. I get it."

Sam studied the scar at the corner of her mouth, tracing it with his thumb. "Families are what you make them."

His touch, light as a whisper, stoked heat to her core.

"Do you want to make one with me?"

Her gaze slammed into his, paralyzing movement.

"Yeah. I'm cuttin' to the chase."

Laughing out loud freed her muscles, and she moved closer to him.

"I don't want to terrify you. I want to love you, Merritt. I do. Love you."

"Yeah, I think I do too."

"Think so?" Pretend hurt washing over his face, he slid a hand behind her neck.

Shivering, she took a deep breath. "I know so. That's why I'm here." Hands traveling up the warm fabric of his T-shirt, she pinned her eyes to his. "I want you, Sam. I want us. And whatever else comes with it."

Touching his forehead to hers, he closed his eyes and smiled. "Hey, that sounds like a hook for a song."

She lifted her gaze to his. "Let's write it together."

Brushing her lips with his, he whispered, "A good plan." He kissed her again like he meant it. "So, are we engaged?"

"I hope so." She teased him. "But am I supposed to have a ring?"

"You are. I wanted to buy one just in case we got to this point, but," he shrugged, "I'm trying to learn my lesson about jumping in without thinking. Trying to be patient."

She cupped his face, the scruff of his whiskers tickling her palms. "Thank you for being patient with me."

"You're worth it." He lowered his lips to hers with a kiss that promised a ring and a song and a home of their own.

DISCUSSION QUESTIONS

1. Millie has already passed when the novel opens, but Merritt keeps her memory alive throughout the story. Discuss ways she honors Millie. How have you found ways to keep your loved ones' memory alive?
2. Family is one of the themes in the story. Talk about the similarities and differences between Merritt's and Sam's idea of family.
3. Merritt says Sam isn't her type because he has too much family. Is that a valid statement? He does come from a close-knit clan, but are his siblings involved in his life too much? Discuss boundaries in families.
4. Pastor Dunleavy speaks about church congregations being family. Do you agree or disagree with his assessment?
5. Including Merritt, Sam, and the minor characters, too, which character is your favorite? Why? What appealed to you most about her or him?
6. Sam is a helper. How is this characteristic both a positive and negative trait for him?

7. Describe Merritt's personality. Is she strong-willed, reserved, spontaneous, courageous? Do you think Merritt is a pessimist or an optimist? Why?
8. Foster care is an important part of the story. Discuss how it shaped Merritt. How did she survive the not-so-good placements? Does she have more scars or strengths from her childhood? Have you ever known someone who is in or was in foster care? Would you ever consider fostering children?
9. Merritt uses her journals to process thoughts and feelings. Do you keep a journal or diary? Why or why not? If not, would you consider keeping one if you knew you'd be the only person reading it?
10. Were you surprised by Merritt's prison visit? Why or Why not?
11. Was Merritt too hard or lenient on Sam when he overstepped with reading the journal and with sending her song to music industry people?
12. Do you agree or disagree with Sam when he says Merritt wants more than a career teaching piano? Why?
13. Music has a starring role in this story. Did it enhance or detract from the story? Were any of your favorite songs mentioned? Do you agree with Sam's assessment of what's called Carolina beach music?
14. Were you surprised by Merritt's sacrifice for Sam? Why or why not?
15. *Forever Home* is the third installment of the Daniels family. Josie was featured in *Forever Music.* Ben's story is "A Hatteras Surprise" in *Candy Cane Wishes and Saltwater Dreams.* Discuss this family in terms of love, character, loyalty, and fun.

ABOUT THE AUTHOR

Hope Toler Dougherty holds a Master's degree in English and taught at East Carolina University as well as York Technical College. Before writing novels, she published non-fiction articles on topics ranging from gardening with children and environmental awareness to writing apprehension. Her published novels are *Irish Encounter*, *Mars...With Venus Rising*, *Rescued Hearts, and Forever Music*. She has a novella included in *Candy Cane Wishes and Saltwater Dreams* and is a member of American Christian Fiction Writers.

A native North Carolinian, she and her husband look forward to visits with their two daughters and twin sons. Hope shares her belief in the God who "has held the dust of the earth in a basket, weighed the mountains on the scales," and "who is able to do immeasurably more than all we ask or imagine" through her actions in real life as well as the words in her stories.

MORE FROM THIS SERIES

Candy Cane Wishes and Saltwater Dreams

A collection of Christmas beach romances

by five multi-published authors including

"A Hatteras Surprise" by Hope Toler Dougherty

***Mistletoe Make-believe* by Amy Anguish** – Charlie Hill's family thinks his daughter Hailey needs a mom–to the point they won't get off his back until he finds her one. Desperate to be free from their nagging, he asks a stranger to pretend she's his girlfriend during the holidays. When romance author Samantha Arwine takes a working vacation to St. Simon's Island over Christmas, she never dreamed she'd be involved in a real-life romance. Are the sparks between her and Charlie real? Or is her imagination over-acting ... again?

***A Hatteras Surprise* by Hope Toler Dougherty** –Ginny Stowe spent years tending a childhood hurt that dictated her college study and work. Can time with an island visitor with ties to her past heal lingering wounds and lead her toward a happy Christmas ... and more? Ben Daniels intends to hire a new branch manager for a Hatteras Island bank, then hurry back to his promotion and Christmas in Charlotte. Spending time with a beautiful local, however, might force him to adjust his sails.

***A Pennie for Your Thoughts* by Linda Fulkerson** –When the Lakeshore Homeowner's Association threatens to condemn the cabin Pennie Vaughn inherited from her foster mother, her only hope of funding the needed repairs lies in winning a travel blog contest. Trouble is, Pennie never goes anywhere. Should she use the all-expenses paid Hawaiian vacation offered to her by her ex-fiancé? The trip that would have been their honeymoon?

***Mr. Sandman* by Regina Rudd Merrick** – Events manager Taylor Fordham's happily-ever-after was snatched from her, and she's saying no to romance and Christmas. When she meets two new friends—the cute new chef at Pilot Oaks and a contributor on a sci-fi fan fiction website who enjoys debate—her resolve begins to waver. Just when she thinks she can loosen her grip on thoughts of love, a crisis pulls her back. There's no way she's going to risk her heart again.

***Coastal Christmas* by Shannon Taylor Vannatter** – Lark Pendleton is banking on a high-society wedding to make her grandparent's inn at Surfside Beach, Texas the venue to attract buyers. Tasked with sprucing up the inn, she hires Jace Wilder, whose heart she once broke. When the bride and groom turn out to be Lark's high school nemesis and ex-boyfriend, she and Jace embark on a pretend romance to save the wedding. But when real feelings emerge, can they overcome past hurts?

Forever Music

Book One in the Forever Series

by Hope Toler Dougherty

A battered heart needs healing.

A community needs rescuing.

A chartered course needs redirecting.

College history instructor, Josie Daniels is good at mothering her three brothers, volunteering in her community, and getting over broken hearts, but meeting aloof, hotshot attorney Ches Windham challenges her nurturing, positive-thinking spirit.

Josie longs to help Ches find his true purpose, but as his hidden talents and true personality emerge. Will she be able to withstand his potent charms, or will she lose her heart in the process?

A rising star in his law firm, Ches Windham is good at keeping secrets.

He's always been the good son, following his father's will to become an attorney and playing the game for a fast track to partnering with a law firm. Lately, though his life's path has lost whatever luster it had—all because of his unlikely, and unacceptable, friendship with Josie. He struggles between the life he's prepared for and the one calling to him now. Opposing his father has never been an option, and spending time with Josie can't be one. The more he's with her, however, the more he wants to be.

When a crisis tarnishes his golden future and secrets are revealed, Ches is forced to reexamine the trajectory of his life. Will he choose the path his father hammered out for him or the path that speaks to his heart?

ALSO BY HOPE TOLER DOUGHERTY

Irish Encounter

After almost three years of living under a fog of grief, Ellen Shepherd is ready for the next chapter in her life. Perhaps she'll find adventure during a visit to Galway. Her idea of excitement consists of exploring Ireland for yarn to feature in her shop back home, but the adventure awaiting her includes an edgy stranger who disrupts her tea time, challenges her belief system, and stirs up feelings she thought she'd buried with her husband.

After years of ignoring God, nursing anger, and stifling his grief, Payne Anderson isn't ready for the feelings a chance encounter with an enchanting stranger evokes. Though avoiding women and small talk has been his pattern, something about Ellen makes him want to seek her—and God again.

Can Ellen accept a new life different than the one she planned? Can Payne release his guilt and accept the peace he's longed for? Can they surrender their past pain and embrace healing together, or will fear and doubt ruin their second chance at happiness?

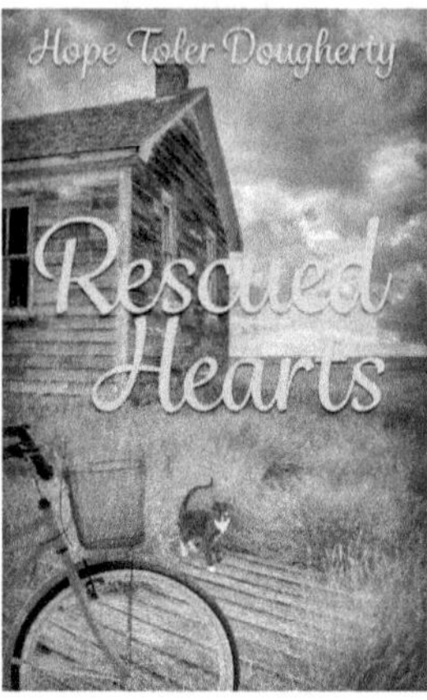

Rescued Hearts

Mary Wade Kimball's soft spot for animals leads to a hostage situation when she spots a briar-entangled kitten in front of an abandoned house. Beaten, bound, and gagged, Mary Wade loses hope for escape.

Discovering the kidnapped woman ratchets the complications for undercover agent Brett Davis. Weighing the difference of ruining his three months' investigation against the woman's safety, Brett forsakes his mission and helps her escape the bent-on-revenge brutes following behind. When Mary Wade's safety is threatened once more, Brett rescues her again. This time, her personal safety isn't the only thing in jeopardy. Her heart is endangered as well.

Stay up-to-date on your favorite books and authors with our free e-newsletters.

ScriveningsPress.com

www.ingramcontent.com/pod-product-compliance
Lightning Source LLC
Chambersburg PA
CBHW071534120726
47907CB00014B/1779

* 9 7 8 1 6 4 9 1 7 2 2 4 2 *